"[A] barrelful of texture... sparkling suspense . . . [
                —Jenn McKinlay, *New York Times* bestselling author

"Piquant, heady and satisfyingly surprising."
                —Carolyn Hart, *New York Times* bestselling author

"[A] good series, with just the right amount of mystery to keep the reader coming back for more."
                                        —*Suspense Magazine*

"The author's experience as a wine specialist shines . . . This novel accurately reflects the pressure, competition and pride all vineyard owners have over their crops. Equally delightful is the truly likable heroine, whose intelligence is matched by her wry humor and dedication to upholding her particular ethics and sense of justice."   —*Kings River Life Magazine*

"A well-rounded mystery that is a welcome addition to the cozy genre. This was a good read and I can't wait to see what happens next in Cypress Cove."   —Dru's Book Musings

"The breathtaking setting and stellar cast of characters—from protagonists Penny and Antonia to their various employees and family members to Penny's pets, gray tabby Petite Syrah and malamute Nanook—made this a sparkling debut."
                —Melissa's Mochas, Mysteries & Meows

Titles by Carlene O'Neil

ONE FOOT IN THE GRAPE
RIPE FOR MURDER

Ripe for
Murder

CARLENE O'NEIL

BERKLEY PRIME CRIME, NEW YORK

**BERKLEY
PRIME
CRIME**

**An imprint of Penguin Random House
375 Hudson Street, New York, New York 10014**

RIPE FOR MURDER

A Berkley Prime Crime Book / published by arrangement with the author

ISBN: 978-0-425-27402-6

PUBLISHING HISTORY
Berkley Prime Crime mass-market edition / March 2016

PRINTED IN THE UNITED STATES OF AMERICA

10 9 8 7 6 5 4 3 2 1

Cover art by Robert Crawford.
Cover design by Danielle Abbiate.
Interior text design by Kelly Lipovich.

**Penguin
Random
House**

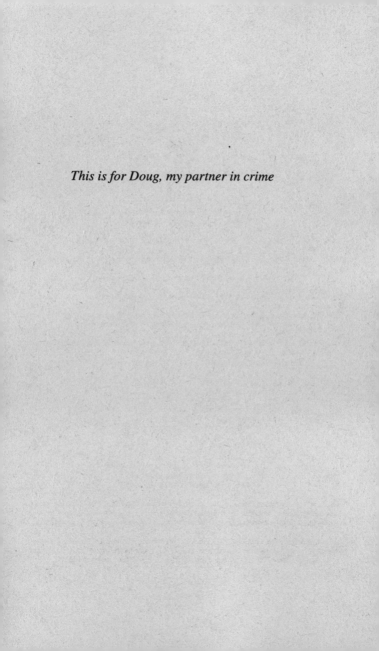

This is for Doug, my partner in crime

One

I'D taken my suitcase out of the closet three days ago, and the only other thing I'd managed to do was trip over it.

"You going to pack that thing anytime soon?" Connor took a sip of coffee. "You leave in two days."

"Tell me again we can handle the extra foot traffic."

"We'll be fine. We might need to add some staff, but we'll manage. It's more a question of what direction you want to take the winery."

I didn't respond. Connor had been running the winery with my aunt for years before I'd inherited, and we both knew I wouldn't make a decision without him.

I walked to the desk, reaching once again for the invitation, the ivory linen paper with raised script clearly designed to impress. A group that specialized in train tours was recruiting investors for a new line in Monterey County. I'd been invited because my contribution would be a narrow strip of land running alongside my vineyards. I invest the land, and the train practically stops at the door of the winery's tasting room.

"It just seems like such a big commitment, and there's no going back once we've agreed," I said.

Connor shrugged. "That's why you accepted the invitation. Just head up to Napa and see what they have in mind."

Joyeux Winery is small by most winery standards and is near the town of Cypress Cove, just south of Monterey. I liked the pace of running a small winery and didn't need to be the next household name in wine. On the other hand, I didn't like how frequently I had to use red ink at the end of the month. I toyed with the invitation.

"Have you talked to Antonia?" Connor asked. "Isn't her contribution going to be a similar strip off the back of her land?"

I nodded. Antonia's my neighbor and a distant relative. She also owns the largest, most successful winery along the central coast. Our relationship has never been easy, especially since as a teen I'd frequently thrown parties in her vineyards. She has a sharp mind and a sharper tongue, and you always know what she's thinking. She has worn long black dresses, her silver hair piled high, for as long as I can remember, and admits to being seventy but must be denying at least a decade. I can't decide if she looked old thirty years ago, or she looks terrific now.

"Antonia is all for anything that helps the wineries in this area grow. She can't wait to go, especially since it comes with an opportunity to snoop on the wineries in Napa Valley."

"I'm sure she'll take full advantage of that," Connor said.

Only 3 percent of California wines come from Napa Valley, but its influence on the wine industry is undeniable. Equally undeniable is the beauty of the area. I was looking forward to seeing it again.

No, the trip itself wasn't the issue; it was what to do about Connor. The invitation included a weekend at a spa hotel just outside of St. Katrina. It was romantic, luxurious and the perfect place to spend time with the man in my life.

My problem was that I didn't have a man in my life. Sure, Connor was the man of my dreams, but *only* in my dreams. He was the best winery manager in the region, and since my return to the winery, I'd managed to contain my growing feelings for him. Joyeux Winery wouldn't be the same without him, and I wasn't sure about mixing business with pleasure, even though I was confident the encounter would be pleasurable, indeed. Like most winery managers, Connor was equal parts chemist, businessman, scientist and farmer. He was smart in a soft flannel shirt. Throw in tall, good-looking and funny, and you see my dilemma.

I took a breath. "The thing is, I think you should be there. If we agree to invest, this will impact you more than me. Hayley can handle everything here while we're gone." Hayley is my niece and assistant manager at the winery.

Connor nodded. "Okay. No problem. They offered two rooms at the hotel if you wanted to bring someone. I'll call them and let them know I'm coming."

He stood and stretched, the flannel shirt riding up to show the trim physique that working outside all day in the fields had given him. Connor had a house in town, but most mornings he joined me in my kitchen to review the day's schedule. He walked over to the counter to pour himself more coffee, the smell of soap and the outdoors lingering as he walked past.

I reached for the cream, adjusted the elastic waistband of my workout pants—otherwise known as pajamas—and tried not to look disappointed. I was ambivalent over my feelings about Connor and didn't want to risk our relationship, but staying with me clearly hadn't even crossed his mind. I adjusted the waist of my pants again. It was only an extra ten pounds, but suddenly it felt like a lot more. I pushed the cream away.

"Sounds good, but don't worry about calling the hotel. I'll take care of it."

Connor poured a last cup of coffee and raised it in a departing gesture. He moved with unconscious ease through the French doors, down the back steps and into the rows of Chardonnay grapes that grew right up to the back of my deck. As I poured myself another cup, the phone rang. I sighed when I saw the caller ID.

"Hi, Antonia."

"I'm bringing Chantal."

I put the cup down and took a seat. "Good morning to you too."

"Yes, well, good morning. I'm bringing Chantal."

"Yes, I heard." Unfortunately. Antonia's youngest daughter, Chantal, had always been a source of irritation, sometimes reaching the level of infuriation, like when she stole my first boyfriend in high school. She was perfectly gorgeous, with luxuriant dark hair and the vibrant green eyes the Martinellis were known for. She lived at Martinelli

Vineyards with Antonia and had recently taken over the marketing efforts of Martinelli Winery. She was surprisingly good at it too.

"Well, I wanted you to know. I realize it hasn't always been easy between you two, but I think it's a good idea that she sees what we're talking about."

"Sure. I understand. Connor's going too."

There was a pause. "Well, that could get a little sticky."

"Sticky? Sticky, Antonia? Anytime Chantal gets around Connor there's only one thing that gets sticky, and it's her." She was like flypaper for any man who flew into her atmosphere. As far as I knew, Connor was the one guy in Cypress Cove who had, so far, resisted Chantal's advances. Not that it stopped her from trying.

"You're exaggerating."

"You want to give her the benefit of the doubt, something I don't have to do, not being her mother."

"I will ensure she behaves and the atmosphere remains businesslike. If not, I will make it right."

"That's something I can't wait to see."

"Don't underestimate me, Penelope."

She only calls me that when she's perturbed.

"Okay, Antonia. I'm relying on you."

"You can't blame Chantal for holding out hope. If you were to remove Connor from the town's list of single men, it would make things easier."

Chantal didn't necessarily care if the man in question was single or not, but I let that pass.

"You forget; I need to work with Connor. The work and the winery need to come first."

There was a pause. "I thought that way most of my life

too, and it cost me good relationships over the years. I'm still playing catch-up with my children, and Chantal's the only one who talks to me. He's a fine man, Penny. You'd be a fool to let him get away."

"Thanks for the advice."

"Besides, you aren't getting any younger."

"Thanks again."

"You just spent so many years away, traveling and taking pictures." She made it sound like an expensive hobby.

"That's what photojournalists do. We travel and take pictures."

"So now you're in your thirties—late thirties, I might add—and alone."

"I'm not alone. I'm single. Bye, Antonia." I tried not to slam down the phone. Photojournalism had kept me on the road nine months out of the year, but I hadn't regretted it then and wouldn't now.

I was, however, glad to have the freedom to choose the subjects I wanted, and now preferred the landscape shots I sold in the galleries that lined Cypress Cove's main street. I was fortunate enough to be living a life that suited me. I reached once again for the wine-train brochure.

Running from St. Katrina to Aqua Caliente, towns a short distance from Napa, the train was owned and operated by the same group that wanted to expand into Monterey County. The tracks were originally laid in the 1800s, when wealthy San Franciscans travelled north by ferry and luxury train to enjoy weekends in the country. After the completion of the Golden Gate Bridge, trains were no longer the fashionable way to make the trip. The train cars were sold off and the tracks slowly fell into disrepair until the 1970s, when the northern sections were restored and Pullman railcars began making the trip once again.

I didn't know much about trains, but even *I* could see their beauty. Honduran mahogany paneling, etched and stained glass partitions, Tiffany lighting fixtures and brass accents throughout. The train had one car for dining, and another car had an antique bar running its length, with a corner fireplace. Even in the photos the richness of the rose velvet fabrics and lead-crystal stemware came through. The slick and glossy brochure covered anything you would ever want to know about the train. It seemed that the only thing not covered was what to do in the unlikely event one of your fellow train travelers turned out to be a killer. That one I had to find out on my own.

Two

"WELL, this is pretty nice." I looked around.

"That's an understatement," Connor said. "It's already surpassed its reputation, and we're still in the lobby."

The Silverado Mission Inn and Spa was, in a word, spectacular. Stucco walls with arched doorways led off the main reception, their umber hue complementing a solid oak–beam ceiling three stories above the lobby. With very simple décor, the space was lit by beaten-copper candleholders and stained glass chandeliers. Hand-turned earthenware in various natural tones added spots of color, and the oversized furnishings were covered in leather and suede. The floor gleamed with polished Mexican tile, and the fireplace with its massive oak mantel was so large I could stand in it. The simple clean design was both powerful and inviting.

A gentleman wearing an Armani suit walked over and picked up my case.

"Sorry, I think you've grabbed the wrong bag. That one's mine."

He smiled. "My name's George. I work for the hotel. I'm the butler in charge of your suite. Once we get you checked in, I'll be taking your bag to your room."

I had a butler. "Good to meet you, George. Nice suit."

We walked up to the counter. The receptionist wore a similar suit, only skirted and in a size two. She took my name and reached for a large book.

"You still use a book for reservations?"

She smiled over the cover. "No computers at the front desk, and we discourage cell phone use in the public spaces. Everything at Silverado is designed to be as welcoming and intimate as an old-world holiday, perhaps with some distant European relative you never knew existed, at a distant villa you'll never wish to leave."

I nodded. "It's working."

She glanced at the book and then at Connor. "There seems to be some mistake. They booked two rooms for you."

"No, that's right." Heat crept into my cheeks. "Two rooms."

"Of course." She recovered nicely, but I caught the look she gave Connor. It was longer than her first glance, and she raised one eyebrow as she turned back to me. Terrific. Even strangers were giving their opinion on my nonexistent love life.

She handed me a real key, a big old-fashioned bronze

one that was satisfyingly heavy in my palm. "Would you like to book any of the spa treatments?"

"I'm not really sure we'll have enough time."

"Go ahead, make time. You've been looking tired lately." Connor stopped. "I don't mean that you've been looking bad or anything . . ."

My cheeks warmed. "I'm fine, really."

She studied my face and passed a menu of services across the counter. "At the very least, book some time in the spa relaxation pools. The water comes straight from the hot springs at 106 degrees. You start at the lower pools and work your way up to the warmer ones. You'll come out completely refreshed and invigorated."

I shoved the brochure in my bag. "Thanks. I'll think about it."

"Yes, well, George will take you to your room now, Miss Lively." It wasn't my imagination. A slight emphasis on the "Miss" echoed through the lobby.

George was both dignified and sprightly, and I had a hard time keeping up. He spoke over his shoulder as we walked to the elevator.

"Another option you might consider is hiking or possibly biking through the mountains and wineries surrounding us. It's a wonderful way to both enjoy the locale and work on your physical activity."

"On the other hand," I said, moments later when we entered the room, "I could spend the entire trip right here." I gave a little twirl around the suite. "This is larger than some of my past apartments."

Lime green and yellows played against the cream stucco walls. French doors opened to a large veranda, and the fireplace was framed with tiles hand painted in a vine motif. The drapes and spreads were patterned in the same motif, the Cabernet hue of the grapes the only other color in the décor.

"Allow me to show you the amenities." He gestured to the wine chilling in an ice bucket. "The bottle of our house wine is complimentary and provided daily. And here"—he handed me a menu from the side table—"are the selections for your breakfast tomorrow. The menu changes daily, but the coffee is always organic French roast. If you want breakfast, please put this on the door with the time you'd like delivery."

I studied the menu. "Is this standard?"

"Well, it does come with the room, if that's what you mean."

"That's what I mean. Fresh coffee delivered to the room. Are you kidding? I may never leave."

George smiled and led me to the bathroom. "Here we have the shower, which is also a steam room that naturally uses the thermal water the hotel is known for." Naturally. He pointed to a cord. "Should you wish a massage in your room, the masseuse will use this to lower the table"—he pointed to the ceiling—"housed above us. And, of course"— he gestured to the far side of the room—"the Jacuzzi tub, large enough for two."

Of course it was. I tipped George, poured a glass of the Pinot Grigio and dialed the front desk.

"Can you tell me if Antonia Martinelli has arrived?" She'd driven up separately with Chantal, as if there were any other option. If I had to spend four hours in a car with Chantal, one of us wouldn't make it.

"Yes, Miss Lively. Chantal Martinelli as well. They should just be reaching their rooms now. Would you like me to ring either of them?"

"No. Let them get settled in. Can you transfer me to Connor Lavigne's room?"

After a click, Connor answered. "What do you think of the rooms?"

"The lobby didn't oversell it. Mine is beautiful." I opened the French doors to the veranda. "So, if I remember the agenda, they're having a reception for us downstairs. Sort of a meet and greet. Do you want to go and then grab some dinner afterward?"

"Actually, they're having a winemakers' dinner at the winery next door. I'd like to attend. One of the things we're both concerned with is the impact to the winery, along with problems the train may cause, that kind of thing. Any issues obviously won't be highlighted in their pitch to you. I think a fellow manager will share with me more quickly than with you as a winery owner."

"That makes sense. I'll miss you at the reception. I mean, I won't *miss* you. I just won't know anybody," I stammered. "Not that you're only good to be around when I don't know anyone else." I bit my tongue. "Never mind. Antonia will be there with me. Have a good time and let me know what you find out." Smooth. Very smooth.

I hung up the phone, grabbed the hotel brochure and stepped out onto the veranda. I skimmed the booklet, stopping to read the history of the hotel. Built in the 1920s, the hotel had always been a haven for wealthy travelers wanting to enjoy time in the countryside. The latest addition was the recently renovated spa, all thirty thousand feet of it. From my vantage point on the third floor, ornate porcelain sea horses cavorted on one side of the outdoor pool. Original to the hotel when wealthy travelers came to "take the waters," these same figurines had been piping hot water from natural springs into the pool ever since, refilling the entire pool several times a day.

Right below my room were the formal gardens, and farther to the left the herb and terraced gardens, shaded with numerous citrus trees. Jasmine scented the air and the sun was that perfect temperature, not too hot on my skin but warm enough to reach deep into my muscles. I released my shoulders, surprised at how tense I was. I rotated my neck, the tightness relaxing, and spotted Connor, several rooms over on the ground floor.

I'd raised my hand to wave when something red flashed in the room next to his. My arm froze. Chantal wore nothing but red. Connor turned to follow my gaze. I think he said something and Chantal came out of the adjacent suite. The ground-floor location gave Chantal the ability to walk just a few short steps and give Connor a hug. Convenient.

"They gave the owners the larger suites on the top floor, with their guests having those down below." Antonia stepped out from her suite and onto the terrace next to mine. "Although I like how the ground floor has direct access to the gardens."

Yeah, that was just terrific. "How are you, Antonia?"

"Better than you, from the look on your face. She's simply saying hello."

"And she didn't even need to open her mouth to do it. Interesting."

Connor and Chantal walked toward the garden together.

Actually, Chantal was pulling Connor by the arm, and it didn't look like he was very comfortable. Good.

I turned toward Antonia, in black as usual. In deference to the heat of the day, her outfit was a lightweight gauze material, with a shimmer of silver thread woven through the fabric. It looked outstanding with her silver hair, and she knew it.

She waved a folded sheet at me. "We don't have long before we're to meet the other potential investors in the Sonoma Room. However, you can take a few moments to tour the gardens, and perhaps rectify any room assignments that may need it."

I rolled my eyes. "If Chantal wants to get ahold of someone, I don't think a simple room change would be nearly enough. No offense meant."

"None taken. I learned long ago my children are responsible for their own behavior."

"Connor doesn't have much time either way. He's attending the winemakers' dinner next door."

"So is Chantal. There, you see? I'm sure that's where they're headed now."

With effort, I shifted my attention from Connor and Chantal to focus on Antonia. "So, what do we know about the other potential investors?"

"The receptionist said a couple from Chicago came in yesterday, and there's a man here from New Orleans. Owns car dealerships. His wife is half his age. They checked in right before me." Antonia tapped her fingertips together. "I wonder how the response from investors has been. You know, we're the only ones contributing land instead of money. It puts us in an unusual situation."

"How so?"

"Even if they raise the money, without our contribution, the railway won't go forward. There simply isn't another logical route for it through Monterey County, one that has the wineries, restaurants, proximity to town and scenery that the chosen route does. This enterprise needs to work for us, and let's remember, we have the upper hand in all this. Beyond that, the number of visitors to both our wineries will increase significantly."

"So you think we should participate?"

"I think we should remain open-minded and noncommittal." Antonia took one last look toward the gardens. "I'll see you downstairs."

TWENTY minutes later I stepped into the Sonoma Room, a large area that featured the same upscale, yet rustic, finishes of the hotel lobby. Walls with a rust-colored suede treatment enhanced the dark brown leather furnishings. A bar ran along one side of the room, and there was laughter and the clanking of glassware. Waiters crossed the room with trays of things that left my mouth watering. As I started to flag one down, a large man in a fitted suit walked up to me and held out his hand.

"Dave Duport. Duport Automotive."

My hand disappeared into his. I'm not small, standing five foot ten, but I felt downright petite next to him. Everything about him was large but seemed somehow to work well together. Not muscle, not fat, just a big solid body topped with a large head covered with plenty of auburn hair. His cheeks had the look of someone who spent a lot of time either outdoors or bellied up to a bar. I'd be willing to bet he'd spent his fair share of time at both activities.

"I'm Penny. Nice to meet you, Dave."

"Call me Big Dave. Everyone does." He gestured around the room. "Mighty fine spread they've put on for us." He leaned in a bit closer. "The bigger the bar, the bigger the hit to your wallet."

"Sounds like you've been to a few of these."

He teetered his head from side to side, almost touching his ears to his shoulders since he didn't have a neck to speak of.

"Not quite like this." He thumbed over his shoulder. "This is more for my darlin' bride than me. Tara's from these parts. I'm just a car salesman down home." He reached into his pocket, pulled out a business card and handed it to me.

I glanced at the card, then took a second look. "That looks like a zebra behind the wheel."

"It surely is. That's Hank when he was just a baby. He lives at my Memphis dealership. Well, one of 'em anyway." He shook his head, the folds on his chin not quite keeping up. "Don't jump to any conclusions. He wasn't smuggled in or anything. Damn people who buy these animals don't have the sense that, well, that Hank does. No, he was a rescue, and believe me, he lives better than most people do."

"Does he really help you sell cars?"

He nodded. "You bet he does. Truth is, it's all about being remembered when people are ready for a new car. And a chance to get the kid's picture taken with Hank just might be the difference between them coming to my dealership or someone else's."

He held a palm up. "God's truth, I give folks the best deal for their money. There's a reason forty percent of my business is repeat business. The rest? Just me having a little fun." His eyes twinkled.

I smiled. I couldn't help it. I liked the guy. "So, you said investing in the train venture is more for your wife?"

He nodded. "Tara. She's around here somewhere. She's a bit younger than me. Just search for the finest-lookin' filly in the room."

"How long have you been married?"

"Couple of years."

When a successful man in his fifties openly admits he has married the young hottie, you can't help but think of the wife he likely left behind. He must have seen something on my face.

"You look like you just ate something sour."

"It's just that as a woman who's never been married, in her mid-thirties—okay, late thirties—I just wonder why people do some of the things they do."

He tilted his head. "By 'people,' you mean men."

I shrugged. "I guess I do."

"You think I left someone else for Tara."

I nodded. "It's a common theme, you've got to admit."

"Well, I'll tell you. Tara's my third wife. The first was after high school—well, not quite after, if you get my meaning—and I've got a son you'll get to meet this weekend." He bit his lip. "That marriage was a mistake her parents insisted on, and it lasted less than a year, although I've always tried to do right by my boy. Shortly thereafter, I met the love of my life, my beautiful girl Sue." He pinched the bridge of his nose for a moment. "For thirty wonderful years she made me whole. Never had any children, but that didn't matter. With her, the world was mine." He paused. "Lost her five years ago."

I took a slug of wine. Lacking a verbal filter has gotten me into this situation more than once. Before I could begin an apology, he shook his head as though to clear it.

"Tara's fun. She keeps me young and keeps the memories at bay."

As though on cue, a high laugh came from across the room, and a smile crossed his face. "There's my Tara now." He put up a hand to the side of his mouth and yelled over the clatter. "Come over here, darlin'."

The woman who turned at the sound of his voice was a few inches shorter than me and curvy. Really curvy. She walked toward me, sporting a big beehive hairdo, the kind they wore in the sixties. The hair came in second for eye-catching. This gal was sporting the largest chest I had ever seen. You couldn't help but stare. It was like they had their own gravitational field. I glanced over at Big Dave, and he shrugged and grinned.

"Having fun, darlin'?"

"Oh, Davey, this is everything I hoped for." She glanced my way. "Who are you?"

"Hi, my name's Penny—"

"Davey, I need another drink." She was either rude or had the attention span of a clam.

I rolled my eyes.

Big Dave caught my look. Again. "Now, Tara, I was having a conversation with Penny here."

Both her lower lip and other physical attributes jutted

forward. "But, Davey." She rolled the name around, like she had a mouth full of marbles.

Again, I felt my eyes disappearing into the back of my head.

"What?" Tara had turned her focus to me, and I got a good look. Pretty but average, except for her eyes, which were a startling shade of topaz. They were heavily made up with false eyelashes and shimmer blue lids. "Well, what?"

"Um, nothing. I just don't know if he looks like a Davey." I was tempted to pronounce it the way she had, but decided to be the bigger person. Yawn.

"Well, when we got married, I stopped calling him Big Dave, and Double D won't work," she giggled. "That could be my nickname."

The server came by with a tray of something wrapped in bacon.

Tara grabbed him by the arm. "Oh, this looks good."

Big Dave leaned over. "Don't take offense. She's just had a little too much of the bubbly."

Lucky her. I polished off my glass of wine. "Oh, look, I'm empty." I nodded good-bye at Big Dave and turned away.

Tara didn't even register that I'd left. She was still engrossed in the waiter, holding him by the arm, her head resting slightly on his shoulder. He seemed to look better than whatever he carried on the tray, but I hoped for Big Dave's sake that wasn't the case. In spite of his question- able choice in current brides, there was something likable about him.

I made my way to the bar just as a tall guy up front

tapped on a glass with a knife. He got the attention of the room, mostly because he was dressed like he'd just stepped off a train. He wore overalls, but they must have been his special-occasion pair because they were dark navy and looked freshly pressed. The shirt was OshKosh, and he had a red bandanna tied around his neck. A little cap in white and blue stripes sat at a jaunty angle, covering most of his jet-black hair, and he sported a moustache to match.

He smiled. "Well, just look at this fine turnout. My name's Bill. I'm the head engineer for the line, and I'll be in charge of making sure your experience on the St. Katrina Express is everything you hoped it would be."

"I'm sure he means everything *he* hopes it will be." Antonia came up beside me. "I read somewhere he's the major shareholder."

"With those overalls, he looks like he belongs in a caboose. I wouldn't have guessed he was the money behind the company," I said.

"I'm sure that's what he had in mind."

Bill continued. "To make this easier, we're going to divide you up into three groups. Each group will have its own car on the train. Now let me get you sorted."

A few minutes later my name was called and I walked to where Bill indicated. Antonia followed me.

"How do you know you'll be with me?"

"It stands to reason he'd put the people that already know each other together."

Sure enough, Bill called her name, and she waved and raised an eyebrow at me. She loves to be right, even over the smallest things. It makes me crazy, although I do the same thing. I just hope less annoyingly so.

"Now that we're sorted, I'm going to get another glass of wine," she said. "Do you want me to get you anything?"

I still had a full glass and waved her off, a move that might have been premature because Big Dave and Tara joined me a few moments later, along with another couple.

"Hi. My name's Jim and this is my wife, Kim."

Good. Even I could remember names that rhymed. Handsome in an understated way, Jim had sharp features with olive skin and a full head of silver hair combed back from his forehead. Kim, in contrast, had a paler complexion, long blonde hair and the prettiest smile I'd ever seen. Like, Julia Roberts pretty.

"I'm Penny, and this is Tara and, um, Big Dave?"

He nodded encouragement at me.

Tara sidled up to Jim. "And where are you from, Jim?"

Jim threw his arm around Kim, who flashed that smile. "Chicago. It's our first time here in California, and I'm taking my gorgeous bride on a dream trip. Beautiful scenery and my beautiful wife. And on a train! Not much could be better than this."

Kim turned her smile on me. "Jim loves trains, which is a good thing, since he's a safety inspector on the Central Pacific line out of Chicago."

Tara put one hand on her hip and rocked to one side. Her chest followed shortly thereafter, as did the peripheral vision of every man in the room.

"How does a person that inspects trains afford the kind of investment we're talking about each of us making here?"

Jim raised his brows and was about to speak, but Big Dave slapped his forehead. I guess he had his limits after all. "Tara, you can't ask things like that. It isn't polite."

Kim's smile didn't falter. "Oh, I don't mind answering. It's crazy, really. My mother had an uncle who did very well. He didn't have any children, and he named my mother his heir years ago. When I lost her, it all came to me."

Jim still had his arm around Kim, and he gave her shoulders a squeeze. "If there's one thing I know, it's trains, so we thought this investment would be a perfect fit."

"Yes, well, that's all very interesting." Tara looked at Big Dave. "It's okay to say that, isn't it?" She whipped that beehive hair around, one hand still on her hip, and walked away.

"Now, honey." He followed her to the bar. The rest was lost as they moved through the crowd.

"Wow, is she a handful," I said.

Jim shook his head. "Then he's the right guy for the job. Did you see his hands? They're huge. I don't see going through life being called Big Dave, but if it works for anyone, it's him."

I spotted Big Dave. He'd reached the bar, his broad shoulders taking up most of the space at the stool on each side of him. Tara was nowhere to be seen.

Jim placed his empty glass on a passing waiter's tray, taking a fresh one. He took a sip and gave his wife a smile. "Not a bad way to live, is it?" He turned to me. "Kim's been good about this whole train business. It's really my interest, not hers."

"I said I'd consider it, Jim, but after the last couple of investments . . . Of course, it's true. Nobody knows more about trains than you."

He whispered something in her ear, and she smiled. "Later, Jim. For now, let's go see the gardens. I can't believe they have so many things still in bloom. It's nearly December!"

The pair walked to the rear doors, Jim with his arm now wrapped around her waist. Antonia returned from the bar a few moments later.

"What time do you think Connor and Chantal will be back?" I asked.

"Not until late. They were having a lecture and then dinner. Care to go for a walk in the gardens? The sun is setting, but the grounds really are quite lovely."

"So I've heard."

Antonia nodded toward the bar. "I met the man that checked in before me, the one that owns car dealerships. A real gentleman. Huge, but solid. I've always liked that in a man." She turned to scan the room. "Simply ridiculous name, though."

"Big Dave. He's married, and he's too young for you."

"I only said I thought he was nice. Very polite, with all that Southern charm." She straightened. "Besides, I can enjoy a conversation with a man, should I decide to do so." She pointed a finger. "I'm not the one choosing to live like a hermit."

"Are you scolding me?"

"I would if I thought it might help. Now do you want to go for a walk and get some dinner or not?"

"Fine. Let's get some air and grab a bite." It was going to be my one offer for the evening. Yippee.

Three

THE phone rang just as there was a knock on the door. The door led to coffee, so it didn't really matter who was on the phone: I let George in.

"Do you do everything around here?"

He set the tray on an ottoman. "I noticed your breakfast was ready to go and I didn't want to keep you waiting." He gave a small nod of his head and let himself out.

I really liked George.

The phone rang again after I'd poured my first cup and grabbed a bagel.

"We need to be downstairs in less than one hour."

"Good morning, Antonia. I'll meet you outside the Sonoma Room at eight sharp." I tasted the coffee. Strong French roast. Yum.

"You haven't talked with Chantal this morning by any chance, have you?"

"No." I put the cup down. "Why?"

"Because I haven't been able to reach her. She might be in the shower but . . ."

I knew what she left unsaid. Chantal sometimes over-indulged. She'd gone to the dinner at the winery last night, but it was unlikely she drank to excess with Connor there to reel her in. Barely tolerable sober, Chantal really upped her game when she drank.

A thought occurred to me and my stomach sank. "Do you want me to call Connor's room? See if she's there?"

There was a pause. "No need. I see her coming now, across the back lawn. See you in a bit."

I hung up and walked out onto the veranda. There below me was Chantal in a red workout outfit.

She looked up, spotted me and waved. "Too bad you don't work out. The fitness center is fantastic."

"I work out," I yelled across the garden. Very mature. "I just don't like to in the mornings." Or afternoons. Evenings aren't that great either.

A chair scraped to my left. Antonia stood on her balcony, shaking her head.

"Don't you start," I said. "I'll be downstairs at eight."

I poured myself another large cup and managed to shower, don my standard uniform of jeans, boots and a sweater, this one in plum, in under twenty minutes. Piling my unruly curls on the top of my head and throwing on a couple swipes of mascara took less than five, and I was out the door with time to spare. Of course, it didn't make a difference. When I got downstairs, Antonia was pacing like she'd been there for hours.

"Chantal said she'd be right out, and Connor is over

talking to the train guy." Antonia tapped her temple with a forefinger. "What's his name? The train guy."

"Bill."

Connor saw me, said something to Bill and walked over. "'Morning. I must say it's fun to take an early run through a vineyard without worrying about all the things I see that need to be done."

"Hmm. Chantal worked out in the gym this morning." I watched his face.

"Too pretty to be inside." If he'd known where she'd been this morning before the gym, he didn't show it, and when Chantal arrived a few moments later, he greeted her without any indication they'd been together earlier.

"What a great morning." Chantal flipped a long pony-tail fat enough to actually be a pony's tail. "I had a terrific workout, which was a good thing since we entirely overate last night, didn't we?" She directed her comment to Connor, who nodded in agreement.

"They really did it up. I got a chance to ask how much the train is actually impacting the business of running a winery," he tipped his head to one side, indicating Bill was coming to join us. "But it can wait until later."

"Good, good. You're all here." Bill rubbed his palms together. "Most of the others have already left. Let's get you in a cab and to the train station."

The taxi ride was mercifully short and confirmed my suspicion that Chantal and I would never have made it in one car from Cypress Cove to Napa. She didn't stop talking and managed to step on my foot twice.

"Now there's a big one," Chantal said when we arrived at the station moments later. Big Dave was sitting on a bench in the sun. As we stepped from the cab he gave a big wave. In the morning light, I was able to study him. He looked like solid muscle, with a full head of wavy hair and a ready smile.

Chantal gave one of those little finger waves. "I wonder if he's here with anyone."

"As a matter of fact, he is, and I can't wait for you to meet her." I spotted Tara across the street. "There she is now."

Tara disappeared into a boutique.

"Where?"

"She just went into that store on the corner. The jewelry store."

"We have a few minutes if either of you ladies wants to join her." Bill wiped his brow with the kerchief from around his neck. "The train should be here shortly." He pulled a pocket watch from his overalls, gave it a little shake and then turned to confirm the time on the clock hanging over the platform. "Yup, should be here any moment."

"I'm going to take a look at the station," Connor said. "Want to come?"

"Sure." I pulled him away before Chantal could join us.

The depot walls were thick stucco, and the temperature dropped several degrees when we stepped inside. It was modeled after a Spanish mission with colorful tile-covered walls lining the main waiting room, and the floor was sanded Mexican tiles in buff tones. Redwood beams ran across the ceiling and supported massive wrought iron chandeliers.

"So tell me about last night," I said.

"The wineries in the region like the train. It has

increased the number of tourists and keeps people off the roads after wine tasting, which is never a bad thing."

"What about noise?" I asked.

"As long as the train runs during the day and early evening, I don't think it would be a problem."

"No, I suppose not."

"I would see how the rest of the weekend goes, but maybe you should consider their offer."

"Fair enough," I said.

We stepped back out into the sunshine. Across the street was a coffee shop, a cute little A-frame with blue-and-white gingham curtains. "I'm going to get a cup. Want one?"

He nodded. "Sure."

Moments later we stepped through the entrance.

"Penny, over here." Kim and Jim stood near the register. "We're waiting for two lattes to go."

"Perfect morning for it." I rubbed my arms through my sweater. "It's chilly."

Kim laughed, showing that perfect smile. "Oh, you Californians. Chicago's looking at a high of fifty today."

The waitress dropped off their drinks.

"See you on the train." Jim held the door while Kim grabbed their coffees.

As they stepped off the curb, Jim guided Kim by the elbow and she smiled up at him.

"They're pretty cute together." I grabbed a menu but a car horn and squealing brakes made me turn back to the window. There was a cry and someone was yelling.

Connor ran to the door. I followed. A bright red Porsche playing music loud enough to vibrate teeth sat right where Kim and Jim had been moments before, its hood covered in coffee and foam. Jim knelt in front of the car, and I was relieved to see a slim hand reach up to grab his arm.

Thankfully the music was lowered, although not turned off, and the door opened. A man in his late twenties stepped from the car. He ran his hand through his hair and pushed past Connor to where Kim sat. "What were you thinking? I could have killed you!"

Jim grabbed the driver by the collar and pulled the younger man close. "You were speeding and you almost ran over my wife." Jim looked to be about twenty pounds heavier and at least that many years older than the driver, but something in his eyes caught the younger man's attention. It certainly caught mine. Jim clenched his fist.

"Hey, I didn't mean for this to happen. It wasn't my fault. She walked right in front of me."

"He's right, you know." Kim reached both palms to the sky. "I don't know what I was thinking. It really was entirely my fault. And it looked worse than it was. He didn't even hit me. I somehow lost my balance and fell all on my own." With Jim's help, she got to her feet. "In fact, I'm lucky you were paying as close attention as you were, Mr.—"

"Duport." Big Dave had walked over from the platform. "His name is Vance Duport. He's my son."

I looked at Vance more closely as he turned to his father. Vance was going for preppy in a peach polo shirt and tailored beige shorts, with Sperry boat shoes. He was blond, and had his father's height, but not his massive frame. He looked like he could be athletic in a sport requiring speed and precision. This was confirmed when I spotted a tennis racket in the backseat of the convertible.

The car looked brand-new and was obviously expensive.

A Porsche Carrera S. I suppose it paid to have a string of family auto dealerships. The license plate was "KissMyS." Charming.

I walked to the front of the car. Kim was right. The car hadn't hit her. Her bag was several feet from the front bumper. Coffee dripped down the hood, but that was the only contact she'd made with the car.

Big Dave stood talking to Vance a short distance away. Vance had his arms folded and looked to one side. His face was red and he wasn't speaking.

A few moments later he walked over to Kim. "I must have been going too fast. I apologize."

"No need to apologize. You're right. I did walk right in front of you." Kim smiled and touched Vance briefly on the shoulder.

He turned and flashed his father a look as he jumped back into the car. "I'll be back. Right after I run the car through the wash."

"You don't have time," Big Dave said as the train whistle announced its arrival. "Just park the damn thing. It's only coffee."

"There's a gas station right there. I'm going to rinse it off at least." Vance slammed the door, threw the car into gear and sped across the lot.

Connor joined me. "If he wasn't driving too fast before, he certainly is now."

Big Dave apologized to Kim again over her refusal of any more help. He then walked over to us. "That boy's always driving too fast." He tugged at his shirt collar and then undid the top button. "You know how I told you I had him while I was still in high school? His mother wasn't the biggest disciplinarian, and I wasn't around enough to have much of an influence."

"I'm sure you did the best you could."

Inadequate, but Big Dave's shoulders relaxed and he seemed to take comfort in my response.

Vance rinsed and carefully wiped the hood.

"I'm not sure that's the right car for someone who can't obey the speed limit," I said. "Maybe you should make him drive a Ford."

Big Dave shook his head. "I wouldn't have bought him a car like that. He got it on his own. Besides, he's in his thirties. Not much I can do at this point. He's a man."

"I'm surprised he's here. It just doesn't seem that a leisurely train ride through wine country would be his type of entertainment."

"I'm surprised myself. He was in California already, down in Palm Springs for a tennis match. When he heard what we were doing, he asked to come along. At the time I thought it was a good idea, but this hasn't been a very good beginning."

"Do he and Tara get along?"

"They don't really know each other. That's why I thought it'd be good for them to get better acquainted."

"Where is Tara, anyway?"

Big Dave shrugged. "Doing a bit of shopping. I'm not sure how any woman who has so many darn clothes could want more."

He really was cute. Naive, but cute.

Bill the train guy crossed the street. "You folks all right?" He nodded to Kim. "From where I stood, it looked like you were gone for sure."

"Honestly, he didn't hit me." Kim laughed, a slight crack in her voice the only sign she was shaken from the experience. "I'm fine, really, and I don't want to hold up the party."

Bill straightened his cap and hooked his thumbs in the straps of his overalls. "A woman with spunk. I like that. If you're interested, we're serving mimosas this first leg of the trip. Just follow me, folks."

We made our way to the train platform where Antonia waited.

"That young man nearly ran her over. Damn fool."

"That damn fool is Big Dave's son. We get the pleasure of his company." I hoisted myself up the metal steps, stopping at the entrance of the car. The interior was paneled in polished mahoganies and rich burgundy brocade. Graceful bronze shelves ran above rows of plush oversized armchairs. Crystal lighting sconces blazed, and the air was scented with lemon oil. Champagne corks popped from somewhere and added to the festive air.

"It's certainly lovely," I said.

"Yes, well, appearance is only part of it. We need to remember this is a business. Look around. Other than our group, this entire car is empty." Antonia lowered herself into the seat ahead of me and flagged Bill down.

"There seems to be a lot of extra room. Has investor interest been low?"

"We had a group of potential investors that needed to reschedule. We're running a bit light today is all."

Antonia raised her brow. "Any particular reason they cancelled? This isn't exactly a good sign."

"Not cancelled, ma'am, rescheduled for next week." Bill took off his cap and wiped his brow with his forearm.

"They're planning on coming down next weekend. We'll have a full load that day."

Bill walked away and Antonia turned in her seat to whisper to me. "The train was half an hour late and now this car is only half full. Not a very strong beginning."

Chantal turned sideways in the aisle to let Bill go by and slid into the seat next to Antonia. Her red cashmere sweater looked terrific with her long brunette curls and fire-engine-red lipstick. She gave me that little finger wave. Placing one knee in her seat, she leaned over the backrest. Her cleavage was eye level with Connor seated behind her.

I pretended to read a magazine and listened to them chat until I heard tires screech. I looked out the window as Vance parked, closed up his car, and hopped on the train. He looked at us in the rear of the train car, Jim and Kim a short distance ahead of us, and flopped down in a front seat.

A few moments later I looked up. Big Dave was running from across the street, with Tara right on his heels. For a big guy, he moved pretty well, even holding several shopping bags. Tara was quite a sight. She wore a gold-sequined sweater that reflected the sunlight. As she ran, her beehive and other things bounced all over the place. She was loaded down with more goodies and a garment bag from Louis Vuitton.

Antonia sniffed from the seat in front of me. "Looks like she bought out half the town."

Chantal stopped talking to Connor and swiveled in my direction. She pointed through the window. "Who's that?"

"His name is Big Dave. You asked me about him before, remember?"

"No, the girl."

"That's his wife. Tara."

Big Dave and Tara climbed onto the train and chose seats in front, across the row from Vance. Big Dave stuffed boxes and bags onto the brass overhead shelf, while Tara casually threw the Vuitton bag over the seat behind her.

"You've got to be kidding. He's married to *her*?"

I looked at Chantal. "I know. I've never understood what some men find attractive. Stupid is never appealing, even in a tight sweater."

The sarcasm was wasted. She nodded agreement and swiveled back in her seat. Connor's face came into view and he was smiling.

Four

"WE sure are going slow." A short time later Chantal turned once again in her seat to face Connor. "What time do we get there?"

"This isn't a destination thing. It's supposed to be leisurely so you can enjoy the countryside." I gestured out the window. "This is something people travel from all over the world to see."

The sky was vibrant blue and capped rolling vineyards of Cabernet grapes, their leaves a blaze of yellows and bronze.

"This is what we have at our winery." She shrugged. "I'm not sure it's all that different."

"Of course this is different. You don't see these at home." Towering redwood trees marked a forest preserve. "Some of these trees are the oldest living things on earth. You can't find them anywhere but here."

She smirked. "Don't get so excited. They're just trees."

I stood. "Excuse me." I pushed past Connor, grabbed my camera from the overhead compartment, and made my way to the rear door. Bill was returning from the caboose and he held the door for me.

"Be careful when you're going between cars," he said. "This train predates the closed-in vestibules, and it takes a little getting used to."

He wasn't kidding. Between the cars the floor shifted, and the sides were blocked by waist-high gates. It took a few moments to get my balance and anticipate the rocking of the train, but when I did, I stepped across the vestibule. The wind was more than I'd expected and it was noisy, but in a pleasant way; the clank of the train had a rhythm and held the promise of new places.

Standing outside, I felt as if we were going much faster, and the ground flew past beneath me. I put the camera strap over my head and kept a firm grip on the railing. Blocking the sun with my hand, I peered through the window into the car behind us. It was the caboose, and it was being used for storage. Boxes lined the walls, held in place with netting, and dining room chairs were stacked toward the rear. I tried the door, and it opened. A few moments later I was on the back platform, the track rolling past under my feet, leaving a ribbon behind the train and across the valley floor.

I tried a few shots but at midday the sunlight is too harsh for most landscape photos, especially without any clouds to diffuse the glare.

After a few attempts and several deep breaths of sweet forest air, I made my way back through the caboose to my seat. A short time later the train rumbled and began to slow. Bill appeared at the front of the car.

"This is it. Berninni Winery. The oldest winery in the valley. Everybody off."

Vance was the first to take advantage of the stop and jumped off the train while it ground to a halt. Chantal's gaze followed him.

"I'm surprised you aren't introducing yourself right now, Chantal," I said.

"To him? He's a boy." She looked up the aisle. "I think his dad's a better catch. Either way, I'm looking for a certain type of guy." The pause hung in the air, as though she was actually waiting for me to ask what type. The way she eyed Connor told me everything I needed to know.

"You should see if Bill's single."

"The train guy?" Chantal eyed Bill, frowning slightly. "I don't think we'd have much in common."

Antonia pushed past Chantal. "Bill is a major shareholder of this train, and a number of other ventures. I'm getting off. Connor, would you mind grabbing my bag?" Connor and Antonia walked toward the front of the car.

"Hmm." Chantal eyed Bill. "Those overalls are kinda cute, actually."

She started up the aisle, and I followed. We were at the front as Big Dave stepped into the aisle. Tara was still in the window seat.

"Wait, Davey." Tara rolled it around in her mouth again, and I bit my lip. "I just need a bit of fixin' up." After digging around in her Gucci bag, she pulled out a small vial and twisted the cap. The strong scent of gardenias drifted through the cabin as she dabbed it on her wrists.

"Pretty easy to tell you haven't done much of this, have you?" Chantal glared at Tara. "You never wear perfume or cologne when you're going wine tasting. It ruins the wine's aroma, not only for you but for everyone in the room."

I rolled my eyes. Chantal had never shown a scrap of interest in her family's business. Now suddenly she's Miss Proper Wine Etiquette. Tara glanced up, then took a second look.

Big Dave still blocked the aisle, not that I would have left. Chantal might have met her match in Tara, and I, for one, was going to stick around and find out.

Tara eyed Chantal, taking in the red sweater, the lush ponytail draped over Chantal's shoulder, and those Martinelli green eyes. Slowly Tara replaced the perfume and pulled out a lipstick. "Who are you?"

"Chantal Martinelli, of Martinelli Winery. We own the largest winery on the central California coast." Chantal nodded out the window at Antonia. "That's my mother."

"So, technically," Tara paused to smack newly painted lips, "your mother's the owner. Now isn't that right?" Tara stood and they eyed each other.

I thought Chantal was going to explode, but when she spoke, her voice was soft. "And you are . . ."

"Tara Duport." She nodded at Big Dave. "This is my husband, Dave Duport. We own a string of car dealerships throughout the South." She patted her beehive as Chantal took a step closer.

The two women glared at each other.

"So, technically," Chantal said, "he's the owner. Now isn't that about right?"

Tara's eyes grew wide, and I thought she was going to slap Chantal.

Big Dave must have thought so too, because he stepped in between the two of them. "Ladies, ladies, we're here to have a good time. Come on, darlin', let's go have us some fun."

I took Chantal by the elbow and steered her around the sputtering Tara. Chantal looked behind her when we'd reached the door and gave Tara her standard finger wave.

"Boy, is she a piece of cheap goods, huh?" Chantal did a little shoulder bump against me, like now we were the best of buddies. "Compared to her, I look pretty good, right?"

"Uh, sure." Compared to Tara, who wouldn't?

We walked up the drive to the main entrance of Berninni Winery, still housed in the stone mansion built by the Berninni family at the beginning of the last century. With its original Tiffany windows and lighting fixtures, the building was a landmark in St. Katrina.

We entered the tasting room located on the ground floor, and I joined Jim and Kim at the bar.

"What are you trying?" I asked.

"The sparkling wine," Kim said. "It tastes just like Champagne."

"It basically is. At least they're made the same way. Champagne is just the name for sparkling wine made in a certain region of France."

"Well, this is really good." Jim clinked his glass against Kim's. "To us, Kimmie." He leaned over and gave her a kiss.

They were sweet. I watched for a couple of seconds, then started to feel lonely. Then like a peeping tom.

"Okay, I'll be going." Get a room already.

I couldn't find Antonia, and Connor was in the corner with the winery manager. Chantal stood at the bar and waved me over. So far this trip wasn't what I'd had in mind, but I joined her.

"Don't worry." She waved a bottle at me. "Water, plain and simple."

I nudged in alongside her at the bar. It was crowded and there was loud laughter from the back of the room.

"Sounds like someone else should consider switching over to water too."

Chantal craned her neck to see, a movement that caused every male in the room to shift his gaze in our direction. "It's that Tara person. She was hitting the mimosas pretty hard on the train. Oh, great." She tossed her ponytail. "She's coming our way."

I turned toward the giggle.

Tara held a glass of wine and waved it around. "You seem to know a lot about all this. Why don't you fill me in?"

"I'd be happy to share wine-tasting etiquette with you, but would you follow it? I think I'd be wasting my time." Great. Chantal was the voice of reason. This wasn't going to end well.

"Big Dave mentioned you grew up here," I said. "You probably did some wine tasting when you were young, didn't you?"

Tara swung the glass my way. "Not likely. I grew up here, but on the other side of town. My daddy was a picker, and when your daddy's a picker, the wineries"—she stopped to empty the glass—"let's just say the wineries don't necessarily encourage you to come taste what your daddy's out back picking."

"That must have been difficult."

The wine business is a world of extremes, where the haves and have-nots often collide.

"You don't know the half of it." She waved to the waitress from across the room, the bitterness evident in the lines etched around her mouth.

"Some people have it made." She glanced at Chantal. "Not everyone is born with a silver wine goblet in their hand."

Chantal tossed her hair and took a deep breath, but before she could get a retort out, the waitress arrived.

"Take Barb, here." Tara put her arm around the waitress. "Barb and me both attended the same high school. Didn't we?"

Barb nodded, filling the glass Tara held out. Barb's nails were bitten down and looked raw.

"'Course, we didn't see much of each other. I was out with the smokers behind the gym, and poor Barb here was always . . ." Tara stopped. "Where did you hang out?"

Barb's cheeks reddened and she shrugged her thin shoulders. "Usually the library."

Tara studied Barb. "Barb was a pretty little thing back then. Married Seth, the high school quarterback. How's that going?"

Barb glanced back to the bar. "Fine. He's working the bar here. Works part-time on the train tour too. We both do."

"Seth's a bartender? He was the catch of our class."

Barb turned to face Tara, a spark in her eyes. "He still is a catch."

"Sure, sure. Don't get upset." Tara patted her beehive. "Just that back then, he was really something." Tara took a hard look at Barb. "Hard to believe we were in the same class."

"Why is that?"

Tara laughed. "I'm just fighting back a little harder than you, honey. Other than diamonds, of course, a little bit of makeup and a good hairstylist are a girl's best friends."

"Sure. That and a good surgeon," Chantal whispered.

For once I agreed with her. Tara had more plastic in her than a toy factory.

"You haven't changed a bit, have you?" Barb moved away. "Still say anything you feel like saying."

Tara watched Barb go. "It's done me good so far." She looked around the room. "How do I get some food?" She looked at Chantal. "They're pretty chintzy with the portions. You see the itty-bitty snacks? Jeez, a shindig like this, you'd think they'd be a little more generous."

Chantal sniffed. "This isn't supposed to be your lunch, and they aren't being stingy. The purpose of the crackers and cheese is to cleanse your palate and help you decide how the wine pairs with food." Chantal turned to me. "Honestly, why am I even bothering?"

Oh, please. I turned to Tara. "Where's Big Dave?"

"He's around here somewhere." She spotted him across the room and cupped a hand around her mouth. "Hey, Big Dave, get on over here."

The yell startled most of the room. Several people jumped, and the man next to Chantal spilled wine on her sleeve and chest. He started to wipe it off, but his wife swatted his hand away. He began sputtering that he was only trying to be a gentleman, and she was always saying he didn't know how to act in public half the time. She grabbed his arm and they disappeared into the crowd.

"Well, this is just great." Chantal dabbed at her sleeve with a napkin. "This is cashmere."

"Relax. It's red. You can't even see it." Tara yelled again, "Big Dave, where are you?"

People started to back away, and I wanted to crawl under the bar. "Inside voice."

Tara turned to me. "What?"

"Use your inside voice."

"Why are you talking to me like I'm a child?"

I'd had enough. "Because apparently I need to. Do you understand you need to keep your voice down, or should I find a simpler way to say it?"

Chantal nodded. "Damn straight. This isn't a honky-tonk dive where you just yell across the room."

Without warning, Tara slapped her.

Chantal gasped.

I grabbed her by the arm. "Chantal, be the bigger person."

"Like hell."

Chantal dropped her glass and launched herself at Tara. Tara screamed and threw her own glass of wine. She missed Chantal but managed to get half of it on me. When I'd wiped the wine from my eyes, Chantal had Tara by the hair. She swung her around by the beehive, and Tara went flying into a group of tasters.

"Get it off! Get it off! For the love of God, somebody get it off!" Chantal danced around the room, flailing her arm. It looked like she was trying to shake off a Pomeranian.

Tara sat on the ground, screaming, her head covered with her hands, and I realized the Pomeranian was Tara's hairpiece.

I grabbed Chantal by the shoulder. "Stop! Let me get it." I pried at the wig. "It's tangled in your ring."

"I'm going to kill her!" Tara screamed as Big Dave pulled her up off the floor.

Five

"THAT'S enough!" Nobody moved as Antonia walked to the center of the room. "Sir, if you would, please take your wife outside."

"On my way, ma'am." Big Dave pulled Tara, still screaming, toward the front door.

"You." Antonia pointed at the hairpiece dangling at my side. "Give her back her . . . give her that back."

I held the hair by two fingers. "I didn't start it, you know. She slapped Chantal and it just sort of fell apart from there."

Chantal nodded. "That's exactly what happened. Penny came to my defense."

Antonia suppressed a grin. "You came to her defense?"

"Tara's drunk and was entirely out of line. You heard her yelling. We all did." I looked around the room for backup.

"It's true." Barb, the waitress, stood to one side. "Tara was the instigator."

The door opened and Connor walked up to me. "What'd I miss? Tara's out front crying how you and Chantal beat her up. Most of her makeup's running down her face, and she's missing half her hair. What the hell'd you do?"

"Nothing! She slapped Chantal. Chantal went after her, and her hair got caught on Chantal's ring."

"So how did you end up with it?" Connor asked.

"I got it off Chantal."

Chantal walked up. "She came to my defense."

"You came to her defense?"

I shrugged. "Lesser of two evils."

Chantal looked puzzled. "Two evil what?"

Antonia stamped her cane. "Enough! Connor, would you kindly tell that train person, Bill, that we have surely outstayed our welcome at this establishment?"

"He just reboarded the train to put the finishing touches on lunch. He said to have everyone meet in the dining car."

"Would you tell him we'll be right out? And please take Chantal. Seat her as far from Tara as you possibly can."

Antonia turned to the stylish man next to her. "Olympio, we should continue our conversation later, and I can't tell you how sorry I am for the disruption."

Olympio? I caught Antonia's eye and raised a brow but she ignored me. I studied the man at her side. He had a full head of silver hair and smooth dark skin. Maybe Italian.

"Indeed, we should, Antonia. The wine train has been a wonderful addition to the valley, and I cannot say enough about what it's done for my winery." His winery?

He moved in closer. "I would be happy for the invitation to travel to your winery and discover our newfound friendship under more informal terms."

Antonia's cheeks colored. "I'll call you."

He kissed her hand with a slight bow at the waist, and we walked to the front door.

When we'd stepped outside, I turned to her. "His winery?"

Antonia blushed even further. "Well, of course. That was Olympio Berninni."

"What do you mean, 'of course'? I didn't know you knew him."

Antonia waved her hand. "I met him years ago when I was still married. I remember him being very nice."

"Is his wife still alive?"

"No, she died the same year as my husband. I think a visit from Olympio would be lovely."

"Yes, I can tell by that look in your eyes. Don't be thinking any saucy thoughts, young lady."

Antonia raised herself up. "I've known you your entire life, Penelope Lively, but that doesn't mean I'll allow impertinence." She stopped and put her hand on my arm. "However, I want to thank you for defending Chantal. She can be difficult, and I appreciate your interjecting on her behalf."

I raised my hands, palms to the sky. "What can I say? This time Chantal really was the innocent party. That Tara is nothing but trouble."

We entered the dining car.

I turned to close the door, and Barb the waitress stood behind me. "Sorry, I didn't see you there. You said you worked on the train, but I didn't know you were joining our group."

She nodded. "We pick it up at Berninni, work lunch, then get dropped back off in the afternoon." She peered around the train car.

Tara dabbed at her eyes next to Big Dave in the far corner, while Chantal sat in the back of the compartment talking with Kim and Jim.

"Looks like things have calmed down for now," Barb said. "With Tara around, there's never a shortage of excitement."

"How long have you known her?"

Barb chewed on her lower lip. "My entire life. At least as long as I can remember. We grew up in the same neighborhood, the side of town where the people that work on the farms and vineyards live. I mean the people that work in the fields on the farms and vineyards. Tara got that part right. There is a distinction."

She glanced through the door to the car behind us, at the man behind the bar. "That's Seth. The three of us lived on the same street and were in the same class at school."

"And then after graduation Tara moved down South," I prodded.

Barb nodded. "It was right after Seth and I got married." She lifted her head. "I think she just stuck around to see if the star quarterback really would go through with it." She raised her thumb to her mouth as though to bite the nail, and then, with effort, lowered her arm. "Well, he did. And here we are."

She had a note of triumph in her voice, but there was a veiled look in her eyes as she glanced again at her husband. He stood behind the bar watching us, a frown on his face.

He was tall, with a two-day beard and a muscular build going to pot. He had a full head of thick dark hair and stunning blue eyes, and there was just enough left of his looks to see how he'd been the star on the football field or back in the halls of high school. Clearly he'd peaked early in life. He leaned against the counter, crooked his finger, and mouthed, "Come here."

Barb shivered. The thin blue sweater didn't look sufficient for the cold morning, and there was a mend in the shoulder sewn in neat little stitches. Mousy brown hair shot with gray hung limp to her shoulders. She tucked her hands behind her back out of view and rocked back on her heels.

"I need to get the wine poured for lunch."

I nodded, and she moved through the door to stand briefly between the cars, her lackluster hair barely affected by the wind. She pushed open the next car door and went to stand in front of the bar. I couldn't see Seth's face, but she nodded and took the bottles he handed her.

"What are you watching?" Connor stood behind me.

"I'm not sure." I turned. "Just a feeling."

There were tables for six along the train's windows. One side of the nearest table was occupied by Tara, Big Dave and Vance, and across from them sat Antonia and Chantal.

"Over here. I saved you a seat," Chantal said.

Sure, one seat between her and the window, and she wasn't looking at me to fill it. I rolled my eyes as Connor hesitated.

"I can decline and sit with you somewhere else."

"What, and make a scene? I'll be fine." I walked to the next table and took a seat right behind Big Dave.

Bill stood in front of the car while servers moved down the rows of tables. Passengers from other cars had joined us, and the car was full. Bill removed his hat and hooked a thumb into the shoulder strap of his overalls.

"Let's see what the chef has in store for us today." He pulled a pair of glasses from his pocket and studied the menu. "For appetizers, you have a choice of either eggplant and roasted garlic in crisp pastry with goat's-cheese cream, or a delicious lobster pâté with a dill mustard sauce." He peered over his glasses. "That last one's my personal favorite."

I was surrounded by a party of five travelling together, so as the servers took our orders, I let their conversation carry on without me. I picked up Big Dave's voice above the hum of chatter and clanking silver as our appetizers arrived.

"Now, I'm not sayin', darlin', not to have a good time. I just think maybe we need to have a little water with lunch, maybe some coffee."

"What's this 'we' business? Unless you got a fish in your pocket that wants your damn water, mind your own self. I'm fine."

This was great. I could be as nosy as I wanted and nobody could tell. I eased my chair back a few inches.

"All I'm pointing out is that you may have a little more fun if you can actually remember some of it tomorrow." Big Dave sounded a bit testy.

I glanced over my left shoulder at Tara. She still had puffy cheeks from her cry earlier, and the beehive clung to the top of her head at a weird angle. *Very* attractive.

Barb stopped at my table. "Can I offer you a taste of

Berninni's Fumé Blanc? It goes really well with the lobster pâté."

"Yeah, sure. Whatever." I leaned back a bit in my chair.

"Well, Dad, have you had enough?" Vance's voice came from over my right shoulder. "How long are you going to let her embarrass the family name?"

"She hasn't come close to the messes I've cleaned up behind you, and you know it." Big Dave's voice held none of the humor I'd come to associate with him. "She's harmless. Which is more than I can say for you. You almost hit that lady."

"Don't start in on that again, okay? I'm telling you she walked right into the street, or maybe she tripped on the curb. Either way, she was on the ground in front of me without my even touching her."

Big Dave lowered his voice. "Too bad you can't say that about the last person you hit."

Did Vance make a habit of running people over? I pushed my seat farther back.

"Even with today's behavior, Tara's got a long way to go before she matches your track record."

"Look, I understand having a little fun," Vance said. "A man your age deserves to sit back and enjoy all his hard work. I just don't see why you had to marry her, and I really don't get letting her spend all your money on this crazy train bull—"

"That's enough." Big Dave's voice was low, and he spoke each word with precision, the anger behind them clear. "Tara grew up here. This means something to her. If this is what she wants, it's what she gets."

Big Dave dropped his voice even lower, and I strained

to hear. "And your screwups over the years have cost me a lot more than this, so sit back and be cordial to Tara, or I'll have you dropped off and you can drive that car of yours right out of here."

"Okay, okay. Just relax. It's your money."

"Just so you remember it."

I turned in my seat, pretending to enjoy the view. The vineyards are never dull, even toward the end of the season. Today the sky was a clear blue, a shade I've only seen here and in Tuscany. Wild mustard, a carpet of golden yellow, grew across the vineyard and over the distant hills.

Big Dave turned to Tara and rubbed her arm, but she had her eyes pasted to the window. "Come on, darlin', this is for you. I want you to have a good time."

Tara pushed his hand away. "I think maybe owning a winery would be fun." She turned to Antonia at the far end of the table. "Is it fun?"

I turned my chair almost entirely around and gave up any pretense I wasn't listening.

"You have to believe in your bones it's what you want to do," Antonia said. "If it is, then it can be very rewarding, but you must remember, it's a tremendous amount of work. You don't take it on without deep consideration."

"Well, we'd have people for the hard stuff," Tara said.

Antonia raised a brow. "It isn't quite that simple."

"Sure it is." Tara signaled for more wine from the server. "I know better than anyone that wineries have people for the tough work. From what I remember, the owner just threw lots of parties and travelled." She turned to Big Dave. "We should think about it anyway."

Vance snorted, stood and made his way toward the bar at the far end of the car.

The spot next to Big Dave was now empty, so I poked him on the shoulder. "Mind if I join you?"

"Sure. Glad to have you."

Antonia pointed across the table at the untouched plate. "Are you sure he won't be coming back? He didn't touch his lunch."

"Ladies, he can figure it out for himself." Big Dave gestured to Barb to remove the plate.

Six

AFTER lunch we made our way forward to the bar, where Vance sat at the counter.

He spotted us and stood. "I'm going back to my seat." He pushed past Big Dave and left through the rear doors.

Big Dave gestured to a sofa. "Tara, why don't you wait here a minute. I want to clear things up with my son, one way or the other."

"Sure. I'll be here." She plopped down as Big Dave followed Vance from the car.

I moved to sit next to Antonia on the sofa opposite, while Chantal joined Connor at the window.

Bill walked up to me. "How was lunch?"

"Excellent."

Antonia nodded in agreement.

"It's amazing what they can do on a swaying train."

"Our chef has worked his entire career on the rails. He's used to it."

I ran my hand down the arm of the sofa. "I love this burgundy velvet. It looks original, but it's in perfect condition."

"We took pains to match the original fabrics and all of the woodwork. The mahogany walls to the carved sofas, like the one you're sitting on, are all unique to the Pullman line." Bill ran his palm across the bottom of the crystals that dangled from the chandelier, and a soft tinkle of glass filled the room. "We tried to keep everything as authentic as possible."

"Right down to that adorable outfit you're wearing." Tara eyed the overalls. "You look like a cartoon character. I just can't remember which one. Maybe Elmer Fudd."

Bill tried to laugh it off, but his cheeks flamed. He removed his cap and twisted it in his hands. "Well, I've got to be going. I need to get some more wine for the bar." He turned and walked through the door and out onto the vestibule.

"That was really mean and unnecessary," I said.

"You would think he'd heard it before," Tara said.

"What an unspeakable bitch you are," Chantal said from across the room.

I nodded in agreement. Chantal and I had our share of quarrels, but there was a big difference between the annoyance I often felt with Chantal and Tara's intentional cruelty.

"I'm not concerned with what you think, and I'm done with this conversation." Tara walked to the bar.

Kim and Jim were deep in conversation at the far end, and Tara settled on a stool just a few feet from us. Seth stood behind the counter wiping glassware.

"Well, Mr. Quarterback, you still look as good as you did back in high school. How about pouring me a glass of red." Tara tipped her head, twirling a curl that hadn't made it back into the reattached beehive.

"Sure." Seth poured her a glass and leaned against the back counter to watch her. He crossed his arms, cupping his fists behind his biceps, which made the muscles strain against the tight-fitting shirt.

"I wonder if he practices that pose at home in front of the mirror." Antonia didn't miss much.

"I'm sure of it."

Seth grabbed a bar towel and rubbed the counter around Tara. She leaned in, resting her top section against the railing as Seth bent over the bar. Tara whispered something in his ear and Seth laughed.

"If Big Dave comes back while this is going on, it'll get real interesting," I said to Antonia.

Seth dropped the cloth on the counter, and his hand slowly made its way to Tara, his fingers running down her arm.

"It appears something even more interesting is about to happen." Antonia nudged me and I shifted my eyes. From the rear of the car, Barb hurried forward, a tray in her hands.

"Stop it! Stop it right now!" Barb threw the tray on the counter and turned to Tara. "You think you can just come back here and start it up all over again? You can't. I won't let you!"

Seth reached across the counter and grabbed Barb's wrist.

"Please, Seth. You're hurting me."

"Then stop making a scene. You go back to cleaning tables, and we'll talk about this later."

"Let her go," I said.

Seth just held her by the arm as Barb tried to pull away.

"Let her go," I repeated, louder this time. I admit I wanted Connor to hear. I wasn't about to take Seth on alone and was grateful to catch Connor turn in his chair at the sound of my voice.

Seth saw Connor as well. "Everything's fine." He let go and raised both hands in mock surrender as Barb hugged her wrist to her chest. "No worries over here."

Tara gestured with her now-empty glass. "I like that. No worries. Ya know what would help that? Another one of these." She rested her elbows on the bar, cupping her chin in her palm.

"Anyway, you don't have anything to worry about now, Barb," she said a few moments later as Seth refilled her glass. "Seth and I had our fun a long time ago. Besides"—she took a sip—"these days I can afford much more expensive toys."

Seth froze behind the counter. One hand tightened on the wine bottle. He gripped the edge of the bar with the other. "Don't ever refer to me as a toy again." With effort, he released the bar and stepped back.

"Barb, I'm going to get a bin for these dirty glasses. Keep an eye on things."

Barb nodded.

Tara tipped her glass and finished the wine in one gulp. "Mr. Sensitive. I'm tired and going back to my seat."

"Good riddance," Antonia said as Tara walked from the car. "She's nothing but trouble."

Connor moved to follow her. "She may be trouble, but in the condition she's in, I don't want her moving between cars by herself. The vestibules are a little tricky. When I'm done, I'll come back for you, Antonia."

"Oh, for heaven's sake. I hardly need help." The train gave a lurch as it rounded a corner, and when it straightened, Antonia held up her palm. "Very well, I see the logic. We'll wait here for you."

"A real gentleman," Chantal grabbed Connor by the arm. "I'll head back with you now." They moved through the door, Chantal liberally using Connor to help her across the vestibule.

"You should have told Chantal to stay here for now," I said. "The farther we can keep her and Tara apart, the better."

"My daughter's a grown woman. The days she'd listen to me on matters such as this are long gone. And anyway, if I had a suspicious nature, I just might think Connor is the one you'd like to keep her away from."

I sniffed. "I have no idea what you're talking about. Although she did seem to need a lot of Connor's help to walk three feet across a vestibule she managed alone just fine a few moments ago."

Antonia smiled. "Well, as long as it doesn't bother you any."

"Can I get you anything?" Barb stood next to me.

"I'll have a glass of whatever you're pouring."

Barb nodded to the back where Kim and Jim sat. "I'll be back in a minute. I'm going for a bottle of Caymus Cabernet for them, if you'd like a glass of that. Aren't they cute? They've been holding hands and looking at each other more than the scenery." Barb's voice held a wistful note. "Here they come now."

"Isn't this beautiful?" Kim gave us that high-wattage smile. "I love Chicago, but we don't have mountains like this. And these redwoods! I love the smell too, all earthy and fresh, although," she rubbed her bare arms, "it is a little chilly. Jim, would you mind grabbing my sweater? I left it on my seat."

Jim kissed her forehead. "I'll be right back."

After he left, Kim turned to us. "I understand you both own wineries. How wonderful."

"It can be," I said, "when the rain holds off, and the summer is just hot enough, and some new pest doesn't come along, or the vagaries of the market don't change, suddenly making the Merlot you've been banking on less desirable for some inexplicable reason . . . Sure, other than that, it's a ton of fun."

"What Penny is doing a poor job of saying is that we're basically farmers, with all the same concerns that haunt most farmers. We hope for good weather, heavy production, excellent timing and a little bit of luck. It's when we turn the fruit into wine that the magic really happens."

I nodded. "Don't get me wrong. It's difficult but worth it. It's something you do for love."

"Well, I think it's just—"

Whatever Kim would have said was lost in the squeal of brakes. The train swayed to one side and somewhere a whistle blew. Its shrill cry went on for several seconds. Antonia held on to the sofa arm, and I braced against the windowsill as Kim grabbed my arm. Dishes hit the floor in the kitchen, and wineglasses flew across the bar. Finally, the train lurched to a halt.

"What on earth?" Antonia was on her feet and heading for the door just as Connor stepped through.

"Is everyone okay?" Connor caught my eye.

"Of course we're okay. Why are you looking at me?"

"Well, I've seen your reflexes and those catlike movements of yours."

Antonia hid a smile behind a small cough. "Everyone's fine here."

He nodded. "I'm going back to our car if you don't need me. I thought I heard somebody scream."

"Go, go. We'll be fine," Antonia said. "So far this trip hasn't been what I anticipated."

"Let's just see what's happened before we panic," I said.

"I never panic." Antonia straightened. "Come with me."

Kim and I followed Antonia through the dining area.

Barb stood next to the dish cupboard holding a plate. When she saw us, she set it down. "The entire stack went flying."

Broken dishes covered the floor around her.

"Do you know what's happened?" I said.

She shook her head. "We've been stopped before, but never like that. Usually it's engine trouble and the train comes to a slow stop. This time it was like somebody threw the brakes."

I turned at the clank of bottles. Seth stood right behind me. "You can pick that up later. Get the door for me."

Barb scooted around me, keeping her eyes down. "Sorry. I have to go."

"He really is an odious man," Antonia said after the door closed.

We crossed the dining area and stepped through to the vestibule. Bill was standing there looking down the side of the train. He opened the door for us.

"Somebody pulled the emergency cord. I need to check around and make sure everything's okay. No reason to be alarmed."

"Um, well, we'll see." Antonia said as Bill moved to the front of the car.

"Did any of you pull the cord?" As we each shook our head in denial, Bill took off his hat and wiped his forehead. "I can't understand it. None of the passengers up front admit doing it either. What in the blazes is going on?"

"I'm beginning to wonder that myself," Antonia said. "Well, let's take our seats."

Big Dave stood up from his seat in front and looked down the aisle. "Where's Tara?" He looked at Vance.

Vance shrugged and turned to the window.

Jim handed Kim her sweater and looked around. "I just saw her a couple of minutes ago. She was standing by the back door."

"Wait a minute," Antonia said. "I don't see Chantal either."

"Oh, great." I pinched the bridge of my nose. "That's just what we need. The two of them together somewhere."

"That's strange." Jim moved through the car. "The last I saw Chantal, she was near the back door also."

"This just keeps getting better and better." I walked

to the rear of the car, stopping at the storage closet. "Big Dave, can you check in there?"

"Got it." He pushed open the door and stepped inside.

I moved out onto the vestibule between our car and the caboose, with Connor close behind. I peered through the door window. Boxes stacked earlier along the walls behind netting were now scattered among toppled dining chairs, and the door leading out to the rear platform stood open.

"Things are a mess in there, but I don't see anyone. We need to go in to be sure." I shoved against the door. "It won't open." I pressed my face against the glass and looked down. "There's something against it."

"Here, let me try," Connor said.

I gave him room and he pushed against the door as I reached through the opening.

"It's a bunch of tablecloths. Let me move them." I shoved the pile to one side and Connor stepped into the car.

"We need to get these boxes out of the way," I said.

"Somebody's purse is here." Connor held up a Gucci bag.

"That's Tara's," I said. "She had it earlier. You don't think she's under this stuff, do you?"

"I hope not, but I don't know where else she'd be. Last time I saw her, she was sitting in the cabin. She isn't there, and she didn't go back past us. This is the only other choice."

I walked to the rear door leading to the caboose platform, moving boxes as I went. "I don't like this door being open. Where can they be?"

I had reached the door when I heard a moan from the floor. I lifted the chair nearest me. The first thing I saw was a red sleeve.

"Help me. It's Chantal." She was on her back, with her head to one side. She moaned again and turned her head.

I took one look and felt dizzy.

"She's bleeding."

I turned away as Connor came up beside me.

"It looks like somebody hit her pretty good, but there isn't much blood at all."

"It doesn't matter. It's enough." The familiar sour taste filled my mouth as the world started to tip.

Connor pushed me down. "Just sit there for a couple of minutes. Looks like your blood phobia hasn't gotten any better."

"It's only been a few months since, well, since it started." A late-night discovery involving a body and a lot of blood was responsible for this reaction.

"It's only a little cut above her eye," Connor said. "I've cleaned it off. You can look now."

I turned so I could see her.

Her eyes fluttered open and locked on mine.

"Can you move?"

"I think so." She cautiously straightened her limbs. "Nothing's broken, but I'm not sure I can stand." Chantal held her arm out to Connor. "I think you might need to help me."

"Put your arms around my neck." Connor picked her up as if she were featherlight. She was pale, but a soft flush of color tinted her cheeks as Connor pressed her against his chest. "I'll get her back to her seat, then come back."

My head was clearing. "I'm going to look around. This just doesn't feel right. Chantal, why where you here?"

"When she's feeling better we can ask her. I'll be back in a minute. Don't move."

Chantal's ponytail bobbed as she rested her head on Connor's shoulder. He must have left her in the nearest seat because he stepped back into the cabin a moment later.

"This is wrong." I walked to the rear door as he came up behind me. "This shouldn't be open."

"Maybe the train coming to such a fast stop swung it open."

"That's just it. Everything on the train went flying forward." I moved the door back and forth. "This opens to the outside. If anything, the braking would have slammed the door shut."

Connor stepped out onto the platform. "Well, these gates are all closed, and the safety chains are in place. At least we don't have to worry about anyone having fallen off."

A reflection some distance behind the train caught my eye. I couldn't look away even as the sour taste returned and I went numb. "No, we don't have to worry about that."

"I just said that." Connor looked closely at me. "Are you all right? You look terrible."

I tried to push air into my lungs as sweat dotted my upper lip. Tara was stretched across the tracks. I couldn't see her face but I recognized the sweater. She didn't move, and even from that distance it was easy to see why. Her body had rolled and now rested on one side, but her head lay at an odd angle. Necks weren't supposed to do that, and the buzzing in my ears got louder. I pointed to her.

"I'm fine. But that could be a problem."

Seven

Y heart was banging around in my chest, and I knew Connor was saying something because his lips were moving.

"I can't hear you. What's making all that noise?" Everything started to tilt and slow down.

Connor caught me right before I hit the ground. We stayed like that until the roar in my ears stopped.

"Are you going to pass out?"

I shook my head.

"Are you sure?"

"Let me just stay here for a second. Did you see how she was? How she's turned? She's facing the wrong way." My hands were clammy and, once again, the world tipped. I closed my eyes.

"Just breathe and try not to think about it."

After a few deep gulps, I grabbed the railing and pulled

myself upright, keeping my back toward Tara's body. Connor stroked my hair and I concentrated on getting air into my lungs; breathe in, breathe out.

When I'd calmed down, I stood and headed back into the caboose. "We need to tell somebody. The train can't leave this spot now."

Bill entered the cabin and heard me as he picked his way through the caboose. "What a mess, but I don't see why the train can't leave." He pulled at the visor of his cap. "Nothing here is broken or can't be fixed."

"That isn't exactly true." I pointed back over my shoulder.

Bill gazed out the door. His face went white, and he wiped at the sweat that dotted his upper lip.

"Oh, this is bad, this is really bad." He took off his cap and crushed it in his hands. "I need to call the police. Don't know what I'm going to tell the other passengers." He swallowed. "Jeez, I've got her husband looking all over for her. How do I tell him?"

Connor stepped forward. "I'll go. He needs to find out before we tell anyone else in the car. I don't want him to hear it from one of the other passengers." He turned to close the door. "Don't let anyone in here."

Bill nodded then turned to me. "We don't actually have a procedure for this kind of thing."

I was calmer now and able to think. "For now, I'd just keep everyone in their cars. Whatever happened back here, no one from the front cars was involved. If they were, we'd have seen them pass through our car."

Bill nodded. "Makes sense. We can be fairly certain nobody from up front was back here. But it sounds like you think it wasn't an accident. Tell the truth, I'm inclined to agree with you. I'd like to hear what you're thinking."

I tapped at the rear door with my forefinger and it slowly moved. "We found this door open. As hard as the train stopped, it should have been slammed shut. Did someone go through the door after the train stopped? Also"—I pointed to the rear platform—"all the gates are closed and locked. If she fell through, wouldn't one of them be open?"

"These are safety gates," Bill said, "something we take mighty seriously round here." He stepped out onto the platform and rattled the gate nearest him. "No, these are all still securely locked. This wasn't an accident. I need to call the police."

"There's something I don't understand, though," I said. "Who pulled the brake cord? Wouldn't a murderer want as much room as possible between us and the body? And when we first tried to get into the caboose, the door was blocked. Tablecloths fell against it when the train braked. Nobody went out that door after we stopped. Wait a minute," I closed my eyes and swayed. "Nobody went in or out that door after the brakes were hit. I need to talk to Chantal."

"WHAT do you mean, you can't remember anything?" I asked. "Come on, Chantal, think."

She shifted in her seat and stared at the ceiling. "Don't you think I'm trying? All I know for sure is that someone hit me over the head. I don't remember anything after that."

"What made you go into the caboose to begin with?"

"There was a note. It said 'Meet me in the caboose.'"

"What note? Who left it?"

"I don't know. I went to get some water. When I got back, there it was, folded on my chair."

Antonia raised her brow. "What on earth would possess you to follow through on something like that?"

"I thought I knew who it was from." Chantal glanced up, searched out and settled on Connor. "I thought it would be fine."

"Yes, I see," Antonia said. "Well, the police should be here shortly."

"Where's the note now?" I asked.

"That's what I'd like to know." Chantal shook her head. "I swear I stuck it in my back pocket. I've looked everywhere. It's gone."

A muffled sob filled the air. Big Dave sat in the corner seat earlier occupied by Tara. He appeared to have collapsed inward. His head rocked from side to side, and his broad shoulders shook with silent tears.

Vance sat next to him, his hand on Big Dave's shoulder. He murmured something to his father and turned away, reaching into his shirt pocket to remove a phone. He flipped through and texted with one hand.

"Vance doesn't look very upset," I said. "Although he does seem nervous about something. Look how he's tapping his foot."

He returned the phone to his pocket and drummed his fingers against the arm of the chair, stopping only to down the glass of wine that rested on the tray table before him.

Across from him, Kim and Jim sat with their heads close together. Kim wiped her eyes every few moments as

Jim brushed the hair off her face, giving her a small kiss on the brow.

Connor pulled me to one side. "I saw the look Chantal gave me. She thinks the note telling her to go into the caboose was from me. I'm sure I don't need to tell you I didn't ask her to meet me anywhere."

I nodded. "It would be better if she could find it. The handwriting might tell us something, and without it . . ."

Connor picked up the conversation. "Without it, there's just Chantal's word someone wanted to meet her. Without it, it looks like she followed Tara into the caboose all on her own. The crucial thing is to prove Tara's death was an accident. That would lessen the impact of Chantal being there."

I rubbed my temples. "That's going to be a problem then. The safety gate was closed and latched, which means someone had to lock it after Tara was, well, off the train."

"You mean pushed."

I nodded, thinking of the way Tara's twisted body rested just a short distance away.

"Also, remember when we entered the caboose?" I said. "The pile of tablecloths blocked the door. If someone else had been in there when the brakes were hit, those would have been moved when they left. Remember we had to push them out of the way to get in."

"Maybe someone from one of the other cars killed her, pulled the brake, and when the train stopped, actually got off the train and ran back to a different vestibule, say, in front of the dining car."

I shook my head. "I thought of that, but it only works if the person left the caboose when the train was stopped.

You certainly can't get back here from the outside while the train is going. No, they'd need to go through this car, and nobody from the front of the train has been back here. That means someone in this group killed her."

"There must be something we're missing," Connor said. "It couldn't be Chantal. It just doesn't make any sense."

"We both agree on that. She's a pain, but nothing more." I scanned the room. "The Chicago couple don't seem to have any reason to want Tara dead. They said they've never been to California before. That leaves Tara's husband and stepson and, for my money, I'm inclined to think it's the stepson. It was pretty clear Vance didn't like her, and Big Dave seems genuinely upset. For all Tara's craziness, I got the impression he was infatuated with her at the very least."

Jim walked over to Barb, who stood silently in the corner.

"Can I get some tea for my wife?"

Barb nodded.

I did a mental head slap. "Things just got more complicated. Barb and Seth come and go between this car and the dining and bar cars. They were in here earlier."

"So they had access, but we still need to answer why either one of them would want to kill Tara."

"We both saw how jealous Barb got when Tara was flirting with Seth in the bar. If she could have, she would have thrown Tara off the train right then. As far as Tara and Seth, there was a lot of sexual tension between them."

Connor held up his hand. "Okay, I'll buy that, in a fit of jealousy, Barb could have pushed Tara. Love triangles have always been a great motive for murder, but Seth wouldn't kill Tara just because he's still attracted to her. That's not a motive."

"Tara made him furious later in the same conversation. You couldn't hear it from across the room, but he was enraged."

"Enough to kill her?"

"It's possible. Tara dismissed Seth when she saw that Barb was jealous. Said she could buy better toys now. The look Seth gave Tara was chilling."

"That must have stung his pride," Connor said. "Guy like him, doesn't have anything going for himself now, still grasping that illusion of being the one all the women want. I bet he didn't much like being called a toy, and a second-rate one at that."

"It wasn't just that one incident. Seth has this anger right below the surface. You can feel it when you're around him. When he grabbed Barb's wrist, you could tell it wasn't the first time. She doesn't ever quite look him in the eyes, and she shrinks away when he's around. Her nails are bitten to the quick."

"And yet you said she defended Seth to Tara."

"I think she's holding on to the past as much as Seth is," I said, "still pretending that landing him back in high school was a good thing. In reality, she should get away from him, as far and as fast as she can."

"So there are several people who had possible reasons to fight with Tara."

I nodded. "Better reasons than Chantal had."

"Still, her being in the caboose doesn't look good. We know her well enough to dismiss the idea she had anything to do with Tara's death. I wouldn't be so sure the police will be as quick to give her the benefit of the doubt."

A large man walked down the aisle toward us. In the heat of the day, he wore a three-piece dark wool suit. Standing well over six feet, he towered over the two uniformed officers who flanked him.

"I think we're about to find out," I said.

Eight

A N hour later I had a good idea of exactly what Police Chief Lawrence Harding thought.

"I understand you live near Chantal Martinelli. Has she ever been violent in the past?"

"Absolutely not." Crazy, sure, but violent? Never. "Mr. Harding, Chantal didn't kill anyone. She just met Tara. Why would she kill her?"

"Actually, my title is Police Chief Lawrence Harding, and I understand from the others on the train, and specifically from those in your car, that Miss Martinelli and the victim had a physical altercation shortly before the murder. I believe you were there."

"Yes. There was a bit of a disagreement." He'd focused on Chantal much too early, and I didn't like it. Alarm bells started going off in my head. "It wasn't anything, really."

"Maybe, maybe not. Sounds like a catfight between a

couple of women who maybe had a bit too much to drink. Normally I wouldn't put this much weight on an altercation like that."

"So why are you?"

He narrowed his eyes.

"I mean, it was a silly little argument, certainly not worth killing someone over."

He rocked back on his heels. "The person in charge of the train pointed out that nobody else could have gotten in or out of the caboose after the brake was hit."

"That must have been Bill."

The chief consulted his notes and nodded. "He said you went back there and found the door blocked by tablecloths."

Terrific. I breathed deeply, forcing my voice to remain calm. "We found Chantal unconscious with blood coming from a cut on her forehead."

"I only have your word for that."

"It sounds like you think I'm lying."

"Not at all, but perhaps you were fooled." He stroked the small moustache that lined his upper lip. "You're possibly too close to the suspect to remain neutral."

"So Chantal's a suspect? It sounds like she needs to talk to an attorney."

He waved his hand dismissively. "At this point, technically, everyone on the train is a suspect but, of course, I'm paying greater attention to those of you in the rear compartment."

"That makes sense," I said. "The only people who knew Tara before today were all in that last car. And no one from the front of the train came into our car, which is the only way to get into the caboose."

Chief Harding continued as though I hadn't said a thing. "No, someone in that last car is my target. I don't mind saying, however, that Miss Martinelli is of special interest to me at this point."

"If it makes a difference, Chief Lucas of the Cypress Cove Police Department knows Chantal Martinelli personally. You might want to give him a call."

Chief Harding wrote the name down. "Cypress Cove. Where is that?"

"Just south of Monterey, along the coast."

"Well, I might give him a call, or I might not. This is my investigation and I'll take care of things my way." He smoothed his moustache. "That whole central coast area. Lots of wineries down there too?"

I nodded. "The Martinellis own the largest winery in the region. Antonia Martinelli is on this trip with her daughter. I own the winery next door to them."

Harding smacked his notepad against his palm. "I don't mind telling you the wineries and the folks that clog our streets coming to see them are a pain in my side. The politicians let them do whatever they want because they bring in tourists and their money. I, for one, wish we had fewer wineries and more peace. This winery train has been nothing but a nuisance. I can't tell you the amount of time I've lost at the rail crossing waiting for the thing. And when it goes by, people are waving and laughing, like I give a damn how much fun they're having. I've got work to do."

"It seems pretty quiet around here. How much crime actually occurs?"

"Enough. For example, I've got a murder to investigate, so if you'll excuse me."

That was it? He hadn't asked anything that might point to motives or suspects beyond Chantal. "Um, Chief Harding, before the murder I observed—"

"You observed?" He chuckled. "I think someone has been watching too many made-for-TV movies. If I have anything else I need from you, I'll let you know."

I ground my teeth. "What should we do in the meantime?"

"In the meantime," Police Chief Lawrence Harding placed his hands on his hips, "you all return to your hotel and get comfortable. You aren't leaving town anytime soon."

"THIS is quite impossible." Antonia paced. We'd just returned from a quick trip to the hospital with Chantal, and the four of us now sat in the hotel lobby.

"The good news is that your injury wasn't serious," I said.

"It still hurt." Chantal lay back on the cushions. Very dramatic. "I mean, I was attacked by an unknown assailant."

"You're right, of course," I said. "I'm just glad you're okay."

Antonia tightened the grip on the silver handle of her cane and thumped it hard against the tile floor. "She's hardly okay, Penny. According to that police chief, she's under suspicion for murder. He's made up his mind Chantal is responsible." Antonia waved her cane in Chantal's general direction. "Why in heaven's sake did you have that altercation with that . . . that person? You've given this police chief exactly what he was looking for: a motive."

Chantal looked up, the glitter of unshed tears in the corners of her eyes. She'd been crying earlier, but without the blotchy red skin, swollen nose and running mascara that accompany me when I have a good cry. There was fear in her eyes, but they weren't red; they shone a startling green. She chewed at her lower lip as she tugged on the end of her ponytail.

"Tara hit me first. I was just trying to protect myself. Right, Penny?"

"She's right. Tara just hauled off and slapped Chantal. She needed to be locked up."

"The only one I'm concerned about being locked up is Chantal." At Antonia's words, Chantal paled.

"Do you think the police will arrest me?"

Antonia sniffed. "I wasn't overly impressed with this police chief."

Connor nodded. "I think we all agree he's no Chief Lucas. He strikes me as insecure, and insecurity can make a man dangerous."

He turned to me. "I hate to say it, espccially since I've told you often enough you should leave these things for the police, but this guy doesn't appear to be looking at anyone other than Chantal."

"I thought the same thing," I said. "He didn't even ask about any of the other passengers."

Connor tapped his chin. "We all know of your, um, proclivity for finding bodies and the murderers that cause them."

"Two. I've found two bodies. Well, three, if you count Tara today, but anybody could have spotted her."

"My point is that nobody is looking very hard at

anyone else for this murder." He looked at Chantal. "We might be her best shot."

Chantal looked at me and broke into a fit of crying, the kind that really leaves its mark. Mascara streaked her cheeks and tears left darkened spots on her cashmere sweater. "I'm going to jail!"

Before I could thank Chantal for her vote of confidence, Antonia pulled her up by the arm. "Come with me. Let's get some room service." As she passed by me, she leaned over. "I'm relying on you, Penny. My girl didn't do this."

I caught her eye and nodded. Antonia was right. Chantal was a lot of things, but she wasn't a killer. We watched them leave, turning the corner to Chantal's ground-floor room. When they'd disappeared, I turned to Connor. "Want to get a bite?"

He nodded and we crossed the lobby to the restaurant. In contrast to the old-world charm of the hotel, the restaurant and bar were cutting edge. Clean lines of glass and chrome, with black leather barstools and polished onyx floors. The music in the background was a hip jazz-fusion sound. We were seated and had just given our drink order when Vance entered the bar. He still had on the polo shirt and shorts he wore earlier in the day. Taking a seat at the bar, he ordered a drink and pulled out his phone.

"Here, switch sides with me," I said to Connor.

"Why?"

"Vance is on the phone and I can't hear what he's saying."

Vance laughed about something and I nudged Connor.

"He sure doesn't seem upset about losing his stepmother. I'm missing it! Change places!"

"I think I'm going to regret supporting you getting involved in this."

"Oh, like I need your blessing? Please."

"You won't be able to hear him. I can't make out what he's saying as it is, and if we get up and switch places, he'll notice and lower his voice."

"Fine." I put my napkin on the table.

"Where are you going?"

"To see what they have on tap, or get something at the bar. That is, if I need to. Hopefully he won't notice me." I stood.

"That's doubtful. You're hardly stealthlike."

"Don't be sarcastic. Maybe I'll surprise you."

"Sure. You're five-nine. You'll stick out like a blonde thumb."

I held my finger to my lips. "Shhh. It's all in the attitude." I pushed my chair back and positioned myself against a pillar.

Connor held his hand up to his face. I think he might have been laughing. I moved to the corner and watched Vance. His elbows were propped on the bar. He picked at a bowl of peanuts with one hand and held the phone with the other.

"Give the old man a few days. He'll be fine."

I crept a few feet closer, stopping behind a potted palm.

"Nah, they weren't married for very long. And at least this way she won't be spending any more of Dad's money." Vance listened, then laughed into the phone. "It leaves more for me, that's for sure."

As Vance hung up, I backed away from the palm. I was fine until I felt a solid nudge right in my waist. I turned just in time to realize it was the edge of a tray loaded with wineglasses. The little bitty thing carrying it didn't stand a chance. I had a good ten inches and forty pounds on her. I grabbed for the tray but only succeeded in slowing the inevitable cascade of glassware that went flying across the bar floor. I glanced over at Connor and he had his face covered. I was pretty sure he wasn't laughing any longer. I froze as Vance looked up at the ruckus. The poor waitress waved away my offer to help with alarm, and I joined him at the bar.

"Nice move back there," he snickered.

Wow, I really didn't like this guy. I took a seat. "You seem to be having fun. Not at all upset about losing your stepmother, are you?"

Vance shrugged. "I didn't even know her. Dad thought this trip would change that. Oh well, not a chance of that now."

"But still." I remembered Big Dave's tears. "For your father's sake, I'm surprised you aren't at least putting on a show of grief."

"In front of him I will be." He pulled out a packet of cigarettes and offered me one.

"You can't smoke in here. You pretty much can't smoke indoors anywhere in California."

"Damn crazy state." He put the pack away.

"I'm surprised you smoke, being an athlete."

"You follow tennis?" He leaned in. Apparently the topic of conversation was now to his liking.

"Not really. I'm not very coordinated."

He snorted. "Yeah, you pretty much confirmed that a couple of minutes ago."

Such a charmer. "So, do you play professionally?"

"Nah, just the club tournaments. I didn't get to the pros. I have the talent, but my dad wouldn't let me play full-time. Put me to work in his dealerships. With a little bit of sponsorship, I'd have had a real shot."

I guess that was my cue to feel sorry for him. Oddly enough, I couldn't muster any sympathy.

"Please give your dad my regards. I'd offer them to you as well, but it looks like you're just relieved Tara isn't spending any more of your dad's money."

"So you listen in on phone calls too? Nice."

"I wouldn't be so quick to judge. After all, you think it's great news that the woman your dad loved has been murdered. He must be heartbroken."

"What do you mean murdered? I thought she got drunk and fell off the train. That sounds like her."

"Well, she didn't. She was pushed."

"How do you know?"

"Because of the safety chain on the platform gate. Someone pushed her and then reattached it. The part I don't understand is the emergency cord. If it hadn't been pulled, the train wouldn't have stopped within sight of Tara's body. It might have been hours before she was found."

"You don't say." Vance signaled for another drink.

"You know, whoever pushed her must have had a motive. Her wasting the family money sounds like a pretty good one to me."

His hand stopped over the peanuts. "Whoa. You don't think I had anything to do with it, do you?"

"It doesn't matter what I think. The first thing the police look for is motive, and I'd say yours is better than most. I heard you at lunch with your dad—"

"Eavesdropping there and now here." Vance shook his head. "You might want to reconsider where you're sticking your nose."

"Maybe you should reconsider what you say in public, especially with a murder to solve. You made it pretty clear at lunch you thought your dad investing in the train was . . ." I rested my chin on my forefinger. "I think you referred to it as bull. Tara also said that owning a winery would be fun. If something like that were to happen, well now, we're talking about a real drain on your—I mean your father's financial resources."

Vance stood and I got a good look at him. He seemed larger than I remembered, maybe because now he was pressed close to me. He gripped the back of the barstool, his wrists thick and muscular from years of gripping a tennis racket. Veins bulged in his tanned neck. I could feel his breath on my cheek.

"But now that isn't going to happen, is it?" he said. "I don't like your line of thinking, and you won't be sharing it with anyone, will you?"

"Sharing what?" Connor came up beside us. All the times I've been glad to see him paled compared to the joy I felt at finding him at my shoulder. He was the same height as Vance and equally matched in strength. What gave Connor the edge was the anger that drew his brows together, his jaw trembling as he clenched his teeth.

My money was for throwing Vance over the bar, but I didn't get a vote. Vance had the sense to diffuse the situation. He took a step back. "No problem here. Penny and I were just discussing a theory she has on why I might be glad my stepmother is dead." He placed a hand on his chest.

"I'm not glad, of course. Not at all, and that's why I was telling . . . I mean asking Penny not to share her theories. People sometimes get the wrong idea." Vance turned to go. "I'm going down to the pool. Catch you later."

He walked away.

"You still going to share any of those theories?" Connor asked.

"Of course. To you and the police and anyone else who will listen."

Nine

"WHAT was that about?" Antonia walked up to the bar.

"Vance trying to pretend he's sorry Tara's dead. No matter what he claims, he's relieved she's gone, especially since she was busy spending his inheritance right out from under him. I heard him talking with Big Dave at lunch on the train before storming out. It doesn't matter what he says now, he was really angry with Tara then."

"It's not going to be easy to prove Vance had anything to do with Tara's death," Connor said. "It's one thing to say something offhand during an argument. Quite another to be incensed to the point of pushing your stepmother off a moving train."

"Either way, you certainly rattled him. Good." Antonia gripped her cane, her hand etched with blue veins stark against the white skin. "He's entirely too flip for my taste. Nice to see him taken down a peg."

Her voice cracked when she spoke. Determination shone in her vibrant green eyes but, at that moment, Antonia looked every bit her age.

Seeming to sense the direction my thoughts had taken, Antonia stamped her cane. "I hope you aren't tired, Penny. I'm certainly not. Let's get something to eat and discuss our next move."

"I thought you and Chantal ordered room service."

"We changed our minds. She wasn't hungry, so I insisted she go and get a massage in the spa. Help her relax."

"She's got to be upset," Connor said.

"She is, of course. But the reality is that Chantal has lived most of her life in a sheltered environment. She hasn't grasped how much trouble she could be in over this."

Antonia has always been overly protective of Chantal, but, for once, I managed to keep my mouth shut.

Antonia gestured to a back table. "That will work."

When we'd settled in, Antonia continued, "Truth be told, I can't imagine anyone on the train having more to gain from Tara's death than Vance."

"Well, it's possible Big Dave wanted her gone. She was a real flirt and maybe he'd had enough. My gut tells me that isn't the case, though. As for suspects, don't forget about Seth and Barb."

"The waitress and that terrible husband of hers?" Antonia shook her head. "I don't understand. Explain yourself."

"You saw them at the bar when I did," I said. "Barb was

jealous of Tara, and Seth didn't like Tara turning down his advances and referring to him as a toy."

Antonia nodded. "And a second-rate one at that. I'd forgotten." She steepled her fingers and rested her chin on them. "It's hard for me to see Barb pushing Tara off the train, but you never know. On the other hand, I have no problem seeing Seth responsible for this. I get the feeling he's had some experience pushing women around."

"I know," I said. "I felt it too. I wouldn't be surprised by anything I learned about him."

"Well, that gives us four people that might have a reason to want Tara dead." Connor ticked them off on his fingers. "Big Dave, the husband; Vance, the stepson; Seth, the insulted and recently scorned ex-lover; and Barb, the humiliated wife." He stopped and thumbed over his shoulder. "I don't suppose those two had anything against Tara. They just met her, right?"

I peered through the dim light and spotted Jim and Kim in a corner booth. "It doesn't look like they knew anyone here before this trip. I think they said they've never been to California before. Tara headed South right after high school. That's where she met Big Dave. I would also say Bill, the train guy, is in the clear. No reason he'd kill someone who wanted to invest in his company as enthusiastically as Tara did."

"Not to mention murder can't be very high in the plus column for potential investors," Connor said.

I spotted Big Dave through the back windows overlooking the garden. He sat under a rose arbor, looking pale even in the twilight. His shoulders shook and he buried his face in his hands.

"Order me the roast chicken. I'll be back in a few minutes." I walked to the glass doors and stepped out into the evening air. The warmth of the day hadn't survived the setting sun, and I buttoned up the light sweater I wore. Stopping a few feet from Big Dave, I waited until he spotted me.

He wiped his eyes without embarrassment and sighed. "They tell me I can't leave. Not that I'd go without Tara. She doesn't belong here anymore, and I won't go without her."

"I guess she doesn't have any family left?" I took a seat next to him.

"None that matter. She's got an aunt over in Sonoma, but she didn't even invite her to our wedding."

"I wish I knew how to tell you how sorry I am for your loss."

"What I wish you could tell me is how to make sense of it." He pushed his palms against his eyes and his voice cracked. "Tara didn't mean no harm. She just wanted to enjoy life. She had a sharp tongue, I'll give you that." He took a deep breath and let it out slowly. "But she always reminded me of a stray, desperate for love but used to fighting for everything she had. She never felt completely safe. I think that insecurity caused her to act the way she did sometimes."

I turned up the collar of my sweater. "In what way?"

Big Dave looked into the clear evening sky. "She craved attention, sometimes from the wrong people. And she was so afraid to be alone."

"She had you."

He sighed. "There was only so much I could do, and sometimes it just wasn't enough. I knew who she was. I knew some of the things she did. She was a flirt, sure, but so much of it was just this insecure little girl still trying to get attention."

She got attention from someone, all right. I hugged my arms against me, remembering once again the twisted neck, the vacant eyes.

Big Dave seemed to understand who Tara was, and it sounded like he'd sincerely loved her, faults and all. On the other hand, I wasn't sure I'd ever met any man that forgiving. His pain seemed genuine, but I couldn't leave him alone yet, not if I wanted to know who killed her.

"So, help me understand. Tara needed attention. She needed to be admired and loved. But not many men would have been that accepting of her behavior. I'm not sure why you put up with it."

He shrugged. "I loved her. Like I told you before, she was fun. At some point in life you stop worrying. I mean really stop. Losing my second wife did it for me. Watching her suffer. I was tired, just plumb wore out, and nothing mattered anymore, until I met Tara. With her I remembered what it felt like to laugh. I wanted to live again. For the first time in a long time, I wanted to have fun again."

He covered his face with his hands and I dipped my head to hear. "I fell in love with Tara because she gave me back my life after I said good-bye to Sue. It isn't right that I have to bury both of them. It isn't right."

Ten

THE next morning started early with a knock on the door.

"Want to go for a run with me?" Connor stretched out his Achilles or ligaments or something else runners tend to use.

"I wouldn't want to slow you down."

"We can take it easy."

Connor's easy run is a death march to most people. Certainly to me.

"Go ahead. I've got coffee coming up and a nice spot on the veranda."

"Suit yourself." He stretched, limber as a cat, and headed down the hall while I tried not to stare at his muscular thighs. The phone rang as I shut the door.

"Care to walk into town?"

"You too, Antonia? What is it with everyone?"

"I have no idea what you're talking about. Do you want to go into town and perhaps get some breakfast?"

"Oh, well, if that's what you're thinking."

"Now that food is on the line you're amenable?"

"Well, yeah. Give me five minutes."

"Of course, I'll give you longer than that. You've never been on time in your life."

It was hard to argue with the truth, and when I arrived fifteen minutes later, she stood at the front door of the hotel pulling on gloves.

"It isn't cold out. It's beautiful. I love crispy fall air."

"These aren't for the cold." She held up her hands to show me. "They're lightweight but block the sun." She took a closer look at my face. "You did inherit good skin."

"I've always been good with sunscreen."

"It's a woman's hands and neck that really give her away."

I pulled my collar up and stuffed my hands into the pockets of my jeans. "Can we go?"

"Don't get testy. We can pick up the walking path right next to the hotel." A few moments later we joined walkers and bikers on the paved trail that ran nearly twenty miles through town and the surrounding vineyards.

"You know this path cuts right across the valley floor, away from the streets and even the train tracks. This way it's just a short walk past town to Berninni Winery."

I stopped. "You want to head back over and see Olympio again, don't you? You sly thing."

Her cheeks reddened. "I really hadn't thought of it. We certainly could stand to apologize once again, given the debacle that occurred there last time. I still can't believe you came to Chantal's rescue against that terrible person. Although," Antonia picked up her pace, "I do suppose now that she's deceased, I should refrain from voicing that opinion about her."

"Especially around the police. Chief Harding wouldn't be heartbroken to hear the mother of his main suspect refer to the victim as a 'terrible person.'"

"Him!" Antonia quickened her pace once more. It's times like this when it's easy to forget Antonia's age. "The pompous fool! What kind of boor goes around insisting people use his entire title?"

"The kind that can charge your daughter with first-degree murder. Be careful of Police Chief Lawrence Harding. He's determined to pin this thing on someone. Don't make it easy for him to have it be Chantal."

I looked around. Rolling hills in browns and grays surrounded us. The grape canes, gnarly with age and trimmed back for their winter rest, weaved across the landscape.

"Look around, Antonia. Take some deep breaths and let's slow down a bit. We need to think carefully of our next steps, for Chantal's sake."

She slackened her pace. "You're right, of course. Sometimes the truth is right in plain sight."

She picked up one of the shoots that lay strewn between the rows of sleeping vines, twisting the cutting in her hands. "This is a perfect example."

"I'm not following you."

"A lot of California wineries started with cuttings just like this, slipped in from other countries."

I nodded. "Suitcase smuggling. A lot of varieties came in that way. So did some of the pests."

Antonia waved the twig in the air. "I'm not advocating it. I'm simply trying to make a point."

"Sorry. Go ahead."

"In one story, the vintner just walked onto the plane. When asked by customs what he was holding, the winemaker simply said, 'This? Just a stick.' That's all it was, then. Just a stick. Just a cutting of Roussanne from a vineyard in Chateauneuf-du-Pape. That stick, and others like it, changed the course of California."

"How does this help with the mess Chantal's in?"

Antonia clenched the cutting, bending it in her hands until it snapped. "There's something we aren't seeing yet. Something we've dismissed as simply a stick that's much more."

"I agree we're missing something. That has to be it, otherwise Chantal would be . . ."

"Exactly." Antonia threw down the cutting. "And we both know my daughter isn't capable of murder. She might inspire it in some people on occasion"—I kept my face averted—"but she isn't guilty of this terrible crime."

"So we need to take another look at the facts and examine them one at a time. But first"—I pointed to the nearest building—"I need coffee, and that place looks as good as any."

We approached the entrance and Antonia grimaced. "I don't know about this. I'm not sure I want to eat at any place called The Diner."

"What do you mean? Look." I pointed to a plaque by the front door. "It's been here for sixty years. How bad can it be?"

The Diner was in an old stone building with red-and-white-checked curtains, mismatched wooden tables and chairs, and, in one corner, a jukebox full of forty-fives.

Two short-order cooks slid plates of bacon and eggs, partnered with mountains of hash browns, through the serving window, dinging a bell every time an order was up.

A waitress with dark permed hair, wearing a white uniform, moved between the customers with a coffeepot in one hand and a cream pitcher in the other. She knew when to add cream without consulting the customers, and they barely noticed her. Most of the diners wore flannel shirts, jeans and work boots, and there wasn't much talking going on.

"This looks perfect. It's full of regulars, which is always a good sign."

"Sit anywhere you want," the waitress said as she walked by.

A few of the steady crowd looked up to see who didn't know the routine before they went back to nursing their cups.

I scanned the room for seats when a wave came from the back of the room.

"Antonia, look, it's the couple from Chicago."

"If we sit with them, we won't be able to talk about Chantal's predicament."

"I disagree. Maybe they know something or saw something."

"I don't think they see much of anything but each other."

I was inclined to agree but weaved my way through the regulars. Kim flashed me that dazzling smile as I reached their table.

"Have you ever been told you look just like Julia Roberts?"

"Somebody tells her that at least once a day. Personally, I think she's prettier." Jim pulled out a chair for Antonia. "Come join us."

"Yes, please," Kim said. "We're trying to decide what to do with our extra time. We were supposed to be flying back home to Chicago today, but that inspector doesn't want us leaving yet." She shrugged. "I can't imagine we were the only ones he ordered to stay put."

"You weren't," I said. "Police Chief Lawrence Harding made it clear to all of us nobody's going anywhere until he's ready to let us leave."

"From what I heard, it sounds like they have a suspect." Jim scooted his chair in closer. "Sounded pretty cut-and-dried to me."

"Now, Jim." Kim subtly moved her head back and forth. "We aren't sure what the police are thinking at all." She gave his arm a discreet squeeze. "I'm sure Antonia's daughter has simply nothing to worry about."

Jim slapped his forehead. "Don't mind me. I forgot Chantal was your daughter. The police will figure out for sure what happened. It was probably an accident, although . . ."

"Although what?" I pulled my chair in closer.

"Well, I'm not sure I want to be talking out of turn."

"Young man, my daughter might very well be accused of murder, one that she didn't commit," Antonia said. "If you know something, I'm asking you to please tell me what it is."

"Thing is . . ." Jim turned his coffee cup in circles on the table. "The problem is that what I have to say may not help your daughter."

Antonia's chin trembled a bit, and there was brightness

in the corners of her eyes. "I want to know the truth, wherever it may lead."

Jim nodded. "Well, then, it wasn't an accident. I know for sure." He paused as the waitress poured him more coffee. He waved off the cream and continued, "I think Kim mentioned when we met that I work for the train and transportation division in Chicago?"

I nodded.

"One of the areas I'm in charge of is safety measures. Now, these trains are old, classic Pullmans, but by law they're required to have the latest safety features, and they do." Jim took a sip of coffee. "That safety latch was still intact. It closes automatically when the train is in motion and would need to be opened manually."

"So there's no way," I said, "even though Tara had had too much to drink, that she fell off."

Jim shook his head. "Not a chance. She would need to intentionally open the safety latch and then accidentally fall off."

"What if she jumped?" Antonia was grasping for anything and Jim gently shook his head.

"Sorry, ma'am, but that doesn't make any sense. She wouldn't have been able to lock the safety gate again behind her. No, the only reason Tara ended up the way she did was because somebody opened the latch, pushed her off, and then latched it shut behind her."

OUR conversation with Jim did nothing to dampen Antonia's desire to revisit Berninni Winery. We finished breakfast and were standing back outside in the morning sun.

"Of course I still want to go," came the reply when I posed the question. "We could certainly apologize for our behavior once more—"

"I'm not sure I have anything to apologize for."

Antonia ignored me. "There may also be some clue as to what happened later on the train. That waitress and that person she's married to might know more than they've let on. I believe they do."

"That's actually a good idea."

"Of course it is. We can cut through town. Let's go."

"Hold it." I took a good look at her. Those snappy green eyes were bright and without a trace of cloudiness the years sometimes bring. She stood ramrod straight in a black cashmere sweater, her silver hair piled high on her head, held in place with silver combs. Her makeup was subtle, but it was there.

"You look pretty nice just to grab breakfast. Heading out to Berninni wasn't brought up until I met you downstairs. When did it occur to you?"

"What a ridiculous question." Antonia turned onto Main Street. I followed. "Are you sure stopping by the winery didn't come up this morning when I phoned you?" She kept her voice light, but I wasn't fooled.

"It didn't come up and you know it, but I don't mind the detour. You're right. It's a good chance to talk with people who were there when Tara and Chantal had their argument. Even getting confirmation Tara started the fight would help."

"I'm not sure he'll want us interfering," Antonia said.

"Who?"

"*Him*." Antonia nudged me in the ribs.

Chief Harding stood on the other side of the street.

"Then we won't tell him what we're up to." I grabbed Antonia by the arm. "Let's go talk to him."

"What exactly do you think he's going to share with us?"

"Nothing, if we don't ask." I started waving at him from the center of the street, and he waited until we reached him.

With thinning hair emphasized by a part just slightly above one ear, the chief had seen better days. A paunch belied a love of food, and his skin was slightly gray. He hooked his thumbs in his belt.

"Thanks for waiting for us," I said.

"I only waited to tell you it's illegal to jaywalk. I could write you a ticket for that."

I can pretty much find something to like in most everyone; this guy had me stumped.

"Well, as you can imagine, we've been wondering if there's been any progress on finding out who killed Tara." I thought of Jim's comments at breakfast. "I mean, the safety gates were all closed, so it was murder, right?"

He rocked back on his heels. "You know, up here in Napa Valley, we have a tradition: The police ask the questions. We don't answer them. You may find things a little different than from where you come from. Oh, by the way, I did speak to the chief of police down in Cypress Cove—"

"So you did call Chief Lucas," Antonia said. "I'm sure he vouched for all our characters, including my daughter's."

"Sounds like you have a pretty informal arrangement with the law down along the central coast. We don't play things quite so easy up here."

"Now really, I don't think—"

The chief held up his hand. "However, I will say that he did tell me he's known you and your family his entire life, and it seemed unlikely to him that Chantal is capable of murder."

"There, you see?" Antonia beamed.

He shook his head. "This will in no way interfere or influence my investigation, and I must tell you that, at the moment, I don't see how anyone else could have been back in the caboose." He looked at Antonia. "As of this moment, your daughter continues to be my main suspect."

"Young man . . ."

Whatever she was about to say wasn't going to help, and I interrupted. "Thank you for the update, Chief, I mean Chief Harding."

"Hold up there. I learned something else from that call with your local guy down in Cypress Cove."

"Yes?"

"It seems this isn't the first time you've gotten involved in a police matter. He said you seem to have a nasty knack for finding bodies." He paused for effect. "Dead bodies."

Of course they were dead. What other kind of bodies are there? "I didn't ask to be the one to find her." I thought of Tara and swallowed hard. "It wasn't something I was looking for."

Harding put his hands on his hips. "I don't want to hear of you meddling or nosing around in my investigation."

"As a matter of fact," Antonia smiled, "we're on our way to do a little wine tasting right now." She stepped around him and signaled for me to follow. "Good day, Chief Harding."

I waited until he was out of earshot. "Why were you

so nice? I have zero confidence in that man. He's made up his mind about Chantal, and I don't think he's going to do anything to find someone else."

Antonia nodded. "I agree. He doesn't strike me as particularly bright. However, antagonizing him at this particular moment does nothing to help us. Going to Berninni will."

"I know we're mainly going to look for clues, but I'm telling you right now I'm having a glass of something when we get there."

Antonia nodded. "You and me both."

Eleven

"YOU are now standing seventy feet underground."

"Olympio, I can't thank you enough for this private tour," Antonia said. "And after the commotion we caused during our last visit."

"Believe me, madam, it's my pleasure to share with you the secrets of my winery. I'm sure I can trust you not to use them against me."

If Olympio trusted Antonia with any secret that might benefit her winery, he didn't know Antonia at all. I caught his smile and realized he had no intention of sharing any information proprietary to Berninni Winery. Vintners were a closed lot and carefully guarded their expertise and knowledge, especially from one another.

The door to the wine cave was just a few steps behind me. "How can we be so far underground that quickly?"

"You can't tell when looking at the front of the winery,"

Olympio said, "but the hill rises sharply behind the buildings. It gives us direct access to this naturally air-conditioned environment. My grandparents built here for that specific reason."

We walked behind Olympio, following the track of dim overhead lights that ran down the center of the arched cave. Tunnels several yards wide, and high enough to stand in, branched off from the center aisle. All of these were lined with oak barrels.

Olympio walked to the wall and ran his hand down its length. "Feel it. It's volcanic rock, from our Mount Saint Helena. She's friendly at the moment, but once, this valley was covered in volcanic ash. It was also underwater at one point. That combination is what gave us our *terroir*, our soil, which is unlike anywhere else."

Antonia sniffed. "Yes, well, just because you have soil unlike anywhere else doesn't mean it's the only soil that grows great wine grapes. Nor is it the only factor. Some would say the combination of weather we have along the central coast, foggy mornings and hot summer days, gives us the edge in producing excellent wine. Some would say you just got an earlier start."

Olympio laughed and took Antonia's hand. "Please, my lovely guest, let us for the moment agree that we both produce exceptional wine."

"Yes, I can certainly agree to that."

I walked to the wall, running my hand over the uneven surface. "This is so rough. How were all of these tunnels built, by dynamite?"

"It was impossible to use dynamite, because volcanic rock shatters when you try. No, these were all dug by hand.

The account I've heard is that after the railways were completed, there was a surplus of Chinese labor. They weren't wanted in America and were poorly paid. Some of them found work digging these tunnels." Olympio shook his head. "Not work to be taken lightly. Hard, backbreaking work. Not the finest hour in the story of California. Still, they completed something truly remarkable here, and helped shape the history of this region."

"I take it the temperature remains consistent," I said.

"Always within a couple of degrees of sixty-four, even on the hottest days." Olympio walked to the wall. "Let me show you something." He reached for a switch, and a moment later we were plunged into complete darkness.

It was so dark I couldn't think, couldn't breathe. The silence was deeper than any I'd ever known.

"Antonia, where are you?" My voice sounded muffled.

"I haven't moved, but where have you gone off to?"

"She hasn't moved either," Olympio said. "It's the walls. This substance deadens sound. Without visual references, the impact is stronger, which is why you didn't notice it before. You could be down here for days, and no one would ever hear you."

"Lovely thought," Antonia said. "Olympio, come stand by me."

"I must turn the light back on first. Otherwise, I would have a hard time finding it again."

"Then, by all means, please feel free to turn the lights back on," I said. "This is giving me the willies."

"No problem." Olympio threw the switch, but the faint glow didn't hold the charm of moments before.

"My dear." Olympio peered into my face. "You look pale even in this light."

"She hasn't had the best trip so far, all things considered," Antonia said.

"Well, no, I can understand why. We will only talk about other, more pleasant matters." He took me by the arm, Antonia on his other side. "For example, do you know how the wineries in the Napa Valley survived Prohibition?"

"Well, I know a big use was medicinal," I said.

"Of course, of course." He winked at me. "Which is exactly the use we will avail ourselves of when we reach the tasting room. Put the bloom back in your cheeks." He turned to Antonia. "When did your grandfather begin your winery?"

"Nearly seventy-five years ago."

"So you were spared the struggle to survive those years, when drinking even wine was considered illegal."

"Oh, please, Olympio. You weren't around then either. I think you're perhaps using surviving Prohibition as a way to mention how old your winery is. It's older than mine. I get it."

Olympio clutched his hands to his chest. "My honored guest, I am crushed. That you would think I would for a moment consider your winery less worthy than mine simply because we've been around since 1879 and are, in fact, the oldest winery in the Napa Valley . . ."

"Now I really do need that drink," Antonia said. "But go on with your story. Medicinal was one use, but that wasn't the widest use, was it?"

"No, no. Thank heavens," Olympio said. "Or perhaps

thanks to the church directly. We had the largest national contract to make sacramental wine for the Catholic Church. Many smaller wineries survived this way."

We reached the door. "There was one other way most people don't know about." He held open the door for us. "Berninni and most of the other wineries sold our grapes during that time. We sold them in packages and on the package was a warning," he winked at me, "not to be taken seriously, of course. A warning saying that whatever you do, don't follow the next seven steps in their precise order, otherwise you will be making an alcoholic beverage. What people then did, in the privacy of their own homes, is lost to history."

"I had no idea," I said.

"And he loves being the one to tell you." Antonia nodded toward the bar. "Now I, for one, would appreciate having a taste of your family's efforts."

"This way, my lovely guests. This way."

We walked between the tourists already well into the day's tastings. Most stood at tables scattered about the room with tour maps and various brochures spread out in front of them.

Seth was pouring and Olympio joined him behind the counter. Seth looked the same, wearing another form-fitting white shirt with a black apron around his waist. He laughed at something one of the visitors said and poured her a glass of white.

"Look how personable he is when he needs to be. It's all just an act," I said. "I wonder why Olympio keeps him around."

"Let's ask him," Antonia said as Olympio rejoined us.

"Penny's asked why you have that 'person'"—she signaled with a nod of her head—"in your employment. He is without a doubt one of the most repugnant people I've come across in quite some time."

"That's why." Olympio sighed and nodded across the room. Barb stood adding flowers to a vase in the entry hall. "Her father worked many years for me. I know he would want me to help."

"You could keep her on and get rid of him," I said. "That's what she needs. A way to support herself and lose him."

Olympio nodded. "You are right, of course. That is a solution I've offered many times. She won't do it. She won't leave him, and I know if I were to fire him she would quit out of misplaced loyalty to him. The lack of income would make it even harder for her in that home." He sighed. "This way I can keep an eye on her, and on him, at least part of the time. Here, he won't try anything."

"Well, I commend you for trying to make a deplorable situation better," Antonia said. "Hopefully when Barb is ready to make a positive move, knowing you're there will make the difference."

"I'll be back in a moment." I darted my eyes toward the bar and Antonia gave a slight nod. If Seth knew anything, now was a good time to ask.

He was alone when I reached him. He studied my face for a moment. "I've seen you before. You were on the train yesterday, weren't you?"

I nodded. "Terrible what happened to Tara."

"Yeah." He grabbed a towel and polished the bar. "What can I get you?"

I wasn't going to be put off that easily. "You grew up near her, didn't you?"

"Yes, but it's been a long time since I've seen her."

"Yesterday you sure looked ready to renew acquaintances."

He stopped wiping. "Can I get you anything to drink?"

"Sure. I'll have a Merlot."

He pulled a bottle out from under the counter and showed me the label. "This is something you can only get here, at the winery."

"That's perfect. I had some yesterday."

He paused, bottle in hand. "That's right. Before the train left yesterday, you were here too. You were in the fight."

"I wouldn't really call it a fight."

"The hell it wasn't. It was you and Tara and that other one, the one in the tight red sweater. The sexy brunette."

"It wasn't a fight."

"Sure. Call it whatever you want."

"It was a misunderstanding."

Seth laughed. "Tara had a lot of those."

"So her having fights with people was pretty common?"

"I thought you said it wasn't a fight."

"Fine," I said. "Let's say it was. Did Tara have a lot of them?"

"You didn't know Tara before this weekend, did you?"

"No, I just met her two days ago," I said.

"Then what concern is it of yours?"

"I found her body."

That stopped him.

"A friend of mine might be accused of killing her. I'm going to make sure that doesn't happen."

"Let me guess. Red sweater. I saw them get into it. Then you stepped in." He pointed across the room. "It started right over there. They really went at it. Wish I'd thought to record it."

"For an old friend, you don't seem very shaken up about Tara's death."

He shrugged. "Like I said, it's been a long time since I've seen her."

I remembered his hand trailing down Tara's arm. "Still, I know you two used to be pretty close. Yesterday it didn't look like you would have minded resuming your 'friendship.'"

"We had our fun a long time ago. She's married to the old guy now, or was, and living the life down in Dixie with the king of car dealerships. That's what was important to her. Being rich. It always was."

"Looked to me like you got pretty upset with her yesterday. You didn't seem to like being called a toy."

He froze and flexed his hands, the knuckles white. Behind me, the tourists chatted and glasses clanked.

I took a breath. "Looked like you wanted to resume right where you two left off, only now she was just messing with you. She didn't have any real interest. Why would she? You're still doing the same thing with nothing to show for it."

Seth's face was pale and a faint sheen of sweat covered his upper lip. "Lady, you should stop while you still can."

"That's some temper you've got. I wonder if it got away from you yesterday, after Tara rejected you."

"What are you talking about?" Seth took a step back. "You think I killed her?"

"The thought has occurred to me. You could have followed her after she made that toy comment. Maybe you tried again in the caboose to renew your relationship and she didn't like it. I bet you don't handle women saying no very well, do you, Seth?"

"Lady, I don't know who you are or what you're playing at, but you better stop. I didn't kill her. I don't care what you say. I didn't kill her, and you don't have anything to prove I did."

I pressed. "If you didn't kill her, who might have wanted her dead?"

"Red Sweater's looking pretty good for it to me."

"Chantal didn't do it. You want me to believe you didn't either? Give me someone else."

Seth stacked glasses for a moment. "I'd start with that husband, or the stepson. They had money on the line. That's always the best incentive there is. It almost always comes back to money."

"Okay, I'll buy that, but I bet Big Dave had a prenup."

Seth laughed. "You really didn't know Tara, did you? No way would she sign a prenup. I've known her my entire life. She'd never sign something like that. Never."

Twelve

"DID you get anything out of him?" Antonia asked when I rejoined her.

"He swears he didn't have anything to do with Tara's death. Of course, he's not above lying to save his own skin. We should get going, and besides, I'm getting hungry."

"Again?"

"I didn't eat much at breakfast."

"You had biscuits and gravy."

"What are you, the breakfast monitor?" My jeans felt a little tight and I avoided my reflection in the window. "I'm hungry. I always get hungry when I travel." I waved Olympio down. "Can you recommend a good place for lunch?"

"Ah, you are in luck. The Northern California Dungeness crab season kicks off this weekend. Downtown St. Katrina always celebrates with a crab festival, and all of the restaurants along Main Street make different dishes featuring crab." He glanced around the tasting room. "I cannot join you, as I hope to be busy here, but our crab is something not to be missed."

Antonia sniffed. "Yes, well, you do know we also have crab along the central coast of California as well."

"Yes, but our waters are much colder up here. It gives the crab, I don't know, something special."

"So your dirt gives the grapes something extra, and your cold water gives the crabs something special. I'm beginning to think—"

I wasn't sure he needed to know what Antonia was thinking. "Olympio, you've been a marvelous host, but we are about to overstay our welcome."

Olympio smiled at me as he kissed Antonia's hand. "I would enjoy having the pleasure of comparing our different regions at a later time. As a matter of fact, I would be honored if you would join me for dinner with the rest of your party, say, tomorrow night? We will eat in the cave cellar."

"What's that?" I asked.

"A special room in the caves where my winery has hosted private dinners over the years. Teddy Roosevelt enjoyed the Berninni hospitality in that same room before he was president."

"Humph. Yes, well, that does sound nice," Antonia said.

"Excellent! Tomorrow at eight." Olympio held the door and watched as we made our way down the drive and back onto Main Street.

"He likes you," I said. "He really does."

"What nonsense," Antonia scoffed, although she glanced back several times.

The street was full of tourists shopping the boutiques of specialty kitchen gadgets, designer clothes and garden items. Window boxes brimmed with pansies and most of the stores had water bowls out for visiting dogs. Restaurants spilled out onto the street, offering a respite and a glass of crispy Pinot.

"I really like it here," I said. "It's got an old-world feel to it. I love some of these buildings."

Antonia nodded. "There was a family of Italian stonemasons who built a lot of them in Napa and Sonoma counties after the San Francisco earthquake in 1906. The entire three blocks of downtown St. Katrina are a designated historical site."

"How do you know that?"

"Olympio told me." Her cheeks reddened. "I suppose he is rather charming. He certainly is proud of this place."

"He has every reason to be. You feel the same way about Monterey and Cypress Cove."

She nodded. "I suppose that's true. Now where would you like to eat?"

We settled on Main Street Hotel, managed to snag an inside window seat, and had just ordered crab fritters and the crab soufflé when I spotted Vance outside the window.

"Look who's parking," I said.

Antonia turned. "You can't miss that monstrosity he drives. Of course it's red. And that license plate: 'KissMyS.' Honestly."

Vance turned off the car and jumped from the seat. Pulling a mint-and-white-striped sweater out of the back, he started to walk down the street but was stopped by someone I recognized.

"That's Bill, the train guy," I said. "I wonder what they're doing together."

"It's probably a coincidence, their meeting."

"Maybe, but Bill's got his hand on Vance's shoulder, and Vance is shaking his head. I wish I could hear them." I tried the window. "No luck."

Vance knocked Bill's hand off his shoulder and pushed past him. Bill stood and watched him, twisting his cap in his hands, before he turned and walked across the street.

"I wonder what that was about. Bill seems really upset."

"Well, Penny, he did just have someone murdered on his train."

"Look, he's going into that office." I studied the sign above the door. "I wonder what type of attorneys Gilbert and Ryan are."

"We can look online."

"There's an easier way." I stood.

"What are you going to do, just walk in?"

"Why not?"

"What are you going to say?"

"Not a clue. I'm hoping something comes to me between now and the front door."

When I entered the lobby, Bill was still there.

He stopped pacing, a look of surprise on his face. "Penny, I didn't expect to see you. I mean, this is my attorney's office. What are you doing here?"

Really good question. "Actually, um, this attorney was recommended by, ah, I forget who Antonia got the recommendation from. Anyway, it sounded like a good idea to have an attorney review any contracts you might have for us to sign. I mean, if we decide to invest."

"Why wouldn't you use someone down in Cypress Cove? Someone you know?"

Right. Why wouldn't I? "Well, I thought someone local, someone who maybe knew the history of the train up here, and how things have gone subsequently, might also have a useful perspective. But enough about me. Are you okay?"

"Sure, why wouldn't I be?"

I took in the fine sheen of perspiration and the cap mangled in his hands. He followed my gaze and loosened his grip, slapping the cap on his thigh.

"I know this weekend hasn't been what you wanted for us," I said.

"Events certainly took the luster off your trip. In spite of the way things have turned out, I hope you can see how entertaining the train is for the guests and how lucrative for the investors. Just keep an open mind on investing is all I'm asking."

Hard to imagine how. The train was late, half-full, and included a dead body. It was a total disaster as far as I could tell. On the other hand, Tara's death had nothing to do with the train line, and maybe the lack of passengers and late arrival really were just a fluke.

"I promise to give it due thought before we make any decision on investing. In the meantime, won't Tara's death negatively impact your business? I mean, what about your insurance?"

Bill's shoulders relaxed. "Actually, that's a spot of good news. My insurance won't be going up. As bad as it was, Tara's murder doesn't have anything to do with the train. We weren't technically responsible, like we would have been with a collision or an accident, that type of thing."

"Well, that's a relief." I moved closer. "Did your attorney just give you the good news?"

"No, I haven't seen him yet." A furrow gathered on his brow and he went back to twisting the cap. "It's not easy to keep things running smoothly. If I were just able to concentrate on the trains, I'd be okay. As it is, the paperwork and dealing with investors takes up most of my time. I mean, I've got people trying to pull money out that I've already spent."

I understood the argument on the street. "It wouldn't be Vance, would it?"

Bill stepped back. "How did you know that?"

"Well, it just stands to reason. I know Tara was an enthusiastic investor, and Vance felt she was spending all of his father's money—all of his inheritance, really. It makes sense that Vance would see if there was any way to pull out of the deal."

Bill relaxed a bit. "It's him all right. He's threatening to have a lawyer see if the contract can be broken. I don't think he has the authority to do anything, but the last thing I need is to spend money on attorneys for something like this."

"Was the contract in Tara's name?"

Bill nodded. "I'm sure her husband gave her the money, but she's the one who signed it."

"Well, then, I can't imagine what Vance thinks he can do. I'm sure the contract is binding."

Bill nodded. "Airtight."

"Then I guess Vance will just have to live with it." I turned to go. "I'll leave you to it then."

"Didn't you want to see an attorney?"

Right. "Actually, now that I know this is your attorney, I should look for someone else. More of a neutral third party." I gave him a small wave and closed the door, scooting back across the street to where Antonia waited.

"The soufflé was delicious. It was going to fall, and I knew you wouldn't mind."

I flagged down the waiter, ordered another soufflé, munched on a crab fritter and summarized my conversation with Bill.

"I suppose Bill's right," Antonia said. "It isn't the train line's fault someone picked that location to murder Tara. The wineries seem to love the increase in visitors, and it does keep people from drinking and driving. Interesting that Vance is trying to get out of the deal. I wonder if his father knows." She reached into her purse and pulled out a notebook. "Let's make some notes."

"Good idea. First there's Vance, especially after what I just learned. He has the best motive, namely trying to protect his inheritance. Big Dave also needs to be on the list."

"He seemed so fond of her," Antonia said.

"He was, but Tara liked to have fun and Seth is positive she wouldn't have signed a prenup. Big Dave could have lost half of everything he's built over the years if she decided to run off. The spouse is always at the top of the list."

Antonia wrote his name. "Got it. Who else?"

"Speaking of Seth, he certainly needs to be included. He and Tara have history, and he didn't like it one bit when he felt she was leading him on the other day. He could have gone looking for more. If she scorned him again, there's no telling what he'd do."

Antonia nodded. "And then there's his long-suffering wife. She might have killed Tara out of pure jealousy, especially if she caught the two of them together. She made it clear she wasn't going to put up with it." Antonia continued to write. "I can't believe that chief of police hasn't looked at these people more closely. Any one of these reasons is better than that silly fight Chantal had with Tara."

"The problem is where Chantal was found unconscious," I said. "If she hadn't gone back to the caboose, if someone hadn't slipped her that note, or if she'd only realized the note wasn't from Connor, she wouldn't be in this fix."

"Lots of what-ifs." Antonia held up the list. "Vance, Big Dave, Seth and Barb. What about that couple from Chicago, Jim and Kim?"

"Well, Kim was with me, so she's in the clear. Jim went to the back to get Kim her sweater right about when it happened, but he didn't say two words to Tara the entire time before she died. It doesn't make any sense. The same with Bill. He was in the back, but Tara was a big investor. The last thing he needed was to have this happen on his train, especially to one of his biggest supporters."

"So Bill was better off with Tara alive than dead, and Jim didn't know her. That leaves the four: Vance, Big Dave, Seth and Barb." Antonia tapped the pen against the list. "I left Chantal alone this morning. She finally fell asleep around four, and I didn't wake her, but I think it's time we spoke."

"She slept in your room last night?"

"I slept in hers." Antonia caught my eye. "As difficult as she can be, she's still my little girl."

*   *   *

"I can't remember anything else," Chantal wailed. "Don't you think I would tell you if I did?"

We'd arrived back and found Connor and Chantal in the center courtyard. Connor was taking long laps in the spring-fed pool, the heat rising off the surface in soft curls of mist. Chantal wore a one-piece red suit with a matching skirt of some type of see-through netting. The bodice was a series of folds, as if she needed something to draw attention to her chest. George, the butler, was staring out the back window, and I shook my finger at him. He blushed and vanished, but he wasn't the only one. Every man who came by found a reason to pause.

"Chantal, you've got to think." Antonia stamped her cane.

An oxymoron if ever I'd heard one. I kept a straight face, but that didn't stop Antonia from shooting me a look.

"Helpful comments only, please," Antonia admonished. She's always known what I'm thinking. It can be a little scary at times.

I sighed. "You aren't speaking her language."

"Well, then, you try."

I pulled my seat up to Chantal. "Okay. Let's break this down. Do you remember where Connor was?"

"Of course. He'd just walked me back a couple of minutes before. Right after that I found the note saying to meet him"—she snuck a quick glance at the pool—"I mean, whoever wrote it, in the caboose."

Antonia huffed. "Why are you asking her about Connor? We know he didn't kill Tara."

"I'm starting with the easy ones. Okay, Chantal, now what about Big Dave?"

Chantal nodded. "Sure, he was sitting in the front when I got up to go to the caboose. Trying to talk to Vance."

"What about Seth?"

"He came in a few minutes before I went to the back. He did a quick check for dirty glasses."

"Did he leave before you went into the caboose?"

"No, he was still there." Chantal chewed her lip. "I guess I remember more than I thought."

She was remembering exactly what I thought she'd remember: the location of every man in the room. She was like a man radar.

"Where was Tara?"

"I think she was near the back too, but I really don't remember."

Shocking. "So, what happened next?"

"Exactly what I told the police. I got a note telling me to meet, um, whoever in the caboose. I went, but nobody was there. There were chairs stacked in the back, so I took one down and waited."

"Did somebody come in while you were there waiting?"

"They must have. Honestly, Penny, I didn't knock myself out. Some detective."

I rubbed my eyes. "Maybe something fell, hit you and knocked you out when the brake was pulled."

Chantal tapped a red-tipped finger against her chin. "That didn't happen, though. I remember waking up with my cheek on the floor and then, a few moments later, hearing the brakes squeal and the train shuddering and stopping."

"Think very carefully, Chantal. Who came in while you sat there waiting?"

She shook her head. "I've been trying but it's no use. I was facing out the rear of the train, with my back to the door."

Chantal grabbed my hand and there was panic in her voice. "You believe me, don't you? Someone came in and hit me. I didn't have anything to do with Tara's murder."

I nodded. "I know you didn't. Someone planned this, though. Someone planned to get you back there. It's lucky you were only knocked out, but I'm guessing you weren't in danger of being murdered. You had to be found alive to take the role of prime suspect."

Chantal grew a shade paler, and Antonia's hand trembled slightly on the cane.

"Don't scare her unnecessarily, Penny. Chantal cast as the killer could have been a spur-of-the-moment decision on the murderer's part."

I shook my head. "If that's the case and Chantal's being there wasn't connected to Tara's murder, the note would still have been on her."

I turned back to Chantal. "Someone went through your pockets while you were unconscious. Without that note, it's just your word that it ever existed."

Thirteen

"T HERE was a note. There was a note!" She stood and, for the first time, didn't seem to notice the appreciative glances she received. "I'm telling you there was a note!"

Her voice carried across the garden and Connor swam to the pool's edge.

"Of course there was a note," I said. "Nobody is questioning that. Otherwise there wouldn't have been any reason for you to be in the caboose."

"Okay. I'm glad you believe me." She shivered. "It's getting cold and I want to change out of this wet suit." She glanced at Connor. "See you later." She walked through the lobby, every man in sight watching as she disappeared down the hall.

"Thank you for reassuring her," Antonia said.

"I believe her about the note," I said. "It's another matter whether the police do."

"Yes, well, thank you nonetheless." She stood. "I think I'll be going in as well. Maybe I can find something to read in the library." She walked slowly, and for the first time her ramrod posture was missing, the worry heavy on her shoulders.

"I need a break from all of this. Want to grab a bite?" I asked Connor as he dried off and pulled a T-shirt over his head.

"I already promised Chantal I'd go for a trail run with her."

"Tonight? In the dark?" My voice sounded high and squeaky, each word dripping accusation. Very attractive. "I just mean," I dropped the pitch, "I'm surprised Chantal is up for it."

"A good workout is the best thing for reducing stress. At least I think so, and I know Chantal does too."

I knew exactly what kind of good workout Chantal would like to engage in with Connor. She might be accused of murder any time now, but she had her priorities, after all.

"So that's what she meant when she said she'd see you later. She meant literally for this moonlight-run thing. Well, you need to eat afterward."

"We plan on going right through town. We'll pick up something there."

"Of course. How nice." The words came out so hard I almost chipped a tooth. I sighed. "Look, you know I have history with Chantal. She stole my high school boyfriend just because she could and didn't look back. She brings out the worst in me and every other woman that meets her. I know in my heart she isn't capable of murder, and

I'll help her, but she isn't the easiest person for me to be around sometimes."

Connor rolled his eyes. "Really? Your high school boyfriend? That's all childhood stuff. A long time ago. She's actually not a bad person."

"I realize that." I fought to keep my voice calm. "She isn't evil. She's just, uh, a pain." I threw up my hands. "The way she puffs up, swells or melts when a man is anywhere in the room."

"I'm curious, Penny, if you've asked yourself why it bothers you, my spending time with Chantal."

Was it that obvious it bothered me? "It doesn't bother me. It doesn't bother me in the least. I just know she chews up guys and spits them out."

"Your lack of confidence in my ability to navigate the dating world is remarkable. How I've managed to survive all these years without your advice is amazing." He stood.

"Well, since my spending time with Chantal doesn't bother you, I need to go get ready for my run."

He draped his towel around his neck and cut across the lawn to his room. After the door slid shut behind him, I stood and stomped into the library. Antonia watched as I paced around the room, running my fingers across the leather bindings.

"All classics. Why don't you find one and settle in?" Antonia said.

"I can't. Doesn't it bother you that Chantal isn't taking this more seriously? She could be arrested for murder and she's out running around." Boy, I bet that's been said a few times. "In this case, I mean she really is out running. Around. With Connor. You would think she'd be more concerned."

Antonia turned a page. "I don't think her getting a little exercise means she isn't taking it seriously. She might as well get some fresh air. I mean, what else can she do?"

"For one thing, she could help us figure out what happened." What was I saying? Chantal would only be in the way. But still. "I'm just not sure why she gets to go for a moonlight run, and I'm stuck thinking about how to get her off a possible murder charge."

Antonia snorted. "Like you've ever in your life wanted to go for a run, at night or any other time. No, I don't think you're bothered by the run. I think you're bothered by the company she has during this run."

"Connor can run with whoever he wants. It's of no consequence to me, and I'm not bothered in the least."

Antonia raised her brow. "Yes, I can tell by the way you're circling the room."

The door opened and Kim stepped into the library. She shut the door with a good swing before she turned and spotted us. "Oh, I didn't know anyone was here. Can I join you?"

"Of course," Antonia said. "How are you holding up?"

"This hasn't been the trip we had in mind, any of us, but there are worse places to be stuck and, considering what happened to that poor girl, I don't suppose I should complain." Kim crossed her arms. "Jim still wants to continue with the investment. He says her death doesn't have anything to do with the train, so why should it change our decision to invest? I honestly don't know what to do. That's why I'm here now. He brought it up again, and I didn't want to listen anymore."

"It looks like the police think it was murder, which lets Bill and the train line off the hook," I said.

"I wonder how much longer they'll keep us here," Kim said.

"Perhaps another day or two," I said.

"I hope it isn't longer than that. Jim needs to get back to Chicago for work. You'd think since he deals with trains all day it'd be the last thing he'd want to invest in."

"Oh, I don't know about that," I said. "Part of this investment is knowing the wine business and if tourists will like the venue. The other part is whether the trains and infrastructure are working. Jim would know that better than any of us."

"Jim claims the land up here alone is worth the investment," Kim said.

"Well, there you are then," Antonia said. "Information like that can be invaluable. I'd like to talk to him about it at some point."

"He loves talking about trains. I'm sure anytime you're interested, Jim would be willing."

"Ah, I found you. What would I be willing?" Jim stood in the doorway and looked around.

"Antonia wants to know more about the trains, and I told her you wouldn't mind."

"Sure, sure. No problem."

"We don't need to do it now." Antonia started to get up.

"Now is as good a time as any." Jim watched as I backed toward the door. "You might be interested to hear about how this model has the advanced coupling system. It was used for the first time on these very trains."

Snore. "Maybe tomorrow." Or never. "I'm going to go on up. Have fun."

I gave Antonia a little finger wave, Chantal's irritating

trademark, and went back out on the patio, taking a seat at the pool under one of the gas heaters. The full moon had settled low in the valley, and I could just make out Mount Saint Helena against the night sky.

Apparently the water was warm enough to swim in, despite the chill in the air. Adults swam laps on one side while children splashed together on the other side, their efforts sending billows of steam off the water's surface.

The heater's warmth and the sound of water splashing were soothing, and I must have dozed off. The next thing I knew, the pool was empty and the night was chillier than when I'd sat down. As I shook off sleep, voices carried across the garden. With the moon and garden lights, it was easy to see the couple coming up the path. Connor wore a white running shirt and dark shorts, while Chantal had on yet another red workout outfit. Her hair was once again in a ponytail, this one high on her head. They were laughing and looked like they were having a good time. They stopped in front of me.

"Penny, what are you still doing out here?" Chantal raised a brow. "Wait, let me guess. Were you waiting for us?" She turned to Connor. "I think you might have a chaperone."

"Don't be ridiculous," I said in a huff. Very adult. "It's a beautiful night and I was just sitting here enjoying it, although your mother did say to ask you to join her in the library if I saw you." Good enough. Hopefully she'd get stuck learning all about train couplers.

After she'd gone, Connor took a seat next to me.

"So, did you have a good run?"

"Like you said, it's a great night to be out."

"How was your dinner and where did you eat?" I didn't

sound causally interested. I sounded cranky. "It doesn't matter. Never mind."

Connor raised his gaze to the sky. "We just grabbed a bite. Some Italian."

I sat in silence until Chantal's laughter filtered outside from the open library doors. I bet Jim wasn't talking to *her* about trains.

"She doesn't seem to be very worried," I said. "If I were all but accused of murder, you wouldn't catch me acting like I didn't have a care."

"Everybody copes differently. Chantal just pretends the problem doesn't exist, whereas you face problems head-on. It's part of who you are and probably why you chose a career in photography. You want to see everything, know everything." Connor knew that I'd been a photojournalist before returning to the winery. "You ever miss it?"

I tried to remember what my life had been like a little over a year ago. At the time I wasn't sure I'd been ready to leave behind a life of travel, living out of a suitcase, and the many nights just like this one in beautiful foreign locations. Now the travel seemed difficult, the suitcase heavy and the nights lonely.

"I haven't missed it for a single minute."

I thought about Chantal. "I'll concede everyone acts differently in these situations. And besides, how often is a person accused of murder? It's not like you can actually prepare for such a thing."

"Then what are you doing out here, really?"

"Believe me, I wasn't waiting for you." Not consciously. "I've just got a lot I'm trying to figure out. This afternoon we saw Bill and Vance in town. Vance is trying to get back the money Tara invested. Bill was worried enough about it to stop in at his attorney's office."

"How do you know he went to see an attorney?"

"I followed him."

Connor raised an eyebrow.

"Then at lunch Antonia and I made a list of suspects. There are plenty of people the police chief should be looking at besides Chantal."

Connor listened while I went over the likely suspects and motives. When I'd finished, he just sat looking at me.

"What?"

"You followed Bill? Into the attorney's office?"

"He was just standing in the lobby."

"If he hadn't been in the lobby, what were you planning on doing?"

"Not a clue. Good thing it didn't get that far."

"Glad to see you're so prepared. Do you think you can figure out who killed Tara?"

"I'm going to try. They've got the wrong suspect, and I'm not going to let Antonia see her daughter arrested for a murder she didn't commit."

"Do you have a plan?"

"Of course I have a plan."

"What is it?"

"I figure Vance is the likely killer. He's the one with the most to lose, and he didn't like Tara one bit. He's shown he's capable of the anger necessary to do such a thing. He has the best motive. I'm going to lean on him. See if I can make him crack."

"That's the extent of the plan?" Connor put "the plan" in air quotes.

"The plan is in the development stages. I'm working on it."

"The first problem I see is that Vance isn't going to take kindly to you trying to make him crack. People get angry at being leaned on, and you just said he's got a temper."

"I can't believe I'm saying this, but we need to help Chantal. She doesn't have a clue how much trouble she's in. I think the police have their minds made up. If we don't come up with someone else for that police chief to sink his teeth into, he'll arrest her. He isn't fond of winery people, and here's a wealthy one from outside his area that looks good for this murder. He gets his killer without ruffling local feathers."

Connor stood and I followed.

"I think Chantal is lucky she's got you on her side. I'm not saying don't lean on Vance or anyone you think may have done this." He rested his shoulder against the pole of the gas heater and turned toward me. "I'm just saying I want to be there."

"You want to be where?" I was too close to the heater and my face felt flush.

"I want to be there when you're leaning on people." He smelled like cinnamon. Who goes for a run and smells even better after?

"Why?" My voice came out a whisper. My best effort. Very sexy.

"Because"—Connor turned his head toward me, his face inches from mine—"at some point you're going to get in over your head. You always do."

I pushed him away and turned right into the edge of the heater. It caught the center of my forehead. I hopped around for a full minute, trying not to fill the night air with expletives.

"Am I bleeding?" I felt dizzy. "I'm bleeding!"

"Here, let me see." Connor tried to remove my hand and I slapped him away.

"Forget it! I won't get in over my head. And if I do, I won't ask for your help."

"You see the problem with that? If you're in over your head, by definition, it's too late to ask for help." He had that playful little smile he gets sometimes. "Come on. Let me see your head."

I rolled my eyes and pulled my hand away. "That really hurt."

"You aren't bleeding. It's a tiny little bump. It'll be gone in an hour."

"I'll be gone much sooner than that." Very dramatic. I turned to go.

"For someone who has a habit of finding killers, you have very thin skin."

I didn't respond, not realizing how quickly that comment would be tested.

Fourteen

I HAD a fitful night. The down comforter, so inviting before, now seemed hot and heavy. It didn't feel as if there was any air in the room. I thrashed around until any real chance of sleep was gone, just about when silver moonlight gave way to a steel-gray dawn. With relief, I threw off the covers, opened the terrace doors and stepped into crisp morning air.

It was too early for the hotel kitchen to be open, so I managed a cup of French roast with the in-room coffeemaker. While it brewed, I pulled on a fluffy turquoise sweater, some jeans and sneakers, and pulled my curls back with two barrettes.

Grabbing the coffee and my camera from its case, I left the room and walked down the stairs and through the silent lobby. One person sat behind the desk as I tossed my empty cup away and slid open the rear doors. Passing the pool, its steam rising into the still morning air, I crossed into the open field of the vineyard.

The camera weight felt comforting in my hands as I snapped a few shots to test my settings. Most cameras today make these decisions automatically, but the results are predictable. Great photography often comes with camera settings that most would dismiss: a longer exposure, the reduction of light. The things that make a photograph extraordinary are sometimes hard to explain.

When I decided to be a photographer, I'd imagined spending my life capturing images of fleeting beauty. However, I'd been offered the chance to travel the world as a photojournalist, and beauty didn't pay. The years I spent behind the camera required me to see far more of the world's suffering than I could have imagined, often with more clarity than I would have liked. More than once I'd hidden my pain behind the lens. When a sense of survival would have softened the memories of what I'd seen, the remaining photos still existed to remind me. I'd been right to leave that behind, returning to the winery and taking the photos I wanted. Now, with some time spent away from that life, I was finally letting go.

I worked my way down long rows of vines, gnarled figures with their arms outstretched toward the sullen sky, waiting for winter to begin in earnest. Dark clouds rolled over the horizon, and from somewhere, thunder echoed through the valley. The starkness matched my mood. I would print the scene in black and white, so I shot it looking for contrasts in the grays. I picked my way across the rows until I hit the bike path. I was alone this morning. No dog walkers, happy tourists or even die-hard fitness buffs joined me. The air was heavy and still when I finally turned back toward the hotel.

Usually mornings spent alone with my camera brought comfort, but this time I carried the unease that had ruined my night. Two days had passed since Tara's death, and the police still seemed focused on Chantal as the likely suspect. There were others with better motives, but finding Chantal in the caboose had moved her to the top of the list. Removing her from that list was going to be a difficult task, and I had no idea how to accomplish it.

I was lost in these thoughts when I felt a chill on my neck. Now, I'm easily spooked. Always have been. Ironic, considering what I've photographed. But behind a lens, I feel invisible. In reality, I'm not particularly brave, so at first I figured it was just my nerves. Nobody was on the path in either direction, and it was quiet. Wait. It was too quiet. I didn't hear a sound. *Any* sound. Nothing, when moments before, birds had chirped and squirrels frolicked in the thicket around me.

With years of practice, I swung the camera to my eye and scanned the brush around me, but nothing unusual appeared in the magnified lens.

I turned back toward the hotel, casting glances over my shoulder. My sneakers didn't make a sound. I strained to hear any movement behind me, and soon deliberate footsteps followed me through the brush. I picked up my pace, only to hear a branch snap.

When I sped up, the steps kept pace. I was in a deep curve of the path, out of sight of both the vineyard and hotel. The steps gained on me, coming from the side. Something in the thicket next to me spooked a flock of birds, and I started to run. The camera banged against my side. Tears ran down my cheeks and my lungs were burning. I wasn't going to make it.

"Miss Penny!"

I looked up and George was standing at the curve. Abruptly the steps stopped, turned and faded. I quit running and bent over, breathing deep.

George walked up to me, wearing his Armani suit and pristine white walking shoes. "I say, it looks like you've overdone the running. I always try to fit in a walk before my shift. Never did take to all the jogging you native Californians love so much."

I didn't answer, mostly because I couldn't. I was still grasping my sides and sweat was trickling down my cheek.

"Perhaps you need to pace yourself."

"Someone was following me."

"Just now?" George looked past me down the path. "I can't see anyone."

"In the forest. Somebody cut through the forest, trying to catch me in the bend. I heard them."

"Maybe someone you know?"

"No, it wasn't like that." How could I explain?

"Wait here."

"No problem." I could barely stand.

George worked back down the path some distance before he retraced his steps.

"It looks to be empty now." He raised a brow. "Maybe it was a deer or perhaps the birds. We have a lot of them around here that make unusual sounds."

I shook my head, still holding my sides. "It wasn't a bird."

George took his time answering. He spoke slowly as he

considered his response. "I believe you, indeed, but, um, with all due respect, it's difficult to imagine how anyone would know you'd be here." He turned slightly pink. "You don't appear to be a regular morning jogger. And at this time of day, I don't mean to question you, but are you sure you didn't imagine it?"

"I'm sure. I was in the vineyard for an hour, easily visible from the hotel, so it could have been someone from here. They might have seen me start toward the path and gotten ahead of me." I shook my head. "It wasn't my imagination."

"No, no. Of course not. I am only pointing out the things other people will be asking of you. The obvious comment you'll hear is that these woods are full of deer and rabbits."

He was right. It wasn't a deer, but I didn't have any proof. The forest was again filled with the rustling of squirrels and birds chirping in the trees. How to describe to George how that all went quiet, that a deer wouldn't have caused that terrible stillness to descend?

"You still look quite pale," George said. "I suggest we retreat for a nice cup of coffee. The strongest brew I can get you to drink. Perhaps even with a bit of a kicker, if I may be so bold."

"You certainly may." I followed him back to the hotel with one last glance over my shoulder. It was the same vineyard, the same path. It looked as it had this morning, but now a pall hung over the landscape and I knew, for me, everything had changed.

"ARE you sure you didn't imagine it? You've been a little high-strung your entire life, and this hasn't been the most relaxing trip." Antonia waved her hand. "I'm not trying to dismiss what you felt. I'm sure it was perfectly frightful. I'm just not sure it was actually real."

We sat on blue-and-white-striped recliners out in the gardens. Honeysuckle scented the late-autumn air. Water splashing into the pool echoed around us.

"So you aren't dismissing my fears, you just think they're all in my head."

"It's simply hard to imagine something like that happening. I mean, if someone did try to corner you this morning, what was the motive? You didn't know Tara or anyone else on this trip before we got here, so what would be the point of harming you?"

"The point is pretty obvious to me. Here I am going around basically accusing everyone we've met since arriving of possibly throwing someone off a train. If I've hit a raw nerve, it shouldn't be any great surprise."

"Speaking of raw nerves. No need to get testy with me."

"Nobody's chasing you through the brush, Antonia."

"Yes, well, you know I do appreciate your efforts. Chantal does as well."

"Yes, she looks overcome with gratitude, although it's hard to tell when she's sipping wine and reigning supreme in the Jacuzzi." Chantal soaked in the steaming water with a red-lace-over-black bikini, a cloud of testosterone surrounding her. "She's got every man in the place at attention. They look like a swarm of drones."

"Not all of them." Antonia nodded toward the far end of the pool.

Connor swam laps and, since I'd arrived, he hadn't glanced Chantal's way once. I knew. I kept checking.

"Are you going to tell him about your encounter this morning?"

"No. There isn't anything to be done about it, so why get him worked up for nothing?"

"I agree wholeheartedly. I'm sure it was quite frightening while you were going through it, but in the retelling, some of that is lost. I'm not saying you aren't accurate in your account, I just don't know what there is to be gained by telling Connor."

Antonia closed her eyes and dropped her head back on the recliner. The sun was warm. Every bit of the morning gray had burned away. I didn't blame Antonia for being unconcerned with the morning's events. Here, with the sun playing across my arms, it seemed surreal even to me.

"Why don't you go for a swim and take your mind off it?" Antonia said.

"I don't know." I watched Connor swim laps. "Maybe I'll just read for a while."

"You could go into the spa and take a steam bath. The girl from Chicago, Kim, has been in there every day since we arrived. She loves it."

"That sounds good, actually." I stood to leave.

Antonia held out her hand to stop me.

"What?"

She studied me. "You're looking more like your aunt every day. She had flawless skin, and you have the same big brown eyes. You also have curves where you're supposed to."

"Yeah, a few too many curves."

She shook her finger at me. "Nonsense. You're being too hard on yourself." She tipped her head to where Connor now rested at the edge of the pool. "He doesn't care if you aren't perfect or that you could stand to lose a few pounds. You're beautiful."

"Why, Antonia, you old softy."

Antonia raised her brows and shook her head. "I'm serious. I've spent far too much time alone. I don't want to see the same thing happen to you."

I leaned toward her. "It isn't like you to get sentimental. I'll be fine, I promise."

There was a splash from the pool, and we looked over. The drones had parted and Connor sat on the edge of the Jacuzzi and toweled off. He said something to Chantal and she threw back her head and laughed.

"Stubborn. You've always been so stubborn. And now you've missed your chance. Serves you right."

I shook my head. "Ah, you're back. My world is right once again."

Antonia stood. "Don't forget about our dinner tonight at Berninni Winery. I'm going to take a nap."

"I'm sure you want to look your best for Olympio."

Antonia's cheeks colored. "I just told you I've spent too much time alone. If I can salvage an old flame, more power to me."

"No argument here. I do think it's nice he's invited all of us still in town because of, you know, the accident. I wonder if Tara's husband will come."

"Big Dave? I wouldn't if I were him. Why be reminded of what's happened? I'm sure Vance won't go. He's probably in town looking for action. Nothing but trouble, that young man." She turned to go. "Enjoy your afternoon."

I nodded and spent a few moments watching Chantal

make ten males feel like they were all somehow special. A smile here, a pat on the shoulder there. She made it look far too easy.

Connor was back swimming laps, but I'd lost interest in joining him. Instead, I grabbed a towel and headed toward the spa.

Big Dave sat under a eucalyptus tree farther down the path. I stopped, waiting until he raised his head. His eyes were red and his hands shook as he twisted them in his lap. "Penny, you have a minute?"

"Of course." I sat on the bench next to him. "What a lovely spot to find a little peace. Been here long?"

"Couple hours." He pointed to the book next to him. "I keep thinking I should try and do something, then I realize I'm still sitting here in the same spot."

If he'd been on the path with me earlier, he didn't let on. I couldn't see him running very far. I wasn't fast, by any stretch, but he was a big guy and whoever had been following me kept up with ease.

"Where's Vance?"

He shrugged. "He was hitting balls earlier this morning, and when he finished, he planned to head into town. But I don't really know where he is now." Big Dave swung his head my direction. "Why do you ask?"

I placed my palms on the bench behind me and leaned back. Very nonchalant. "Oh, that's just me. Always being nosy."

"You sure like asking questions. Have you gotten any answers that might explain what happened to Tara?"

I wasn't sure how to respond. He looked distraught, but how else would he look? Either he was genuinely desolate or he needed to come across that way. Not many husbands would put up with Tara's flirtatious ways, and I wasn't ready to believe his easy acceptance of her prior behavior just yet.

"Nothing so far. There are still a lot of things I'd like to know. If you don't mind, I'd like to ask you a couple more questions."

"Ask whatever you want."

"Well, for starters, I heard that Tara wasn't the type to sign a prenup."

Big Dave flinched and his head jerked back. "Who told you that?"

He didn't need to know I'd gotten that tidbit from Seth. "Is it true?"

"Sure, but it never came up. It was never an issue."

"I find that hard to believe. I mean, a man with your wealth . . ."

"That's the whole point. Don't you get it? Even if she ended up with a chunk, hell, even half of it, I'd still have more than I know what to do with. I'm a country boy. There wasn't anything I needed or wanted more than Tara's smile."

"Did Vance know that Tara hadn't signed a prenup?"

"I never said anything to him, but you can't think he would have done this. He's my son."

"He has a strong motive. We all heard him at lunch. He didn't like the way Tara spent your money." I stood. "It isn't anything the police won't figure out for themselves." If they were looking, that is. "I can stop asking questions if you think it might lead somewhere you don't like."

That wasn't going to happen, but the conversation needed an olive branch.

He shook his head. "No, you ask everything you want to ask. I've got nothing to hide."

I couldn't help it, I believed him. But then again, what else would he say?

"What about Vance?"

Big Dave made fists with both hands, placed them on the bench and pushed himself up. "Now, I want to set the record straight. I don't think he's capable of something this terrible. He's far from perfect, but this is a whole new league. However, if Vance has something he's hiding, I hope you do find it. I've been as good a father as I know how to be. Somebody was killed. Someone I love. You find out who."

"I'm planning on it."

"I do ask one thing of you, Penny. Keep an open mind about Chantal. If there's one thing I learned about my Tara, it's that she could make other women crazy with jealousy. It might be Chantal did this terrible thing. You can't just discount her being found in the caboose with no one able to get out of there after the brake was pulled."

Big Dave hadn't spent all his time crying over the last couple of days. He'd been paying attention.

"I'll remember to keep Chantal on the list," I said.

"Don't forget, Tara knew both Seth and Barb from living here as a kid. Maybe there's something there."

I nodded. "Maybe."

"How do you find out more?"

"Spend as much time as possible with everyone that has a motive."

"Makes sense. Let me know if I can help."

"You can. Are you planning on going to the dinner tonight at Berninni Winery? Olympio invited all of us still being kept here because of, you know, the investigation."

"I wasn't planning on it. Haven't had much of an appetite. You think I should go?"

"The more time we all spend together, the more likely someone will let something slip. Something that doesn't add up, that sticks out."

"I'll be there."

"I suppose Vance won't want to come."

"Don't worry. He'll be there too."

Fifteen

I LEFT Big Dave, stopping briefly at the tennis courts, which ran between the vineyards and the bike path. There wasn't any sign of Vance at the courts, just a bunch of tots only slightly longer than the rackets they could barely swing. Still, most of them were doing better than I could, so I wasn't much of a judge.

I didn't go to the spa in the end; instead I rested for the afternoon in my room, so for once I was early and waiting in the lobby when Antonia joined me several hours later.

"You look amazing," I said, and meant it. Her floor-length dress was black satin shot through with crystal beading. Her silver hair was up and held in place with ornate black and crystal combs.

"How did you get your hair so perfect? It looks like you had it done."

"I did. You just call down and they send someone to

your room. Or you use the salon right down the hall." She looked at the pile of curls on my head. "You should try something different. You've worn your hair that way for thirty years."

I patted my hair. "I actually thought I was looking pretty good." My dark brown cashmere sweaterdress showcased my cleavage, which is decent; hugged my waistline, which isn't bad; and hid my ample bottom, which is a necessity.

"You look pale. You should try some color," Antonia said.

Bill came up behind us. "Well, I think both of you look fine, just fine."

Antonia nodded her approval. "As do you." Bill had lost the overalls and kerchief, opting instead for a dark blue suit.

"Thank you." He straightened his tie. "So we're all here to have a good time tonight, but I've got to ask if you've given any more thought to investing."

Antonia waved her hand. "Honestly, no."

Bill's response was quick. "Now I know you've had other things on your mind, but if you want a good feel for how things are working, Berninni Winery is an excellent example. You can ask Olympio tonight how much more traffic he gets through his winery since we began stopping at his place."

"As you know, there have certainly been distractions on this visit," Antonia said, "although the train is beautiful."

Bill beamed. "Top-notch. Everything is top-notch. And for tonight, I can drive you over to the winery if you like."

"Where are the others?" I asked.

"Well, that young guy, the tennis player with the fancy

car, just left with his dad. The son didn't exactly seem excited about going but, from the way his father was acting, I'm betting they show up. The lovebirds from Chicago rented a horse-drawn carriage."

"And here come Chantal and Connor now," Antonia said.

Chantal had on a chiffon rose-red dress with a black pashmina draped over her arm, but I couldn't take my eyes off Connor in his black pants with a black mock turtleneck and black blazer.

"Wow, you look great." Heat rose to my cheeks.

"What?"

"What?"

He shook his head. "I thought you said something."

"Not me." I hurried ahead. "Come on. We don't want to be late." I threw myself in the front seat next to Bill, my face burning.

Chantal kept the conversation going until we arrived at the entrance to Berninni Winery, where Olympio came to the door to greet us.

"Welcome, my friends, and a most warm welcome to my special friend Antonia." He reached for her hand and placed it on his arm. "A quick tour of my fermentation room is about to start." His gesture took in Jim and Kim, as well as Big Dave and Vance.

"Our guests from out of state haven't seen one before, and it leads right into the cave where we're having dinner."

Chantal's smile faded. "We're eating in a cave?"

"Ah, my dear, many dignitaries and even a president have done so. I do not think you will be disappointed."

Olympio led us behind the main building and up through the gardens to the entrance of the fermentation area.

"It's part of the caves," Connor said.

Olympio held the door. "We designed it that way. The temperature differences are never more than a few degrees, and moving the wine from the fermentation area to the aging barrels and tanks is very convenient."

He stopped at a bar just inside the door. Seth was behind the counter, polishing a glass. He spotted our group, set the glass down and disappeared around the corner. Barb appeared moments later. She was pale and her eyes were tired, her makeup smudged. "Here, let me get whatever you need," she said.

"Looks like you and Seth work a lot of hours between here and the wine train."

She shrugged. "I work at a restaurant in town too. We need the money. I'm grateful for the weekends here at the winery. Olympio pays us well, and Seth . . . Well, sometimes the environment is easier here."

I knew what she meant: Seth behaved himself under Olympio's watchful eye.

"This is where we have barrel tastings," Olympio said. "Do all of you know what that is?"

"Not a clue," Vance said. "But I'm willing to try it." He pulled up a stool. "This may not be a wasted night after all."

Olympio was gracious in his answer as he pulled out a seat for Kim. "We will certainly try to make it worth your time. A barrel tasting is an event wineries have several times a year, to sample very young wines right from the oak barrels or stainless tanks they are aging in. It's a chance to see how the wine is developing. If you like the direction a wine is going, you may order quantities then and there, sometimes at a significant discount. Collectors often make use of these opportunities to stock their cellars."

He signaled Barb to pour from a bottle into glasses already on the counter. "This is a Chardonnay, one that holds much promise. Remember: you don't collect white wines the way you do reds. There is a saying: 'Red wines age, white wines just get old.'"

"He certainly knows how to make his guests feel welcome," I said.

"Yes, he's always been very hospitable," Antonia said, as Olympio caught her eye.

"To those of you who have knowledge of how wine is made, indulge me while I give a short explanation to our guests from other parts of the country."

I fell behind the group to join Big Dave. "I'm surprised you got him to come." I tipped my head toward Vance.

"I told him he'd be cut off clean if he didn't stop the way he was behaving. I should have been stronger with him before this." Vance leaned on the bar and Big Dave shook his head. "I just hope I'm not too late."

We walked a short distance down the rows of tanks, both steel and oak. The structure was much larger than our building at home. It was even larger than Antonia's, although she would never admit it. We stopped at the midpoint.

"Here is where we add yeast to the grapes, turning them into wine. Fermentation is complete when the sugar in the grapes is turned into alcohol. Carbon dioxide and heat are also produced." Olympio walked up to an oak barrel. "You can hear it, this bubbling of grapes into wine."

Kim strolled down the aisle, looking at the ceiling. "What are all the fans for?"

"Ah, a good question," Olympio said. "One of the hazards in making wine is the carbon dioxide that builds up in the process. It can be very dangerous if the doors are closed and the exhaust fans fail to work, or are reversed."

"What happens?" Kim asked.

"The gas builds up quickly in the caves. Although we've never had an accident here, people have suffocated at other wineries from this. Not a pleasant death."

Olympio walked to the wall and gestured to a control panel. "Everything is easily monitored from here. Lights, power, even the temperature regulators, as well as the exhaust fans, all working fine."

We walked through the fermentation area, entering the main cave Antonia and I had been in the day before. Olympio led us through a maze of turns that ended in a quaint and somehow welcoming hollow, lit with candles and lined with wine racks.

"This is the oldest wine cellar in California, and some of these bottles are older than the state itself." Olympio stood a bit taller. "This is my pride and joy. Welcome, my honored guests."

"Oh, please, they've probably turned to vinegar by now," Antonia whispered.

I kicked her and skirted around to the rear of the table. "It's beautiful, Olympio. Thank you."

A chirping came from the corner where a cage of yellow canaries sang.

"You have birds here," Kim said. "Not something I expected to see."

Olympio went to the cage, and two bright yellow birds came to him at once.

"Usually they live in my offices in a sunny window. I bring them down when I have company here for dinner. Canaries have a long tradition in the caves. If there is a buildup of the carbon dioxide, they will be impacted first. Now they are just my little companions." Olympio gestured around the table. "Sit, sit." He pulled the chair out at the head. "Antonia, you must sit here. Opposite me."

Chantal practically shoved Kim out of the way to get the seat next to Connor, and he pulled her chair out. I faced them from the other side of the table, next to Vance, who jerked out his own chair and dropped into it, elbows on the table, until he caught his father's gaze. The elbows were removed. I managed to slip into my own seat unaided.

Olympio smiled around the table. "Naturally we have a wine selection with every course, and we have ample courses. My chef has outdone himself with an assortment of dishes, starting with peppered tuna tartare with tomato fondant. I hope you are hungry."

TWO hours later I was full, slightly tipsy, and ready to leave. Vance hadn't eaten, drank everything put in front of him, and managed to ignore me the entire meal. Bill was on my other side, and even if I managed to forget most of the conversation, I now knew more about trains than I ever needed to know.

Antonia stifled a yawn and Olympio immediately stood. "It's been a late night and unfortunately it's time for us to say good-bye. Just temporarily, I am hoping."

"Perhaps, Olympio. We shall see." Antonia smiled across the table.

Compliments and accolades were voiced as Olympio led us back into the main cave and out the main doors.

"I must tell Barb and Seth we are finished so they can clear," he said. "I will meet you in the parking lot."

We stepped into the night air and onto the path. Connor and a laughing Chantal passed me, and I fell in next to Antonia. "Did you learn anything?"

She nodded. "Jim is convinced that investing in the trains is a good idea. He might be right. Apparently there are setbacks on both sides of the train tracks where you can't build, anywhere from fifty to more than a hundred feet in spots. The train line owns all of this extra land."

"And?"

"And, my dear Penny, that doesn't mean you can't plant grapes there."

I stopped. "He's right. There aren't any vines along the tracks."

She nodded. "I've heard the land here is worth upward of a million dollars an acre along the valley floor. If that's the case then . . ."

"Investors in the train line could be sitting on a fortune in land that isn't being used. Does Kim agree with Jim?"

Antonia shrugged. "She's the more cautious of the two. Jim's more willing to take risks. I like Kim. She seems to have a good head on her shoulders. Not that Jim is wrong. There may be a real opportunity here."

"Antonia, wait." Olympio hurried down the walk to us. "I was wondering if you would permit me to show you my rose garden by night, and then I will gladly drive you back to the hotel."

She arched her brow. "It's too dark to see anything."

He took her arm. "That's why I had lighting installed. Perfect for special guests and special nights, such as this."

She arched her brow even higher. "Exactly how many times have you used that line?"

Olympio answered in a solemn voice. "You are the first one I've asked to share it with me."

Antonia must have heard his sincerity. She glanced over her shoulder. "See you back at the hotel."

I smiled and caught up with the rest of the group. It was dark on the path, the steps dimly lit. Afraid of tripping, I moved carefully, but it was Chantal who hit the ground. One minute she was standing there, and the next she was sitting in a hydrangea.

"I can't believe I did that." She giggled.

"Well, look at those shoes," I said. "Who wears those?"

Chantal lifted her leg in the air and wiggled her ankle. "Just those of us that want to be stylish." She glanced at my flats. "I don't see you taking a tumble anytime soon."

"Yeah, whatever. Can you stand?"

"Of course I can." She put her weight on the leg and promptly fell right into Connor's arms. Convenient.

"Oops," she said. "I guess not. Funny thing is, it doesn't hurt at all."

"It will tomorrow," I said. With any luck.

"Why am I so cold?" She looked around on the ground. "Wait, I forgot my pashmina. My cover. I forgot my cover." She looked over at me. "Penny, will you go get it?"

"I can go back," Bill said.

"No, you go ahead and bring the car around," I said.

"I'll go back for it," Connor said.

"No, that won't work," I said. "You need to help Chantal get to the car."

Big Dave turned to me. "Would you like for me to go with you?"

"They're fine, Dad. Let's go," Vance said.

As rude as Vance was, I couldn't help but agree. "He's right. This isn't a problem."

Chantal sighed and pulled at Connor's arm. "My ankle really hurts. I think I need to get ice on it as soon as possible."

Oh, please. "Everyone just go. I can get a ride with Antonia and Olympio."

"Well, if you're sure," Chantal called back over her shoulder.

Connor studied me over Chantal's head, but I waved him on. "It won't take any time. Don't worry."

Kim and Jim headed toward the main winery, while Big Dave and Vance turned to the parking lot.

Bright lights glowed as I stepped back into the cave's entrance. Even well-lit, the walk was tricky down the main passageway back to the cave where we'd eaten. All the tunnels looked the same, every one stacked to the ceiling with barrels.

There wasn't any sign of Seth or Barb, and when I reached the enclosure, the dining table was still littered with empty dessert plates and coffee cups. I walked by the canaries, who fluttered in their cage at my passing. The pashmina rested on the floor under Chantal's seat. I grabbed it and smelled the faint scent of Obsession perfume.

I'd just walked back past the birdcage when the lights went out. All of them.

Sixteen

THE sudden darkness caught me by surprise. I dropped the wrap and stumbled into a chair in front of me. Backing up, I hit the corner of the table and tipped to the side, falling flat on the rough floor. I sat straight up and smacked my forehead right into the edge of the table.

"Stop moving." My voice echoed around me as I reached out to find the rough surface of the wall. I tried not to panic, but my mouth went dry and my palms were damp. It was so black I couldn't see anything, and the darkness pressed heavy against my face. Olympio's comment that we were seventy feet underground now came back to haunt me. He'd also said it was soundproof. How many side tunnels had I passed getting here? In this total darkness I could easily take a wrong turn. My only real option was to wait until someone came to look for me, a difficult thing to do when every instinct urged me to find the way out.

The cave felt warmer than at dinner, and my throat tightened. I listened for a moment before I realized the hum of the exhaust fans was missing. That might explain why it felt so stuffy, the air so still.

I took a deep breath to try to calm myself and instead remembered Olympio's words. No fans. Without them, carbon dioxide was building up around me. In these caves, deep in the mountainside, there was absolutely nowhere for it to go. But not enough to kill me before someone found me.

Surely not.

If someone was trying to scare me, they could consider this a success. The silence was oppressive, not that I could have heard anything over the pounding of my heart. I reached for my phone, which, of course, had no signal, but the small light was enough to give me some comfort. Using the glow of my screen, I crept down the center aisle. The fear of taking a wrong turn made progress slow. It seemed I'd walked for hours just to cover the short distance to the main door. Finally, as I neared the entrance, the lights came on. I was standing only a few yards away as Olympio and Connor pushed through the door, Antonia right behind them.

"I leave you alone for five minutes and you get locked in?" Connor's harsh words were tempered by the way he grabbed my arms and gave me a gentle hug.

"I'm fine." I wasn't. Not really. "The lights went off." My voice sounded hollow. "So did the exhaust fans. That's what scared me the most, you know. Not hearing those fans."

"You should be okay. We found you in plenty of time," Connor said.

Olympio walked to the control panel and examined the settings. "That is so very odd," his eyes were dark with alarm. "See here. The light switch was off. Sometimes it happens."

"Then what's odd?" I said.

"Both the lights and fans were off. The light switch can get flipped, maybe. But look." He pointed to the control panel. The exhaust fan lever was bright red and clearly marked. "Someone hit both. That never happens. This red lever is never turned off. The exhaust fans go all the time."

Antonia pushed past Connor and scrutinized my face. "Are you sure you're feeling all right?"

I tipped my hand back and forth. "A little light-headed."

"Did you see or hear anyone?"

"Nothing. I'm pretty sure I was alone in there." I took a deep breath. "Look, it turned out okay. Nothing happened."

"Only because we found you in time," Connor said.

"Yes, that's true. I suppose if I'd spent the night in there . . ." I said it lightly, but Olympio looked grave, his lips tight.

"If we hadn't found you when we did, well, we would be having a very different conversation, if at all. After a full night without the fans on, the gases would have built up." He shook his head. "It would not have ended well."

My mouth went dry and I swallowed with effort.

Olympio shook his head, as though the matter was settled for him. "It simply must have been an accident."

"Maybe." I took several deep breaths. "Why did you even think to come back? How did you know I was in trouble?"

"It took forever to get Chantal to the car. She kept

stumbling, and I practically had to carry her," Connor said.

Big surprise.

"By the time we were ready to leave, Olympio and Antonia were in the parking lot getting ready to drive back to the hotel. When they said they hadn't seen you, I knew something was wrong." His voice cracked at the end. "I grabbed Olympio and we headed back here."

"I'm so glad you did." I took another deep breath. "I'm sure it was an accident." I wasn't nearly as convinced as I tried to sound. "Olympio, I don't suppose you know where Seth and Barb are. The table hasn't been cleared yet."

"I just saw them both in the winery. They are finishing up the bar now."

Where had they both been fifteen minutes earlier? "There wouldn't be any reason for them to turn off the lights, would there? Maybe they accidentally hit both the lights and the fans."

"No, especially because they still needed to bring the birdcage and the last of the dishes up to the winery. Either way, that main exhaust is never off."

Connor caught that I was trying to pinpoint how many people from dinner had time to circle back to the electrical panel. "Big Dave stopped to talk to us for a minute while Vance got the car. Vance had time before he brought the car around."

Olympio frowned. "Time for what?"

I didn't respond. "For that matter, Big Dave could have circled back around before he joined Vance at the car."

Connor glanced at his watch. "They left not five minutes ago. Then there's Bill. He was waiting in the car when we got to the parking lot with Chantal, but it took so long he had plenty of time."

Olympio shook his hands in the air. "This is crazy talk. Next thing I know you will be accusing that lovely woman from Chicago, Kim, of this terrible thing, and I know she couldn't have."

"Why?"

"She is a nice girl. From the Midwest. They don't do things like this in the Midwest."

"You need to give me a better reason than that," I said.

"She was with us in the garden, discussing roses," he said. "Tell them, Antonia."

"That's true. She did join us for a short time."

"Was she with you when I headed back into the cave?"

Olympio squirmed. "Well, not right at first. Just a few moments later, when her husband went to check on the carriage."

He wrung his hands and frowned. "It cannot be anything more than a terrible accident."

"I'm sure you're right." He wasn't. "Someone just pulled the wrong lever. Things like that happen all the time."

We said good-night to Olympio, leaving him inspecting the electrical panel.

"So," I said as Connor, Antonia and I walked to the parking area. "Kim had enough time before she joined you and Olympio in the garden, and Jim was alone when he went to check on the carriage. In other words, either one of them had time to walk back fifty steps and throw the switches." I groaned. "Olympio showed us the electrical panel right before dinner, remember? It could have been any of them."

"You know there's an outside chance it actually was an accident," Connor said.

"It wasn't any accident. At the very least, someone was trying to scare me."

"The police aren't going to be that easy to convince."

"Forget even telling Chief Harding anything."

"Why are you so certain it was intentional?"

"Because it would be too much of a coincidence after what happened this morning," Antonia spoke up.

"Why, what happened this morning?" Connor looked at me.

I bit my lip. "Someone was following me. On the bike path. I'd pretty much convinced myself it was just my imagination."

"I certainly thought she had imagined it," Antonia said. "Now I'm certain both events were intentional."

Connor stopped and turned to me. "You were scared enough to tell Antonia about this, but you didn't think to tell me?"

Antonia kept walking down the path. "I'll give you two a moment."

"When would I have had a chance to tell you anything? Out by the pool when you and every other man in the hotel were fluttering around Chantal in the hot tub?"

"I don't flutter. I'm not even sure what that means. If something has you scared, tell me. You find me and you tell me."

A warm glow travelled through me. "Okay. I don't know what you could have done, though."

"Whatever happens, we'll figure it out together. Now that I know about this morning, I'm more inclined to agree with you. One incident, maybe. Not two. You need to watch what you're doing, Penny. Someone else certainly is."

"Terrific."

When we reached the car, Chantal eyed me. "Where's my cover?"

Damn. "I couldn't find it. We can get it tomorrow."

Bill kept a flow of chatter going until we reached the hotel. Antonia refrained from asking any questions until we were alone in the hotel corridor. "My room or yours?"

I opened the door and ushered her into my room, hitting the gas starter to the fireplace as she poured two glasses of the house wine.

"Now, I want you to tell me once again what happened in there." She stared into the flames, turning to me only when I recounted hearing the exhaust fans go off.

"That was a tough moment. There in the dark, knowing the air was slowly going bad."

Antonia gripped her wineglass, the faint tremor in her hand the only sign of her distress. "Have you thought of how easily you could have been left there overnight? I didn't know you were planning on coming back with me. Everyone else would have assumed you'd arrived back at the hotel."

The room started to tilt a bit. I took some deep breaths. "Now that you put it that way . . ."

"This is getting much too dangerous. We must think of something else."

I shook my head. "It doesn't work like that. How do you suggest I let the killer know we've decided to back off? Not that I have."

She started to speak and I held up my hand.

"We started this, so we need to see it through. We need to get to whoever is responsible before they get to me."

Antonia polished off her glass in one gulp and held it out for a refill. "I concede your point. If I could somehow get you out of this, I would, but I think you're right. They won't stop, and neither can we."

I slept little, and when the pink dawn rolled over the horizon, I gathered up the comforter and moved out onto the veranda. I waved to George as he returned from his morning walk on the bike path. He moved across the patio, looking stylish, even at this early hour, in his Armani suit and spiffy white walking shoes. When I got a knock on my door a short while later, I wasn't surprised to see him standing there with a pot of strong coffee and a basket of bagels and spread.

"I love this hotel. Honestly, George, keep treating me this way, and you'll never get rid of me."

He smiled and moved to the table, setting the tray down. "I like seeing people enjoy the hotel. It's quite romantic. Of course, like in any hotel, you get to see a bit of everything. Believe me, I've seen it all in the years I've worked here. Take last night. There was a terrible row from some couple from the Midwest."

My ears perked up. "From the Midwest?"

George poured a cup of the dark brew. "So I gather. Cream?"

"Black. Where in the Midwest?"

"Chicago, I believe. Now that I think about it, they're

part of the group invited by the train line. You probably know them."

Kim and Jim? Fighting? I didn't believe it. "What were they fighting about?"

"I shouldn't say more. It really isn't very professional." George leaned in, a gleam in his eye. "From what I could gather, however, she has quite the colorful vocabulary."

"I wonder what the problem was." I watched his face.

George rocked back and forth for a moment, his hands held in front of him, fingertips tapping together as he mulled over how to answer. Satisfied, he leaned in. "Apparently there was mention of how much, um, her husband had to drink at dinner. Apparently he let the horses run, which must be jargon for something."

"They rented a horse-drawn carriage to go to dinner at Berninni's last night."

"Ah, that might explain it." George gave a conspiratorial nod.

"Did you hear anything specific?"

George coughed discreetly. "I believe I did hear something along the lines of, 'Dammit, Jim! It's wine tasting, not wine swigging.' She then went on to accuse him of slugging it back, in language most inventive."

So, Kim had a temper. I thanked George, refilled my coffee and returned to my spot outside. Shortly after sunrise, Antonia stepped out onto her adjoining veranda. She sipped from a cup as she studied me.

"What?"

"You look absolutely exhausted. Did you get any rest at all?"

"I've had better nights. Someone trying to kill you tends to set your nerves on edge."

"I was thinking about it," she said. "Someone took a risk going to the control panel and throwing those switches while you were in the cave. Someone willing to chance being seen for the opportunity to frighten you, or worse."

I swallowed, my mouth dry. Then my stomach growled.

"Was that you?"

"Evidently I can be scared and hungry at the same time. Want to walk back into town and have breakfast at The Diner again?"

"Not this morning. I think I'll just relax. I didn't sleep any better than you did." She turned her eyes to me, and her concern was apparent.

"Look at me." I wiggled my arms and shook my head. "Everything's still where it's supposed to be. I'm not that easy to kill. If that were the case, I'd have been finished a long time ago."

"Your reassurance is anything but comforting. I repeat, you need to be careful." She set her china cup down with a clank. "But enough about that. The train company is sponsoring a lunch and wine tasting for us here at the hotel. They're doing all they can to put a positive spin on our inability to leave town. And on that subject, I think it's about time Chief Harding admits he doesn't actually have anything on Chantal. He can't keep us here indefinitely."

"I know," I said. "I'll go have another talk with him."

"You shouldn't be going anywhere alone."

"I'll ask Connor."

"He left for a run a few minutes ago."

"Of course he did." Did the man ever sleep in?

Antonia pointed toward the horizon. "He went that way if you want to find him."

"How long have you known me? What behavior have I ever exhibited that would suggest to you I might possibly take it upon myself to go running across the countryside first thing in the morning?"

Antonia held up her palm. "Fine. It was just a suggestion. Go ahead and wait for him then."

I sighed. "Do you want some coffee? George brought me an entire pot."

Antonia nodded and passed her cup over from her veranda. We drank our coffee in silence until Connor turned into the garden. I flagged him down. He stopped under my window. Antonia stayed where she was, listening to every word, no doubt. I tried to keep from staring at his legs, which were basically perfect.

He peered up at me. "How are you this morning?"

"Tired and anxious. Sadly, it hasn't put a damper on my appetite. Want to walk into town to grab a bite? While we're there, I want to see if the police have any updates. It's about time they let us know when we can go."

"Give me ten minutes to shower."

I bit my lip to stop the imagery that conjured up. "Sure you're not too tired from your run?"

"It was a short one. I didn't even hit four miles."

"Oh, well, sure. Why did you even bother?"

"I'll meet you in the lobby in ten minutes."

I had just enough time to throw on jeans and a sweater, stopping to pick up a coffee in the lobby. Connor grabbed a cup as well, and we started off.

A short time later he looked around the path. "Show

me where you think someone was waiting for you yesterday."

I pointed out the thicket. "I know it's hard to believe, especially now under this perfect blue sky and the crisp, clear air, but yesterday, just around this corner, the birds went quiet and footsteps kept time with mine. Right here is where I met George coming from the hotel. And look at it." I pointed to the brush. "It's overgrown, hard to navigate. Someone had to work at getting through that, all to get me alone out here."

Some of the fear I'd felt yesterday returned. "It couldn't be a coincidence—this and then what happened in the caves last night."

"I don't think it was either," Connor said. "Now we just need to convince Chief Harding."

After our walk, I felt entitled to waffles at The Diner. Connor ordered the same, although he was quick to point out that he'd gone for a run as well.

"I'm planning on hitting the gym this afternoon." I was too, and as a reward, I might get a massage right after. If I was stuck at the hotel, I might as well enjoy myself.

After we'd eaten, the walk to the police station took less than five minutes. The moss-green wooden-frame building looked right out of central casting. A plank sidewalk, worn and uneven from years of use, was framed with a white wooden railing. I could easily imagine lawmen down the years sitting there watching over the town, likely in the same rocking chair that now sat empty.

The front door creaked open and we entered a small lobby facing a waist-high counter. To the rear were two doors, both open. Several deputies moved about in the office on the right. I stepped up to the counter. A woman sat at a desk between the two offices. She was tiny, with shocking white hair, and she was wearing a baby-pink sweater.

When she spotted me, she walked over, peering over her glasses. "Hello, dear. How can I help you?" She flashed me the sweetest smile I'd ever seen. She reminded me of cotton candy.

"We're looking for Police Chief Lawrence Harding. Is he in?"

The smile faded a bit and her fingers started tapping on the counter. "Harding stepped out a while ago. Didn't say when he'd be back."

I glanced at her name tag: Myrtle. "I didn't know it was okay to call him by his last name. I guess he's less formal in the office."

She snorted and gestured with her head toward the deputies. "Wanna bet? Those boys in back know to use his full name, or they better get ready to catch an earful."

I nodded. "I made the mistake of calling him Mr. Harding. I won't be doing that again."

She rolled her eyes. "That sounds like him. Scaring the tourists. Smart."

Connor leaned on the counter. "How do you know we're tourists?"

There was a twinkle in her wide blue eyes as she appraised him. "I bet women remember you. I know I certainly would."

Connor turned the color of Myrtle's sweater, and I hid a smile behind my hand.

"I've lived here my entire life, nearly eighty years. I know everyone in town and all their kin."

"So you must have known Tara when she was growing up," I said.

"The one killed on the train? Sure, I knew her. The question is, how did you?"

I decided to downplay my involvement. "I was on the train when it happened, and I thought of something the police might find useful. I guess working here you hear about everything, especially something like a murder."

"That's about the size of it. This one's the talk of the town. Most of the locals remember Tara. She came from the wrong side. I don't just mean where she grew up. I mean her folks. Her daddy was mean. She didn't have much of a chance."

"Was she ever arrested?"

"She got herself into trouble a couple of times. Silly stuff. Might have been shoplifting." Myrtle rested her chin on one hand. "I've been behind this counter for over fifty years, and I've seen a lot of kids walk through this door. Most are scared out of their minds. Not her. There wasn't much the police were going to threaten her with that was worse than what she'd already gone through."

"Do you remember what happened to her?"

"Sure. Left town as soon as she could. Next thing you know, she's back here and this happens. Should have stayed away."

"I heard she was involved with a local boy," I said. "Played football in high school."

She snorted. "Seth. He's still around. He reminds me a lot of her dad. Just mean. It's a good thing she got away from him. Although it's too bad for his wife."

"Oh," I leaned in. "So he married a local girl, then?"

"Barbara. Sweet as can be. Can't understand how she got stuck with him. It would seem she loves him though. No accounting for taste."

"Well, I should let you get back to work."

She shook her head, sending fluffy white curls in every direction. "I'll tell Harding you stopped by."

"Out of curiosity, how do you get away with just using his last name? I thought he insisted everyone use his title."

She snorted. "I'd like to see him try. I've been through six police chiefs. I'll be here long after Harding's gone. Guarantee it."

Seventeen

"WE'VE got time to kill. Let's take a walk through town. Maybe we'll see Harding along the way," I said to Connor.

The windows along Main Street presented everything from sports equipment, which I easily managed to resist, to a confectioner that specialized in red wine–infused chocolate, which I spotted half a block away.

We strolled to the end of the retail area, munching chocolate, and continued out of town along the river. The road curved ahead into a park and public garden, and classical music drifted through the air.

"Let's see what's going on," I said.

We got to the edge of the party before I spotted the bride. "Oops, nothing like crashing a wedding."

"I see some benches ahead," Connor said. "We can sit for a bit and listen to the music."

We sat, enjoying both the music and the chocolate. I was feeling pretty relaxed, the warm sun on my face, chocolate shooting all those endorphins or whatever through my system, so I wasn't really ready when Connor leaned over and whispered in my ear.

"You ever regret not getting married?"

"What?" Why did I feel so defensive? "Why would you ask me that?"

"I just wanted to know if you wish you'd gotten married."

"No!" The truth is "maybe," but I didn't want to go into it.

"Why are you yelling?"

I felt my cheeks redden. "I'm not yelling. It's just not the sort of thing you spring on someone."

"It wasn't an ambush. It's just a simple yes or no question."

"No woman would ever consider that a simple question. It's complicated."

"What's complicated? Either you wish you'd gotten married, or you're happy with the way things turned out."

I rubbed my eyes. They felt gritty from the lack of sleep. "All right, here's the short answer. I wish sometimes I'd gotten married, I suppose. The problem comes when I try to figure out what I would have given up, because there's always a trade-off. I've travelled the world and seen so much. All of it makes me who I am."

"Was that so hard?" He considered me without saying anything for so long I started to squirm.

"What?"

"I wasn't sure you'd be happy when you came back. I wasn't sure you'd stay."

"Are you glad I did?" I regretted the question as soon as I asked it. It sounded so coy. "Why did you stay? Did it ever occur to you to live anywhere else?"

"Sure," he said. "When I lost the winery to my brother, I wanted to live anywhere but Cypress Cove. Your aunt gave me a job running her winery, your winery, while I decided what I wanted to do. That was fifteen years ago."

"Wait a minute." I held up my hand. "What winery? I didn't know you owned a winery."

He nodded. "Well, my family did. Twenty-six acres east of Monterey. It's where I grew up."

I shook my head. "I never realized."

Connor shrugged. "No reason for you to. We had different friends, different schools."

"So what happened?"

Connor was silent for so long I wasn't sure he was going to answer. "I need to start earlier. My father was French and came from a family of vintners. On his own, he purchased a small winery in the Burgundy region. In his early twenties he married and had one son, but years later, he and his wife divorced. My dad wanted a fresh start, so he moved to California. His son was in his teens by then and stayed with his mother in France."

"That explains why you've never mentioned you had a brother."

"We were never close. He's sixteen years older than me, and he seemed to resent Dad remarrying, seemed to resent me. He's never come to California."

"What happened?"

"The plan was to leave the winery in France to my brother, while the winery here was supposed to go to me."

Connor seemed lost in thought and I waited. Finally he gave himself a little shake and hurried forward. "My dad died unexpectedly. It took a while to figure everything out, but there was only one will found, and it left everything to Paul, my brother."

"Didn't he know the winery here was supposed to be yours?"

He shrugged. "As I said, we were never close. He remembered my father's wishes differently than I did. There wasn't anything I could do."

"That's awful. So does Paul still own the winery here?"

Connor shook his head. "No. He sold it to expand the winery in France. My mom moved into town and I started working for your aunt."

"So you lost your home and your property. What happened to Paul?"

"I have no idea. We haven't spoken since." He stood and reached out his hand to me. "You ready?"

We walked in silence until we were back on the trail. "What about you? Why haven't you gotten married, settled down?"

"I've always wanted a place of my own first. It'll be smaller than where I grew up, and I might need to just keep it a vineyard. Sell the grapes to bottle under someone else's label." He looked at me and smiled. "Maybe Joyeux."

"I would welcome that. You know it."

He smiled and continued. "As for marriage, well, I think there's still time."

"But it goes so much faster when you get older." I kept my eyes straight ahead. "There's also meeting the right person."

No physical reaction from Connor, but his voice was low. "Sometimes you just need to know where to look."

I left Connor at his terrace, threw on a lemon-yellow sundress and sandals, and walked into the Silverado room a short time later.

Antonia sat at the bar, and I slid into a seat next to her, nodding when Seth held up a bottle of Pinot Grigio. Barb stood next to him, washing glasses.

"I didn't know you worked for the hotel too," I said to Barb.

Barb shrugged. "We take the work where we get it. We certainly need the money."

Seth tensed next to her and she quickly continued.

"Anyway, in this case, Bill hired us directly through the train company to work this lunch."

Big Dave sat next to me. Vance sagged into the stool next to him and raised a glass to his lips. Big Dave shook his head, but Vance ignored him and downed the contents in one gulp, gesturing as Seth walked past to refill his glass.

Kim and Jim came into the room all smiles and pulled out stools next to Antonia. Whatever argument had occurred the night before seemed behind them, although Jim stuck with club soda.

Connor and Chantal walked into the room together, and I looked away before they caught my glance.

"Their rooms are next to each other. It means nothing," Antonia said.

"I know. Did I say anything?"

"Volumes. Without actually saying a word."

Bill walked over. "Mind if I join you?"

"Of course not," I said.

"Well, this is nice. It's especially encouraging to see you up and around, Penny."

Vance snorted. "Why is that? Has something else happened on this train wreck of a trip?" He chuckled.

Bill bridled. "Actually, it didn't have anything to do whatsoever with my train, but yes, something did happen to Penny." He looked at me. "Do you mind if I tell them?"

"I guess not, but how did you hear about it?"

"Olympio told me this morning. He asked his staff about it, but nobody seemed to know anything."

"That's right," Barb chimed in. "He asked all of us if we'd seen anything." She glanced at Seth and received an unspoken approval to continue. "We wanted to go back into the cave to clean up from your dinner, but after what happened, Olympio had us wait until this morning."

"What do you mean?" Big Dave leaned his big arms on the bar. "What happened?"

Bill hesitated. "I guess I should have checked with you before I said anything, Penny. That's just like me. Anyway, at this point can I share the story?"

I raised my palms to the ceiling. "Sure, go ahead." I couldn't very well stop him now, and this way I could watch their reactions.

"After we left the Berninni caves last night, Penny returned for something—"

"Chantal's shawl," Kim offered.

"I remember that," Big Dave said. "We were all on the steps in the garden."

"That's right. That's right." Bill paused. "Anyway, while she was back inside the caves, somehow the building's main power switches, including the air fans, were shut off."

Kim shook her head. "What does that mean?"

"It means she was left in the caves in the dark. Worse, given enough time, the carbon dioxide might have been fatal."

Big Dave held up his hand. "What do you mean *somehow* the switches were turned off?"

"That's just it," Bill said. "The switches are clearly marked and everyone at the winery knows what the consequences can be. Nobody knows how it happened, or if they do, nobody's talking."

Vance snickered. "Classic."

Big Dave turned to him. "That's enough."

"Well, come on. You're thinking it. We're all thinking it. She stuck her nose in and look what it got her."

It was clear Seth agreed with him. He smiled as he moved about the bar, pouring Vance another glass of wine without being prompted. Barb didn't raise her head but watched her husband's movements with cautious glances.

"Well, I, for one, am going to believe it was just an accident," Kim said. "People don't go around like that, trying to kill each other."

"What trip have you been on?" Vance said. "Because from my seat that's exactly what has been happening."

"Jim, what do you think?" Kim demanded.

Her husband shrugged. "Hard to say. I don't remember the switches, and it's possible it was an accident. On the other hand . . ."

It appeared he, too, thought I'd pushed the wrong person, and made it clear with his next statement. "It's best, of course, to leave these things to the police. They know what they're doing."

"Well, I don't like it." Big Dave leaned on the bar and studied my face. "You take this seriously. I agree with him." He bobbed his head toward Jim. "Let the police handle it. Now, I understand," he said to Antonia, "that it's your daughter caught up in this and you want to find out exactly what happened. We all do. Just remember it was my wife"—his voice cracked—"it was my wife that was killed. Let the police solve it."

"She can't. That's the funny part." Vance leaned in to look at me. "You don't know when to stop, do you? You're going to keep pushing into people's business, pushing until somebody pushes back."

"That's enough!" Big Dave, his face red, pushed the half-empty glass of wine away from his son. "You'll keep a civil tongue in your head."

"Yes, let's change the subject. I'm sorry I brought it up," Bill said.

The group fell silent until Antonia finally asked Bill some question about the train schedule. I only half listened. My attention was taken with some unspoken energy. Something was very wrong with one of our group. I could feel the fury. Someone who held their wineglass just a little too tight, holding their smile just a little too long. One of them very much wanted me to stop and knew I wasn't going to.

Eighteen

WITH an effort I turned and focused on Bill. "It's so nice of you to host this lunch. Although, I suppose for you it's work."

"Well, we want to make sure your trip is as nice as can be. At least as nice as it can be, under the circumstances. In any event, I'm sure you'll be able to return home soon. In the meantime," he rubbed his hands together, "you're in for a real treat. We're having a Northern California specialty for this time of year. Crab!"

"You know, we do have crab along the central coast . . ."

"Antonia, let it go." I turned to Bill. "That sounds lovely."

An hour of good wine and fresh crab didn't make the day any worse, and I dug in with gusto as the hotel's head chef walked us through the preparation.

"This is exactly how I like my crab. Pulled from the

ocean this morning and a quick cook in hot water. Crack and eat." He pulled the meat from a claw and ran it across his plate. "Butter is never a bad thing. It's rich and that influences the wine selection. Chardonnay's the way to go, but look for something that isn't also rich. The ones with the buttery undertones are too much. Go for something with a fruity bite to it, or maybe try a Riesling." He swirled the liquid in his glass. "This is great Northern California dining."

Antonia threw down her claw. "Yes, because apparently the only crab worth eating—"

I poured more Chardonnay into her glass. "Have some more wine, Antonia."

After lunch, Vance bolted toward the rear door. Big Dave shook his head and watched him go.

Kim kissed Jim on the forehead. "Time for my massage."

"Have fun, darling. Do you want to bring some water or club soda with you, maybe a glass of wine?" He gestured toward the bar. "Seth can get you something."

"I can get whatever I need at the spa. They have refreshments there. Either way, I wouldn't ask him for anything. I really don't like that guy."

She wasn't alone. I stood and walked toward the entrance, stopping by the table where Connor and Chantal still sat.

"I heard the story about last night," Chantal said. "How you were left in the dark after going back for my shawl."

"Yes." I waited.

"You know, I kind of saved your life."

"What?"

"Well, if I hadn't tripped and needed help walking, we

would have made it to the car faster. We might have left before we saw Antonia and realized you were missing. Nobody would have known you were still there. Good thing I twisted my ankle, and it took so long to get me to the car."

I rubbed my temples as Connor turned away to hide his smile.

"Chantal, if you hadn't forgotten your wrap in the first place, I wouldn't have needed to go back into the caves at all."

"Oh. Well, I suppose that's another way to look at it."

"It certainly is," I said. Chantal had on high heels once again. "It looks like your ankle isn't giving you any problems."

"No." She lifted her leg and wagged her foot back and forth. "I guess it wasn't as bad as I thought."

"Gee, I guess not." I took a deep breath and turned to Connor. "And what are your plans for the afternoon?"

"I'm thinking a game of bocce ball." Connor pushed back from the table. "There's a bunch of Italians here and they asked earlier if I wanted to play."

Big Dave sat alone at his table.

"I hate to see him like that," I said. "Too bad there isn't something to take his mind off Tara's death."

Connor shrugged. "It's all the same to me. I'll ask him if he wants to play bocce ball."

"Hey, that sounds like fun." Jim walked by. "Mind if I join you?"

"Not at all."

The two of them walked to Big Dave's table. Antonia was up with the head chef, likely arguing the merits of

Central California crab, and I was left alone with Chantal, who'd straightened up when Connor left her gravitational pull.

She flipped back her masses of sable-colored locks and looked up at me. "Why'd you have to go and scare him off like that?"

"Do you hear yourself?"

"Penny, relax. I'm only joking, trying to take my mind off, you know, everything else."

"Is it working?"

"Some. And worst case, maybe I get lucky and Connor takes me up on my standing offer."

Perhaps I was just tired, or it might have been the wine. I pulled out a seat, dropped into it, and leaned in. "That's enough. Connor's off-limits."

"What?" The vibrant green eyes, so like Antonia's, opened wide. "He isn't like private land. You can't put a sign on him and tell me not to trespass there."

"That's exactly what I'm saying." I shook my finger. "I've got a long memory, and I clearly recollect back in junior high you made off with my first boyfriend. The first time I really liked a guy, and you knew it."

Chantal studied her scarlet red nail polish. "I don't remember any of this."

"Of course you don't! Does the name Bill Davenport ring a bell? I'll never forget coming around the corner and seeing you two kissing in the parking lot."

She tapped the table with her nails. "Nope, I got nothing."

"Well, I'm not interested in a repeat of that experience."

"Wait a minute. Are you saying you and Connor are an item? Why wouldn't he mention it?"

I held up my hand. "I didn't say we're an item." What exactly was I saying? "Look, you don't know what's between Connor and me—"

"So you're saying there is something between the two of you?"

"No! But you didn't know that!"

Chantal scrunched up her forehead and chewed on the inside of her mouth. "But if there isn't anything between the two of you, then why do you care?"

Damn, she was actually making sense. I didn't have a comeback for this scenario. It was just so unexpected.

"Look, forget I said anything."

She did the hair flip. "Okay by me." She took a closer look at me. "You look terrible. Have you been sleeping?"

"No! Have you already forgotten I was trapped in a cave last night in total darkness with poisonous gases building up around me? And all because you left your throw, which became my problem after you tripped and hurt your ankle." I bent over and looked at her leg. "If you even did."

She opened her mouth but nothing came out.

"What?"

"Well, it hurt last night, anyway." She squirmed in her seat. "I'm a fast healer."

"Ha! Come on, it's a lot more fun to trip and have Connor catch you. Then you can let me go back to get your throw—"

"Which I never did get back—"

"Only to get left in the dark."

She shivered. "I didn't know that was going to happen."

"Believe me when I say I didn't either. Otherwise I would have let you go get your own damn throw."

Antonia tapped me on the shoulder. "What are you two going on about? I could hear you from across the room."

"Penny and Connor are an item."

"That isn't what I said!"

Chantal tossed her hair and stuck out her chin. "Did you or did you not just tell me Connor was off-limits?"

"Yes, I mean no! Look, he works with me and you live next door. Let's be honest, we have history . . . I just see this going down a bad path."

Antonia peered into my face. "You look terrible and you're overreacting. You need to get some rest."

Chantal nodded. "That's what I told her."

"I'm not overreacting!"

"I haven't done anything I don't always do, and it's never bothered you before," Chantal said.

"Of course it's bothered me before. It bothers me all the time."

Antonia took my arm. "Penny, I have a treat for you, which appears to be well-timed."

"What?"

"I took the liberty of booking you a massage this afternoon." She looked at her watch. "You clearly need it. You have an hour, but get a longer one if you think it will make a difference."

A massage. The knot between my shoulder blades loosened at the thought. "All right, fine. That sounds pretty good, if you want to know the truth."

"Of course it does. It was easy to get the appointment this early in the day. That nice girl from Chicago, Kim, is getting one, and it sounds like you two will have the place to yourselves. It should be quiet and peaceful. Maybe you can even get in a nap."

I rubbed my eyes, which were gritty with exhaustion. "The spa is supposed to be spectacular. Thanks."

"There, you see?" Antonia said. "A perfect way to spend the afternoon. Something may even come to you while you're relaxing. Things often present themselves at moments like that."

I thanked Antonia, ignored Chantal and went up to my room. On a shelf I found one of the thick comfy robes I'd seen other guests wandering around in. A few minutes later I made my way down the sweeping stairs, across the lobby and through the back doors.

The golden light of an Indian summer afternoon washed over me the moment I stepped outside. Bees flew lazily through lavender, the warm air heavy with its scent. A couple of youngsters sat eating vanilla ice cream cones, sticky drops falling around their bare feet and into the grass. Crickets chirped and laughter drifted from the bocce game.

Connor saw me and sprinted up the hill. "Where are you off to?"

"Antonia booked me a massage. Thought I needed it."

"You do look pretty thrashed. Obviously you didn't sleep last night."

Everyone's a critic. "How's the game going?"

"Jim's a ringer at this. He's beating everyone."

"Big Dave didn't join you?"

Connor shook his head. "He wasn't up for it. As annoying as Tara was, I think he really loved her. He's lost."

Jim shouted it was Connor's turn.

"Gotta run. Have fun at the spa."

I stood there for a while longer, watching the kids finish up their ice cream. The wine had made me lazy, and I didn't feel like moving much. A massage was the only thing that sounded better than staying right where I was. After what Chantal had been putting me through, I was going to let Antonia spring for the whole package. "Heated stones?" *Sure!* "Brown sugar scrub?" *You bet!* "Care to upgrade for another half hour?" *Who wouldn't?*

With this happy thought I shuffled off down the path. Moments later I pushed open the double glass doors and took a deep breath of lavender-scented air. "Wow, it smells great in here."

The bubbly attendant behind the counter smiled and bobbed her head, long blonde hair falling around her shoulders. She must've used a shoehorn to get into the formfitting black smock that was just long enough and apparently counted as a uniform. "We get that a lot, but after a while you get used to it." She pulled out a clipboard. "I'm Sandie, with an *ie*. You must be Penny."

"Good guess."

Sandie shrugged, miles of blonde hair flipping all over the place. "The weather's so nice, everyone wants to be outside. There are only two people, including you, here for treatments today. It was pretty easy to figure out."

I held up a finger. "Let me guess. Is the other person named Kim?"

"That's right. Also, with you I had some help. The lady that booked your massage said you'd be the one looking like you really needed it."

Perfect. "Um, Sandie, any chance of getting some upgrades to that basic massage?"

She smiled, like I'd just announced it was Christmas, and typed something into the computer. "You bet. We're having a special on the seaweed thermal wrap followed by a Calistoga mud full-body mask. You'll love it."

"I'm sure I will." I took a minute to look around the room. Along one wall, from ceiling to floor, water cascaded down a jade face. "What's that surface?"

"Quartz. It was dug up near here over a hundred years ago," she said.

"I love the sound of water. So peaceful."

She moved out from behind the counter. "You have a robe, so all you need is a key to a locker and sandals." She glanced at my feet. "What's your shoe size?"

"Nine."

"Umm." She eyed my feet. "Let's just make it ten to be on the safe side." She handed me sandals and a numbered key, and pointed down the hall. "Changing rooms and lockers straight ahead. You'll find the solarium, steam rooms and heated pools branching off from there."

"The steam room sounds fabulous. I wonder if I have time."

"Take the time." She eyed me. "Trust me on this."

I didn't have it in me to take offense. Anyway, I knew what she was talking about. I'd seen the blue circles under my eyes that morning.

"The masseuse I booked you with has a flexible schedule today. I'll just tell her to find you in the steam room in half an hour."

"Thanks." I gathered my sandals and key and made my way down the hall, entering the solarium a few moments later. The room was furnished in beiges and greens, with big comfy loungers. In the center of the room, under the skylights, was a large round fountain and palm trees. Along one wall was a large stone fireplace and an attendant was adding a small log to the flames. In one corner was a coffee and hot tea bar, with raw almonds and banana chips. The table opposite had a decanter of water laced with sliced strawberries, a bowl of rolled facecloths and another with sliced cucumbers.

Although I've never really understood why, I know you're supposed to drink extra water when you get a massage. I poured a large glass and perched on one of the loungers, sipping away as I munched on a couple of sliced cucumbers.

The attendant had finished with the fire and came to stand next to me. She looked a lot like Sandie-with-an-*ie*, except her hair was jet black. I didn't really notice her until she did a double take.

"I know. I look like hell. I really need to relax. That's why I'm here, to get a massage."

"Uh, no, that's not it," she said.

I faced her, taking another swig of the water. She had on a white smock and her name was embroidered on it: Suzette.

"Well, then, what can I do for you, Suzette?"

"It's just that, those cucumbers," she pointed to the bowl. "We soak them in rosewater first. They're for putting on your eyes."

Terrific. I was eating eye pads. "I wondered why they tasted so different."

She was just watching me.

"Not bad exactly, just different." Please just let me stop talking.

"Here," Suzette said. "Let me take that from you. I can get you some almonds, or perhaps banana chips."

I handed her my napkin with the rest of the cucumber. "No, I'm fine, thanks. Heaven only knows what I'd do with those, right?"

She looked puzzled. "Those actually *are* for eating."

"No, I get it. I'm fine." Completely humiliated, but fine. "I'm just going to go take a steam bath before my massage."

"Here then, you really do want a couple of these." She handed me two fresh slices of cucumber. "Sometimes the heat can irritate clients' eyes, and having your eyes covered can help you relax." She took a closer look. "They also help firm the skin."

"Okay, fine, I'll take them. Which way is the steam?"

Suzette pointed me down the hall to a glass door. Next to the door was a robe rack and a wicker basket of fluffy white towels. I grabbed a towel, ducked into a dressing room and exchanged my robe for the towel, adding my robe to the one already on the rack.

Nothing was visible through the thick wall of steam. When I pushed open the heavy door, a fresh blast of hot mist came from somewhere above me. The vapor was heavy with eucalyptus. I began to relax as I crept forward. Lying flat on the heated tiles, with cucumbers over my eyes, the scented steam soon had me drifting off. I had no way of knowing how much time had passed before I heard someone at the entrance.

"It's time for your massage, Kim. Kim? Is there a Kim here?" It was Sandie from the front desk. She stood at the open door, peering through the dissipating steam. I turned my head and, for the first time, realized I hadn't been alone.

I rolled on my side and took a closer look at the person lying across from me. She also had cucumbers over her eyes, but I recognized the profile.

"That's her. She must be asleep." I reached over and tapped her on the shoulder. "Kim?" Nothing. I shook her lightly. "She must really be a heavy sleeper." I gave her another shake, and this time the cucumber slices fell away and her face rolled toward me. Her eyes were open, but there were dark red marks around her neck, and she was very, very dead.

Nineteen

I SENSED rather than heard Sandie screaming behind me. I couldn't hear her because the hammering in my head was even louder. I shivered in the hot air and backed away from Kim, bumping right into Sandie. She hadn't moved, and I turned to face her. Even though I knew she was right in front of me, my vision had narrowed and she seemed to be in a tunnel. Her screams brought Suzette, who stopped next to Sandie and joined in on the screaming.

My mind couldn't get around what was on the bench behind me, so I just stood there and watched them scream, Sandie with the blonde hair and black smock, and Suzette with the black hair and white smock. Negatives of each other. Was it a coincidence the smocks were in contrast to their hair? What if they hired a redhead? What would she wear?

I took a few deep breaths and tried to calm myself. I

couldn't think with the screams bouncing off the walls, and without hesitating, I slapped the one on the right. Maybe Sandie. They both stopped instantly and stood there in shocked silence.

"Turn off the steam and call the police," I said, my voice loud in my ears.

Without a word they turned, one to the thermostat on the side wall and the other to the wall phone.

I looked back over my shoulder at Kim. I really didn't want to go back in there, but the police would be here within minutes. If I wanted a closer look, this was my one chance.

I took a moment to change into my robe. Knotting the belt tightly around my waist, I crept back into the steam room. The open door and closed vent had cleared the room, and now puddles formed and water dripped from the ceiling.

Kim was on her back in a one-piece green swimsuit. Her long hair was wrapped in a towel, and she had a diamond stud in her right earlobe. Her left ear was bare.

The roar in my ears returned, but I pushed it down and took a closer look at her neck. Angry red marks stood out on her pale skin. Without touching her, I positioned my hand over the bruised skin. It was a wide reach with a hand larger than mine, and I'm not a small person.

I took a step back. There wasn't any sign of a struggle. After she was dead, the killer must have repositioned her, making it look as if she'd fallen asleep. Either that or she was unconscious when she was killed. If they hadn't come to collect her for her massage, she could have been there for a while.

There was one deep mark about the size of a thumb on the left side of her neck and several smaller marks on the right. I tried to move behind her but the roof sloped, making it impossible. If the killer had done this where she was, which was likely, he was probably left-handed.

"What do you think you're doing in here?"

I knew the voice and tried to gather my thoughts before I turned around. It was Chief Lawrence Harding, and I was in for it.

"Wow. You got here really fast."

Wrong thing to say.

He narrowed his eyes. "You! I might have known." He rested one hand on his hip and with the other he caressed the butt of his gun, as though I might be a threat requiring its use.

"Believe me, I didn't ask to be the one to find her. I just took a steam bath and didn't even realize she was, she was . . ." I dropped back down on the tile bench, put my head between my knees, and pushed a couple of deep breaths into my lungs. When my head cleared, I stood. "I'm surprised to see you so soon. I mean, they just called."

"I was in the area. Lucky for me. Unlucky for you. Seems like you've been at the center of all the trouble this week. Why don't you tell me what you were doing? This is a crime scene."

I fingered my locker key in the pocket of my robe, scooped it out, and dangled it in front of him. "I just came back in to get this."

"And you didn't disturb the body?"

"No. Except when I shook it." I stifled a groan. Even I could hear the problem with that one.

"Do you want to explain yourself?"

"We thought she was asleep! Ask Sandie up front. I think she was the one I slapped. She came in to get Kim for her massage, and I tried to wake her."

"You slapped someone?"

"She *wouldn't* shut up."

He looked angry, or maybe he was just uncomfortable in the warm, damp room. His face was bright red, and the paunch he'd squeezed into a uniform two sizes too small bulged over the top of his pants.

"Do you want to continue this conversation somewhere else?" I glanced behind me. "I wouldn't mind moving if it's all the same to you."

He swiped at the top of his head as water continued to drip from the ceiling. "Go for now, but don't leave the spa. My deputy will be along soon. When he can take charge of this room, I'm going to want to have a talk with you."

"Sure." I pulled the robe around me. "I'll just wait out front."

He didn't answer and turned back to the body.

Just out of sight, I stopped. I'd had my locker key in my robe pocket. Kim didn't have a key on her now. The robe from earlier still hung outside the steam room. I peeked around the corner. Harding was bent over Kim, his back to the door.

I ran my hands across the robe pockets and immediately felt the outline of a key. I slipped my hand into the pocket and grabbed it just moments before Harding came out to grab a towel from the stack to wipe his forehead. Before he spotted me, I scooted around the corner leading back to the dressing room.

The locker numbers were etched into the sides of the keys, and I made my way to Kim's locker. Number twelve. The door opened with a small rush of air. In the front were Kim's dress and matching sandals, both in navy blue. To the back was a black Coach shoulder bag. I pulled it out, wrestled it into the folds of my robe and ducked into one of the private dressing rooms. I spread out the towel I had wrapped around my head and set the purse on it.

Kim's purse was perfectly arranged and looked nothing like the inside of mine. A neat little cosmetics bag held just the essentials, and for some reason her powder blush and eye shadow were in one piece. Mine always shattered within a day or two. Another little matching case had small containers of headache and stomach relievers, tweezers, an emery board and a small sewing kit. A small notebook and attached pen fell out, holding flight information and little else. Reading glasses, her phone and a mystery paperback were the only remaining items.

A quick check of her phone showed calls to the Chicago area. Nothing local. Another pocket held a printout of the profits and losses for the train company. It matched the copy I'd been given. Finally, I ran my hand along the bottom of the bag, looking for the missing diamond stud. Nothing. I replaced everything, scurried back to her locker and shoved the bag back where I'd found it.

Using the wall phone, I called the hotel front desk. I told them Antonia would be asking to enter my room and that I gave my permission for her to do so. Then I asked to be transferred to her room.

"Penny, why on earth are you calling? You're supposed to be getting your massage. I must say I wouldn't have spent the money if I didn't think you were going to relax and enjoy it."

"Antonia, I didn't get a massage. What I did get was another body. George is going to let you into my room. Grab me some sweat clothes and get down here."

To her credit, she didn't ask any questions. She didn't even say good-bye. Ten minutes later she walked through the spa front door. For a woman her age, she knew how to move when she wanted to. She practically sprinted up to me, waving off Sandie when she tried to stop her.

"Talk to me," she said.

I summed up what had happened through the changing-room curtain as I slipped into the sweats.

"What did you find in her bag?" Antonia asked.

"Nothing out of the ordinary." I stepped out from behind the curtain. "Wait here."

"Where on earth are you going?"

"To return a key."

The spa girls weren't in sight and, for the scene of a murder, the hall was eerily quiet, although I heard Harding from somewhere within the spa. I reached the steam room, dropped the key back in Kim's robe and was back with Antonia moments later.

"Did anyone see you?"

"Nope. Not that I learned anything from checking her locker. Why would anyone want Kim dead?"

"Well, you must have seen or learned something."

"I saw her neck." I shut my eyes and swallowed hard. "She looked peaceful enough, until I saw the bruises. Someone crossed her arms. She looked like she could have been asleep from a distance." I stared into nothing as the image came back to me. "My first thought when I saw the marks was the killer was left-handed."

"What makes you say that?"

"There was a row of small bruises on the right side of her neck and one dark deep bruise on the left side." My mouth went dry and a cold sweat ran down the center of my spine. "The size of a thumb."

"I wonder if her husband is left-handed."

I shook my head. "It couldn't have been Jim. He was with Connor, playing bocce ball. I saw him right before I got here."

"Okay then, what if it was a tennis player, someone used to gripping a racket all day using both hands . . .?"

I took over. "Someone equally strong with both hands. That would fit, but I don't know why Vance would want to kill her. Of course, the same could be said for Big Dave, Bill or even Seth. Why would any of the men in our group want to kill Kim?" I rubbed my temples. "And yet, it's got to be one of them."

"No doubt," Antonia said. "There has to be a connection with Tara's death. Someone went to the trouble to sneak in here to kill Kim. That's too much work for it to be a random murder." She pounded her fist in her palm. "I just don't understand it. Surely a mistake's been made. Why would anyone want to kill Kim?"

I sat down hard on the changing bench. "What if that's exactly what happened? A mistake, I mean. I just said it myself. Nobody wanted Kim dead. The one they want dead is me." I grabbed the corner. "When I checked in to the spa, Kim and I were the only two getting massages. We were both wearing identical robes."

Antonia tilted her head and studied me. "You could be mistaken for Kim from the rear, especially if both of you had your hair up in towels."

"We did. And it's practically impossible to see in the steam room."

"But at some point, he would have realized his mistake," Antonia said. "He would have stopped once he saw it wasn't you."

"Oh, no," I said, feeling sick. "You're wrong. Once he grabbed her, she was dead either way. There wasn't anything he could have said to explain why he'd attacked her, so he needed to make sure she wasn't around to say anything."

Antonia considered, then took my hand. "You mustn't blame yourself."

"Kim died because of my snooping."

"Nonsense." Antonia stamped her foot. "Kim died because there's a murderer on the loose. It's time the police stopped looking at Chantal. She couldn't have done this. For one thing, she was in her room."

"She doesn't have the strength, for another," I said, remembering the angry marks on Kim's neck. "Let's go find Chief Harding."

Twenty

"I THINK you'd be surprised at how strong someone can be, in the grips of an uncontrolled emotion." Harding sat at the desk in the spa office, his laced fingers resting on his stomach.

"You can't actually believe Chantal did this to that poor girl." Antonia had insisted she be allowed to join me and, to my surprise, Harding had agreed. A determined Antonia is a hard woman to deny.

"What I can't believe is how the two of you fail to understand how police interviews work. I'll be the one asking questions."

"At least tell me you agree that the two murders are connected," I said.

"It's certainly a possibility, which is why I'm keeping my list of suspects open at this point, including Chantal and everyone that had access to this spa." He narrowed his eyes. "The fact that you found the body doesn't mean you aren't on that list as well."

"If I'd known I was in a steam room with anybody, and I mean *any body*, I would have been out the door."

"Not necessarily. Not if you were guilty. What better place to hide than in plain sight? However," he raised his voice over my protestations, "I have other suspects with more motive than you. No, we'll continue our investigation and follow the leads wherever they take us. It could even be a robbery that ended with unintended consequences."

I caught myself before I snorted. "Two days after someone else in the same group of people is thrown off a train? Quite the coincidence, wouldn't you say?"

He ignored my question. "Did you see a diamond earring?"

"No. I saw she was wearing only one. Maybe it was lost when she was killed."

"Maybe. My deputy is searching the victim's bag for it now."

Good luck finding it there.

"We think Penny might have been the target and that the killer made a mistake," Antonia said.

Harding raised a brow and his lip curled faintly. "Really. You're just going to insist on voicing your opinions on this, aren't you? So go ahead, Penny, tell me why you think you might have been the intended victim."

I gave him the quick version of being followed along the bike path and getting shut in the Berninni caves. While I spoke he looked at his watch several times and checked his phone. When I finished, he sighed.

"So you think you might have heard someone on the

bike path yesterday morning." He rocked back in the chair behind the desk.

"I know it doesn't sound like much, but you weren't there. Just the way the birds, everything, stopped. It just *felt* wrong, and I'm sure I was being watched. Followed."

"Right. And then at Berninni Winery someone turned off all the power when you were alone in the caves. It could have been a coincidence."

"It can't be a coincidence that both things happened to me on the same day."

"If something happened on the bike path, and I'm not convinced there was anything to cause real concern, there's nothing to connect the two events."

"Together they could be taken as a warning," I said.

"A warning? About what?"

"Someone doesn't like my asking questions, interfering."

"Well." He rubbed his arm absently. "You've put me in the unusual position of finding myself in agreement with my suspect, whoever that might be. I don't like you asking questions either."

"Indeed, somebody's got to," Antonia said.

Harding focused his attention on Antonia. His jaw quivered, and when he spoke, he worked to control every word.

"I will allow you some latitude since it's your daughter you're trying to protect." He picked up a pencil, tapping it on the desk while he stared into space. Finally he dropped it and laced his fingers. "It looks like you've been asking questions in spite of my admonitions to stay out of it. If that's the case, tell me what you've discovered about your fellow passengers."

I briefly outlined what I'd learned. Harding didn't move,

his eyes focused on the wall somewhere behind me. When I finished, he flattened his palms together and rested his chin on the tips of his fingers.

"Vance was afraid Tara was spending his inheritance, Big Dave didn't have a prenup, Seth was her high school lover and was possibly rejected in his bid for a final fling, and Barb wanted Tara to keep her hands off Seth. That it?"

My spine stiffened. "All pretty decent reasons to want someone dead. Better than that little scrap Tara had with Chantal."

He watched us for a moment, absently rubbing his chin, until finally he shook his head. "This is how we're going to play this. I know you won't stop meddling where you don't belong, and we all know I can't haul you both down to jail. How's it going to look, me dragging winery owners in? Especially you two."

"Why especially us?" I asked.

He leaned toward us, meaty elbows resting on the desk. "Because you're a yapper, and she's old enough to be my mother."

"It's true," Antonia said. "She is sort of a yapper."

I shot Antonia a look and Harding ignored the interruption. "So here's how it's going to work. Everything you hear, and I mean everything, I want to know about it."

Antonia sniffed. "I would have thought you'd be conducting your own interviews."

"I've interviewed everyone who was on that train. It doesn't matter if you believe me. I don't answer to you."

"Surely the reasons I just gave you prove that other passengers had as much motive as Chantal to kill Tara, if not more," I said.

He rubbed the back of his neck and frowned. "The problem is that nobody else could have been there but Chantal." He swiveled his head toward me. "You're the one who pointed out the tablecloths piled against the door. Nobody else entered that room after the brake was hit and the entry blocked."

"Yes, very clever of you, Penny." Antonia raised her brow. "My daughter and I can't thank you enough for sharing that interpretation of the crime scene."

"But." He held up his hand. "There's something about it I don't like." He tilted his head toward the door. "I also find it unlikely Chantal was responsible for this murder here."

"Well, that's something," I said. "What about me?"

He shook his head. "The span of your hands isn't large enough either. Did you notice anything else in there before I found you with the body?"

He made it sound like I'd rearranged the crime scene. "Just that the killer is probably left-handed."

"Of course," he reached for a notepad. "Because the bruises line up with someone's left hand."

"Or it's someone equally strong with both hands. Someone used to manual labor. Or an athlete. Like a tennis player. I should mention that a couple of nights ago, Vance grabbed my arm in the bar. The power in his grip was astonishing." I thought back. "Come to think of it, he used his left hand."

"There is the problem of getting into the spa without being seen," Harding said.

"Not really. This place is huge and the only staff actually walking around are Sandie and Suzette. The massage rooms are on the far side and can't be seen from the lobby."

Harding flipped his notebook shut. "Interesting information about Vance. I'll make sure to talk to him first." He signaled one of the officers by the door, who nodded and then disappeared. "I'm quite confident this murder was done by a man."

Antonia slapped her palm on the desk. "Finally we're getting somewhere."

He snorted. "Don't get carried away. I just explained to you why Chantal is still very much my prime suspect in Tara's murder. Just because I think the fight she had with Tara is weak as a motive, I still have a problem with her having the only known access to the body. If I come up with a stronger reason for Chantal to be Tara's killer, we're going to be having a very different conversation."

"So what happens next?" I asked.

"As much as I dislike your involvement in this crime, you seem to be getting people to talk. I'm not convinced anyone threatened you on the bike path or at Berninni Winery, but it's possible. If they warned you off, they're nervous. And if you've made someone nervous, you're on the right track."

"It seems reasonable that if we're making progress and we've agreed to keep you informed, maybe you can share with us what you've learned," Antonia said.

He toyed with the pencil. "You still aren't getting how this works. Your daughter is my main suspect. Anything you find out and share with me might prevent her from being charged with murder, but I won't be telling you anything about the case. Not a thing."

Twenty-one

"WHAT a horrible man." Antonia stomped down the path beside me. "He refuses to give us any help, yet he practically admitted we're getting to the truth faster than he is."

"And no doubt if we come up with anything, he'll be ready to swoop in and take all the credit," I said. "Not that it matters, as long as we prove Chantal isn't the killer." Although if I were being honest, I wouldn't mind showing up Harding. Antonia clearly felt the same way.

"His biggest fear is that we'll get better results than he does. That ego of his is nearly as big as that paunch he's sporting."

Uniformed police now walked the garden paths and several of the guests stopped to watch. Near the pool an officer led Vance in our direction, and his voice carried over the garden.

"What's this about anyway? I paid for a full hour's session with the serving machine and I'll expect the hotel to replace my time." Vance wore tennis clothes and appeared flushed. When the officer didn't respond, he continued. "If my racket gets stolen, I'm holding you personally responsible."

He looked up and spotted us. "You two. I might have known you'd be in the thick of it."

I gave him my version of Chantal's little finger wave. It was growing on me. Sarcastic, but immune to criticism. I'm waving. It could almost be mistaken for being civil.

"Penny?"

Barb stood a few steps to my right. She wore a shapeless dress in silver, although it might have been blue a hundred washings ago. It fell below her knees, ending just above little white ankle socks. The sneakers on her feet were also white, or had been at one point.

"I'll see you later." Antonia left the two of us.

"Hi, Barb. What are you doing here?"

She twisted her hands together. "I just wanted to find out if you knew anything more about Tara. I mean, I wondered if the police have any new leads that you know of."

"Nope. Not that Chief Harding is going to tell me. He's a real treat to deal with. Taken quite a dislike to me."

Barb swiped her hair behind her ears. "He's never been anyone's favorite person. He keeps his job, though, so I guess he knows the right people. Men like him always do."

"It's hard to say when he'll name a suspect, especially now that there's been another murder."

Barb's hands froze and she squeezed them together. "Another murder? What time, I mean, when?"

"Just a little while ago."

She started to sway a little.

I stepped toward her. "Are you okay?"

A tremble moved across her face. "I'm fine. Really."

"Look, you need to sit down." I gestured to a set of lawn chairs. "Have a seat in one of these." She took the few necessary steps and collapsed.

"Lunch finished up quite a while ago. I would have thought you'd be gone by now." I looked around. "Is Seth still here or are you alone?"

"Alone." She gestured to the bike path. "I'll walk home in a bit. Our house is on the edge of town. Just over a couple of miles on the path. Easy."

"So what are you still doing here? You've been on your feet all day." I took in the thin wrists and the collarbones so prominent above the edge of her dress. "Want to grab some lunch?"

She shook her head. "I couldn't, really. We're working at Berninni Winery tonight, and I, well, I just thought I'd get some fresh air."

I've seen a lot of good liars, myself included, and Barb wasn't one of them. The thin shoulders hunched beneath the worn fabric as if prepared for a blow. I hated to be the one to deliver it, but I remembered the red marks around Kim's neck.

"Barb, when I said there was a second murder, you didn't ask who. Why wouldn't you want to know who was killed? Or maybe you knew already?"

Barb pressed a hand to her cheek. "Of course not! I don't know why I didn't ask who was killed. I was just confused. You can't possibly think I know something. You can't possibly!"

"No, but what was it you asked? Not who the victim was, but what time it happened. All you wanted to know was when the murder took place. Why would that be your only question?"

"Stop it, Penny. I mean it." She stood and jerked down the steps back to the hotel.

I followed close behind. "Why are you up here alone, Barb? You say you wanted to get some fresh air, but you aren't dressed for a walk. And why, when you hear someone is murdered, would your only question be what time it happened?"

"I won't talk about it." She crossed her arms. "Stop asking me these questions."

"Where is he, Barb? Is that why your first concern is what time the murder happened? Because you don't know where Seth is? Did he run off, and now you're afraid he's done something?"

"Stop it! You can't prove anything. I'm telling you I only came up here for some fresh air."

"Let's see if you feel like sticking to that story after I describe the marks on Kim's neck."

Barb stopped and tilted her head. "What did you say?"

"That I'd still like to see you try and protect Seth if you saw the marks on Kim's neck."

"Kim's dead? The one from Chicago?"

I nodded. "Killed in the spa. I found her."

The tension in Barb's shoulders eased and they dropped. "Seth wouldn't have any reason to kill her. He doesn't even know her."

"Then why are you so worried? Where is he, Barb?"

"I have no idea, but I can tell you he didn't have

anything to do with this." She had some color back in her face, and she looked me straight in the eyes as she said it.

"Okay. Let's say you're right. He didn't kill Kim. Did he kill Tara?"

She bit the side of her mouth and some of the color left her cheeks. "Don't say that. He wouldn't have hurt Tara. Why would he?" She tossed her hair, but the attempt fell short. "She was just part of his past. Part of both our pasts."

She started walking away. "I need to go now. I have to get ready for work soon."

I caught up to her. The strength she'd shown defending Seth seemed to have deserted her, and she moved with heavy steps. She wiped her eyes with the back of her hand, the nails bitten and red. Her breath caught, and she stifled a cry.

I grabbed her arm, forcing her to stop. "What is it? You need to talk to someone and maybe my being a stranger will help. Look at it this way. In another few days, you'll never see me again."

She dug the heels of her palms into her reddened eyes. "It's nothing, really. Nothing you can help with."

"Well, you seem confident he didn't kill Kim. If he killed Tara, it's better if you know now. You need to protect yourself. You don't need him."

She shook her head slowly. "You don't know anything about it. I do need him. I always have. I wish it wasn't the case, but I've always known I can't live without him."

"Can't or won't?"

"Same thing." She sagged. "He didn't kill either one of them. I don't have any proof. I just know he didn't."

"Then what is it? Why do you seem so . . . ?"

"Hopeless?" She took a deep breath and slowly let it out. "I'm here looking for him."

"Right, I get that."

"No, Penny, you don't. I'm looking for him. Here. At a hotel. A hotel that I've followed him to many times before. A hotel that's a short walk from town, from our home. Whenever I can't find him, I know he's here. In this hotel. In one of these rooms. With someone else who, in another couple of days, he'll never see again."

Twenty-two

WITH that, Barb turned and walked down a side path. I let her go and found Antonia sitting on the bench Big Dave had occupied the day before. I took a seat.

"What was that about?"

"She's convinced Seth had nothing to do with the murders."

"Well, of course that's what she's going to say," Antonia gave a dismissive wave.

"No, I really got the feeling she doesn't think he's a killer."

"So what's she doing here?"

"At first she said she was going for a walk. Then she said Seth might be here visiting a guest. A female guest."

"Then she's here looking for him. How very sad."

"And it's not the first time she's done it." I stood. "The fact that she doesn't think Seth is capable doesn't mean he isn't. Let's go back to my room. I want to show you something."

A short time later we stood on my balcony looking out over the resort. The sun was low, the sky a vivid turquoise streaked with bronze. Mustard plants and wild clover wove through the vines, the only sound the soft rustle of a light breeze through the trees.

"Not a day for murder," Antonia said. "Okay, what did you want me to see?"

"Take a look at the layout." The gardens were to the far left, the pool directly below us, and the path to the spa was on our right. Beyond the garden were the woods and the walking path into town. The tennis courts flanked the path. Vineyards lay to the right. An officer walked past the garden, heading toward the spa. Jim walked next to him and said something. The officer shook his head and kept walking.

"He doesn't look like he knows anything yet. I hate to think what he's about to go through," Antonia said.

"We know he's been with Connor playing bocce ball. We should try to figure out where everyone else has been this afternoon."

"So we're agreed you were supposed to be the victim instead of Kim."

"It's the only thing that makes sense." The memory of Kim's lifeless eyes made me shudder. "Barb said Seth wouldn't have killed Kim because he didn't know her. The same could be said about everyone here but her husband, and we know where Jim was at the time of the murder."

Antonia nodded. "You've been asking too many questions about Tara. Someone is willing to go to great lengths to stop you."

"The question is how did they get to the spa." I gestured across the landscape. "Barb got here from the bike path. An easy walk from town, she said. Assuming she's correct about Seth's movements, he's here as well."

Antonia frowned. "We only have Barb's word for it that Seth is here at all."

"You didn't see her face. I believe she followed him and he's somewhere in the hotel."

"Okay, I'll accept that, which brings us to Vance. Huh. Someone with strong hands, likely left-handed. I suppose it narrows things down a bit."

"You said in front of everyone at lunch that you were treating me to the massage. Vance could have easily said he was going to the tennis courts and then walked up to the spa."

"He's got a great motive for killing Tara, after watching her fritter away his father's money. If he had anything to do with her death, he'd certainly want you to quit asking questions. And if he's already killed once . . ."

"Then there's Bill and Big Dave. Bill is here, at least he was after lunch, and Connor said Big Dave didn't join them at bocce ball. He could be anywhere."

She threw up her hands. "Both of them certainly are big guys. Plenty strong enough. This is hopeless. They were all here."

The phone in the room rang and I grabbed it.

"The police just came to get Jim. I don't suppose you know anything about that?" Connor asked.

"Actually, I do."

"Of course you do. I was being facetious."

"Meet me by the pool. I'll be down in a minute."

I left Antonia in her room and joined Connor a few moments later. We sat at one of the patio tables, Connor not saying a word as I recounted finding Kim.

"I don't get it," he said. "Why would someone want Kim dead?"

"I'm not sure Kim was supposed to die. I think maybe they were looking for me."

He paled a bit. "I hadn't thought of that."

"The bike path. Last night in the caves. Maybe someone is desperate to shut me up. And at the spa today, we both had our heads wrapped in towels. We both wore the same robes. In the steam room it's hard to see. Somebody could have made a terrible mistake."

He didn't say anything. I waited. And waited.

Finally I couldn't take the silence. "Say something."

"It could have gone either way. It might have been you."

I heard his voice, but all I saw was Kim's face. And her eyes. I would never forget her eyes. I got hot and everything started to spin.

"Penny?" His voice sounded miles away.

"I'll be okay. Just give me a second."

"What are you talking about? You aren't okay. You're as white as a sheet." He grabbed me by the arms, and we stood, walking into the lobby.

"Where are we going?"

"To the bar. You need a drink."

"Good idea." I folded onto a bar bench. "I'll take a margarita."

"I was thinking of water."

"Oh. Right."

As we sat there, my head cleared and I grew accustomed

to the dim light. In the back of the bar I spotted Bill, alone at a round table in the far corner. On the table in front of him was a stack of folders. He took the bandanna from around his neck and wiped his forehead as he eyed the folders, his mouth tight.

I nudged Connor. "He doesn't look very happy."

Connor sighed. "You can't help yourself, can you?"

"Shush."

A waitress walked past and stopped at Bill's table. She set a bottle and glass down and walked away.

"Look at that," I said.

"But then there would be two of us staring at him."

"I'm not staring." I forced myself to look away. "I'm wondering if he's heard about Kim."

"Of course you are."

"Well, if I want to find out, no better time than right now."

"What's your plan?" he said.

"Talk to him. You're right here. You can keep me out of trouble."

"Because I've been so successful at keeping you out of trouble on this trip so far."

I ignored him and moments later I stood at Bill's table. He'd opened the top folder and missed my approach. When he finally saw me, he flinched and looked like he wanted to take flight.

"Hi, there. Can I join you?"

With a small nod he pulled out the chair next to him and gave me a bleak look. He didn't seem in any shape to talk, but I pressed on. I was running out of time; Kim already had.

"I suppose you know what's happened to Kim."

He didn't answer right away. Instead, he twisted the cap on the whiskey, broke the seal, and poured himself two fingers. Liquid courage. He threw back the drink and nodded his head.

"Some of the hotel staff were talking about it. It's awful. And such a terrible coincidence." His color had improved and he rested his arm on the back of the adjacent chair.

"What was?"

"That both of these victims were in our party," he said.

"Really? You think it's a coincidence?"

"Well, sure. Kim and Tara didn't know each other before this weekend, and I can't imagine why anyone would want them both dead."

Not wanting to divulge that I was the likely target, I stayed quiet as Bill poured another glass.

"What are these?" I tapped the large stack of files at his elbow.

"Government red tape. Runs the gamut from our investment offerings to safety on the train. They even spell out how hot the water in the kitchens should be. The regulations are never ending. It's mind-boggling." He tipped his head and downed the shot.

"How has business been otherwise?" I asked.

"Oh, great, great." He brightened somewhat. "Every week we have more guests than the week before, the wineries are happy with the flow of tourists and most of the big expenses are behind us." He gripped the glass. "At least I'm hoping they are." He drifted off for a moment then gave himself a shake. "Look, anytime you want to go over the prospectus, let me know. Be happy to discuss your potential commitment."

"I will. Although, with two murders, I wouldn't expect much participation from our group."

"No, I suppose not." He slowly turned the empty glass on the table. "Murder. Just about the only thing I wasn't expecting. As if government regulators, investor issues and employee problems weren't enough."

Wait a minute. "What employee problems?"

Bill poured another drink. "You know the bartender we use?"

I nodded. "Seth."

"That's him. We can't have people complaining about the behavior of our staff, and I've had enough complaints on him to last a lifetime."

"What complaints?"

"How he treats his wife. He grabbed Barb's arm yesterday in front of a guest—it was Kim, funny enough. I told him after lunch today we needed to let him go."

"You fired Seth this afternoon?"

"That's right. Couple of hours ago. He was steamed, I can tell you that."

"I'll bet. Bill, I want you to think about this. Did Seth know it was Kim that complained?"

He paled. "It never occurred to me not to tell him. You don't think he . . ."

"You bet I do. Look how he treats his wife. If he's capable of that, he's capable of taking out his anger on the person who got him fired for it."

Twenty-three

WHEN I rejoined Connor, I told him about Seth losing his job. He listened in silence until I'd finished.

"So maybe Kim was the intended victim after all."

I wasn't convinced, but on the other hand, insisting to Connor I was the target seemed counterproductive to keeping him calm and having him help me solve this.

The patio was crowded with guests enjoying the last of a beautiful November day.

"You don't need to stick by me like glue, especially with this many people around," I said.

"I want to. It's as much for my peace of mind as it is your safety. It makes me feel like I'm doing something to help."

"I appreciate it and understand how you feel. I keep thinking if I'd gone into the steam room just a few minutes earlier . . ."

"Then it might have been you."

We grabbed a table next to the pool. A short time later, Antonia wandered out the lobby doors and Connor waved her over. Once she was settled, I repeated my conversation with Bill.

"You need to tell the police," she said.

I looked around. The police were gone. Yellow police tape stretched across the spa entry. "I'll call Chief Harding and leave a message. Or better yet, I might walk into town in the morning."

A laugh from the heated waters caught my attention, but I didn't need to turn around to know it was Chantal.

"It must really be nice to be her," I said. "Not a care in the world. I bet she sleeps like a rock." It sounded peevish even to my ears. "Sorry, it's just been a rough day."

"Oh, yeah? You want to talk about rough? I was basically accused of murder because of you." Vance stood next to the table, hands clenched into fists, one gripping a tennis ball.

Connor started to rise, but I caught his eye and shook my head. With an effort, he lowered himself a fraction, remaining perched on the edge of his chair.

"The police asked me who might have the strength to kill Kim the way she was killed," I said.

"How was she killed?" he asked.

"You'll have to ask them if you want to know."

Vance squeezed the tennis ball, shifting it between both hands.

"I figured that as a tennis player, you were a pretty good bet."

"Why would I want to kill her? I've never met her before."

There was an easy way to confirm what hand he favored, if I was able to make him mad enough. "Maybe you mistook her for someone else," I said. "Someone asking a lot of questions about Tara. Maybe you thought she was me."

He clenched the tennis ball in his fist. "So you think I'm guilty?"

"Maybe I do."

"I'd have to be stupid."

"Maybe you are."

In an instant, Vance shifted and threw the ball into the shrub beside me with such force it stuck there. Connor was next to him so fast, I didn't even see him move. One second he was in his seat; the next he had Vance by the arm in a fairly tight grip, if the grimace on Vance's face was anything to go by.

"Leave. Leave now, and leave quietly, while you still can." Connor spoke just above a whisper, which somehow made it all the more convincing.

Vance nodded his head in agreement. As he walked away, I scooted my chair back and reached for the tennis ball. It was lodged deep in the hedge. He'd thrown it with such force I needed both hands to remove it, and he'd thrown it with his left hand.

I slept fitfully for the third night in a row. The wind came up sometime after midnight, causing just enough rustling outside to keep me on edge. The temperature also dropped, and in the morning, gray skies heavy with rain greeted me. I slipped into jeans and a thick sweater in shades of purple heather before going downstairs. No one was about, but the lobby had a coffee bar. I sat in a comfy leather chair and drank cup after cup of dark Colombian until I felt somewhat alert.

I turned at the sound of steps hitting the tile floor.

"I'm having breakfast. Care to join me?" Big Dave stood next to me. His eyes were bloodshot, and it looked as if he'd spent the night running his hands through his hair. I think he had on the same clothes.

"You look like you had a rough night," I said.

"We both do. No offense."

I raised my coffee in mock salute. "None taken." I stood. "I can probably be talked into eating something."

We got a table next to the patio windows. The rain started falling soon after, dancing across the pool's surface and pelting the petals off the season's last roses.

When the waitress came, I took a quick glance at the menu, closing it after I spotted the cheese blintzes.

Big Dave slapped the menu shut when he heard my order. "I'll have the same, along with a Denver omelet and a side of bacon."

He might be missing Tara, but it wasn't impacting his appetite. He caught my expression. "Hey, I'm a country boy at heart. We know how to eat." He smiled at the waitress, but when he turned to me, his look was solemn.

"I need to apologize for Vance's behavior last night. He didn't have anything to do with Tara's or that other poor girl's murder. You got it wrong there, but his behavior was inexcusable. Throwing that ball the way he did, he's lucky

Connor didn't break his arm. I'm surprised how much restraint Connor showed, given how he feels about you."

My face grew hot. "He's a good friend; that's undeniable."

"Hmm. For a smart lady, you're missing something pretty obvious."

That nettled. "If I'm so smart, then why are you certain I'm wrong about Vance? Put aside for a moment that he's your son. He has the strength and the temper, not to mention what the police are looking for—motive, opportunity and means. He wanted Tara to stop spending your money, his inheritance, and maybe Kim somehow knew something or saw something. Even more likely, he mistook her for me. A simple case of mistaken identity, one that cost Kim her life."

He shook his head. "I had a long talk with Vance last night. Told him this attitude of his isn't helping him any and that if he keeps it up, he's going to end up in a heap of trouble, the kind of trouble I can't get him out of. He told me he didn't do it. Looked me in the eyes when he said it, and I believe him."

The waitress came with our food, and he fell silent. When she'd gone, Big Dave pointed his fork at me. "He's far from perfect and he's got issues with his temper to be certain, but he's no killer."

I didn't like him pointing his fork at me that way. "If you know he's innocent, then why did you agree to keep Vance in line and promise he'd cooperate?"

He jabbed the fork in the air. "Because I was confident it would clear him and, at the same time, help you find the real killer. I never thought he actually had anything to do with any of this."

I kept my eyes on the fork, and he followed my gaze. Putting the utensil down, he rubbed his temples with his fingertips.

"First my boy throws a tennis ball practically at your head, and now I, well, I show a terrible lack of manners. I'm really sorry about that."

"I understand." I didn't really, but I needed to keep him on my side, if only as a source of information. I eyed the blintzes. They were covered in fresh blueberries. I took a bite. They were good, but the air was tense and I wasn't going to enjoy them as much as I'd thought.

"Well." I smiled and dug into my plate with feigned gusto. "I'm sure the police will figure it out soon. I know they're talking to everyone, asking where everyone was."

He leaned in a bit. "Is it true you were in the spa and found Kim?"

"That's right." I pushed away the image that immediately came to mind. "I'm sure they asked where you were yesterday afternoon."

"They sure did. I was alone in my room so I didn't have an alibi, as they say, but I guess they believed me when I told them I was watching a movie."

"Which one?"

He was startled, then shrugged. "I can't remember the name offhand. Just one of the old movies they run on the classic channels all day long."

A nonanswer. Big Dave ate, the fork nearly invisible in his large hand. His right hand. A country boy, now a large man—either of his hands certainly strong enough to make the marks on Kim's neck. When he spoke about not having a prenup with Tara, he'd been so believable, but would he really be happy to give away half his fortune?

After we'd finished I excused myself and wandered into the library, closing the door behind me. A large leather wingback chair draped with a throw faced the fire, where a merry blaze crackled and warmed the air. On both sides of the fire, large patio doors confirmed that rain continued to beat down. Occasionally the doors rattled from a gust, but inside it was comfy and warm.

I curled my legs under me and pulled the throw up around my neck. Resting my head on the back of the chair, I watched the flames. Lack of sleep and the shock of finding Kim caught up with me, and some time later I sat up with a start. It took me a moment to remember where I was. The fire had died down, but the room was oppressively warm. My hair felt heavy and damp against my neck, and I pushed the throw off. Rain fell lightly now, and gusts of wind no longer tugged at the heavy doors. The room was still, yet something was different. Voices carried from the reception area, and I turned to the library door. I'd closed it earlier, but now it was open by several inches. Cold trickled down my spine, and I shivered in spite of the warmth. I felt exposed, as though someone had been watching me sleep. I stood and tried to shake the feeling off. Perhaps someone had grabbed a book, something to read on this cold and windy day. Perhaps the chill I now felt in the air had nothing to do with me. Perhaps.

Twenty-four

I FOUND an Agatha Christie novel on the shelves and stayed in the library until early afternoon, when the sun broke through the clouds. Outside the hotel, grounds-keepers worked their magic, and piles of soggy leaves and broken branches disappeared.

"Do you want to get out of the hotel for a while?" Antonia stood in the library doorway. "I thought I'd have the hotel car service drop me in town for a little snack and some shopping. Possibly an early dinner."

"That sounds great, but where's Chantal?"

"Off somewhere. She mentioned going into town earlier, but I haven't seen her since."

"Let's go," I said.

She eyed me. "You might want to freshen up first. You look like you just woke up. You've got creases in your cheek and your hair is tilting to one side."

"Right. Lobby in five minutes."

* * *

"WELL, I can't say this did anything to improve your spirits," Antonia said sometime later. We'd hit most of the downtown specialty stores and, while Antonia carried several bags, I was empty-handed. "Not that I blame you, after what you've been through. Surely there's something that will help."

I considered. "Chocolate. Actually, I need to see Chief Harding. Then chocolate."

We rounded the corner and arrived at the police station just as Harding stepped outside. I could tell he was thrilled to see me by the way his eyes glazed over. Antonia curled her lip and was about to say something, but I gave her a subtle elbow. Like it or not, we needed to work with this guy.

"Hello there, Chief!" My smile was so big my cheeks hurt. "I know you're busy, but I have something you might find interesting."

That caught his attention. Placing one hand on his hip he leaned back against the door frame. "Well?"

"Right here?" I looked around. "Don't you want to go into your office, at least get something to take notes with?"

He rolled his lips around as though looking for a toothpick. "If you tell me anything of interest, Ms. Penelope Lane Lively, I'll let you know. At that point I'll be sure to make a note of it."

"Your middle name is Lane?" Antonia said. "I never knew that. How could I not know that? I've known you your whole life. I was at your baptism."

"Well, I guess it never came up. Can we talk about it later?"

"Wait a minute. Your name is Penelope Lane. Your parents named you Penny Lane? After the Beatles song?"

"They were big fans, okay? Later!"

Harding crossed his arms and watched the exchange. What threw me was that he'd made the effort to learn my middle name, yet I couldn't get him to pay attention to any suspects other than Chantal.

He took my look of astonishment as a sign I'd been impressed. "I guess I know a little more than you thought, wouldn't you say, Ms. Lively?"

Irritating oaf. "It really all depends on if the knowledge is relevant. For instance, I wonder if you knew that Bill had to fire his bartender yesterday, right before Kim was killed."

Chief Harding stopped searching for the imaginary toothpick as he scrutinized my face. "Well, I'm not real sure what one thing has to do with the other. Seth's a surly no-good. Always has been. Not the kind of person most people want to encounter when they're out having a nice evening."

"Yes, yes, we all know Seth is obnoxious," I snapped. "So you might well ask why it happened now. What finally made Bill fire him?"

He'd raised his brow at my tone, but curiosity got the best of him. "Okay, go ahead and tell me. What happened?"

"Seth was being rough with his wife."

Harding raised his hands. "I've heard the rumors and I wouldn't put it past him, but until she makes a complaint and sticks with it, there isn't much I can do."

"Well, he did it in front of a guest, and that guest complained to Bill. He fired Seth on the spot."

He shrugged. "Surprised it hasn't happened before this."

What was wrong with this guy? "Aren't you a little curious who the guest was? The guest that cost Seth his job?" I could hear my voice getting louder, but fatigue and shock took over. "Come on, think! Take a wild guess!"

He grasped the significance at a glacial pace. "So, you're telling me it was Kim that complained."

I waited until I was certain I could control my voice. "Yes, that's what I'm telling you. She's the one that complained. An hour later, she's dead."

"CHOCOLATE!" We hit the nearest specialty shop we could find after leaving the police station. "I really need this." I eyed the upscale truffled delights lined up inside the glass case. "He didn't seem all that concerned about verifying Seth's whereabouts." I paced back and forth in front of the counter. "What was I expecting? That he might actually do his job?"

"Pick out whatever you need, on me." Antonia patted my hand. "Can't let that blood sugar get too low, now can we?"

"Don't placate me, Antonia."

"You're scaring people." Antonia thrust her chin toward a young girl backing toward the front door.

"Fine. I'm going to sit over there." I made a sweeping gesture toward the counter. "I will take one. One of everything in the top row."

Half a dozen truffles later I felt ready to discuss the subject calmly. It didn't hurt that the truffles were chock-full of liquor.

"What I think we should do is try and find out if Seth really was with a female guest like his wife suspected," Antonia said.

"Barb seemed pretty sure. She also said her husband had no reason to kill Kim. 'Course at the time, she didn't know about Kim getting Seth fired." I bit into chocolate heaven. "Yum. Brandy."

Antonia stood and pushed the last few truffles out of my reach. "It seems to me Barb might be more willing to talk now. Bad enough the way Seth treats her. Surely if we stress to her he might be guilty of murder, she'll finally see how misplaced her devotion to him is."

I nabbed one final nugget of melty goodness and popped it into my mouth. "Kahlua. Tasty."

"That's enough." Antonia stamped her cane.

"Okay, fine. Barb said she works at one of the restaurants right here in the center of town. There's only a couple. Let's give it a try."

Within minutes of being back outside, Antonia nudged me in the ribs. "There she is."

"Where?" Dusk had settled in while I was busy eating chocolate.

"There, across the street." Barb stood yards away on the patio of the nicest restaurant in town.

I grabbed Antonia's arm when she moved to wave. "I'm not hungry after all that chocolate, but you said you wanted to grab a bite. Let's wait and see if there's some way we can talk to her alone."

We left Barb still on the front patio and scooted down a side walkway to the rear of the restaurant. There, a second entrance led into the main dining room. We entered and grabbed the first table we found.

Moments later, there was a waiter at my shoulder. He peered at us beneath lowered lids, lips pursed together. "I really must ask you to check in with the maître d'."

"Where'd you come from?" I said. "Honestly, were you waiting under the table?"

He wasn't amused or distracted. "All guests must first check in with the maître d'."

"Okay, then." I started to stand, but Antonia held out her hand and I sat back down.

There was a look in her eyes that I remembered as a teen. Watching her now, I didn't think we'd be moving. The silver cloud of her hair positively glowed in the candlelight. Sitting tall, she proceeded to show the waiter what a good lip pursing really looked like.

"What utter nonsense. Young man, there are only two other tables occupied in this entire room. If the maître d' needs busywork, he is more than welcome to come and introduce himself to me, but I for one will not be going to him."

The waiter's eyes were now open wide, as was his mouth. With a short nod, he disappeared.

When he'd gone I leaned closer. "You were a little hard on him."

"Don't get me wrong. If they were at all busy, I would have happily checked in. But busy rules are just silly rules, and at my age I can't be bothered. Besides, if we'd gone up front to check in, Barb would have seen us and taken pains to avoid us. This way she doesn't even know we're here."

Antonia proved correct when, a few moments later, Barb walked across the room, failing to recognize us until she stopped at our table. When she took a good look, she paled and clutched the round tray to her chest like a shield.

"Hi, Barb, got a moment?" I asked.

"Only to take your drink orders. I'm really busy tonight." She glanced around the nearly empty room. "There are a lot of people on the front patio that need to be served too. What can I get you?"

"Just a couple of minutes. It's important," I said.

She clicked the pen in her hand in rapid succession, eyes darting between us. "Okay, what do you want?"

"Well, for starters, did you find Seth yesterday when you were looking for him at the hotel?"

"I'm not going to talk about that. If he was or wasn't there, it isn't something I need to rehash with you. I'm sorry I said anything to you at all. It's none of your business, if you want to know the truth."

"I'm not asking to snoop. It's important."

"I'm not sure why my marital problems, if I have any, could be important to you." She stepped back. "If that's all you wanted to ask me—"

"He had a reason to kill Kim."

Barb paled and dropped her pen. She ignored it. "What? What are you talking about?"

"I'm sorry, my dear," Antonia gestured. "You look like you need to sit down."

Barb shook her head. "I can't. I'm working." Her voice

cracked. "Just tell me what you're talking about. Seth didn't know Kim. He didn't know her!"

"He didn't have to. All he needed to know was that she got him fired," I said.

"Fired? What do you mean, fired?" She took two steps back and collapsed into a dining chair. "He didn't say anything. I think I'm going to be sick."

"We need to stop," Antonia said. "She's had enough."

"No!" Barb gripped the edge of the table. "Just give me a sec." After a few deep breaths, she stood. "All right. Tell me."

"I'm sorry—"

Barb raised her hand. "Spare me the sympathy, Penny, and just tell me."

"Go ahead and tell her," Antonia said.

I took a breath. "Two days ago after lunch, Seth grabbed you—"

"He didn't!"

"Yes, he did, and you know it. So did Kim. She saw it, she didn't like it and she went to Bill yesterday and complained. He fired Seth on the spot."

"Oh, please, no. He got fired again and didn't tell me." She trembled.

"That's not the worst of this, Barb," I said. "Think about it. After that he had a reason to kill Kim."

"No! He has an alibi." Barb wouldn't look at me. "He was with, with someone, and you know it. I told you yesterday."

"You told me where you *thought* he was, but if the police don't find the girl he was with, he'll certainly be questioned for Kim's death. If you know something and don't tell them, you'll be in trouble too."

"I don't know anything! I only suspect he was with someone. That's what he usually . . ."

Barb stopped and her face crumbled. Slowly she bent over and picked up her pen. "If the police want to ask me something, let them."

"Don't you want to go to them first? Don't you want to be free of him once and for all?" I shook my head. "This is your chance, Barb. Take it."

She turned the page on her pad. "I have no idea what you're talking about. Now tell me, can I get you anything to drink?"

After taking our order for a bottle of Berninni Chardonnay, Barb avoided coming anywhere near our table.

"She can't go on like this for much longer," I said.

"None of us can." Antonia shook her head. "I think the end of this is going to come quickly now. After what happened to you on the trail and at the winery, and then poor Kim . . . I know you were hoping to help Chantal, and I appreciate that, believe me I do, but now I almost wish you hadn't gotten involved."

"I thought by now we'd know something," I said. "I understand why the police want us to remain in town, but they didn't think any of us were in danger. They thought it was Chantal."

"Until Kim was murdered. At least they don't believe Chantal was responsible for that."

"Exactly," I said. "But what is the killer thinking?"

"That he's running out of time."

"I agree. He must be starting to panic. Hopefully it will lead to a mistake. Either way, you know I can't stop now. Even if I wanted to. I find out who it is—"

Antonia steepled her fingers. "Or they try and kill you. Again."

I took a swig of wine. "Dinner's on you."

"At least you're keeping your sense of humor. Now, what sounds good?" Antonia eyed the menu.

"I just had a pile of chocolate. Honestly, I'm not very hungry."

"Nonsense. You need some nourishment, something besides alcohol-injected confectionary."

"Fine. A salad."

"Have the chicken."

"Fine, I'll have the chicken."

The waiter came and took our orders. A different waiter than before. This one eyed Antonia warily and kept his distance. We ate in relative silence and had just finished when Seth walked into the dining room. The people at the two other tables had gone, and we were now alone. He spotted us and strode over to our table.

"I suppose you're going to have after-dinner drinks now. Congratulate yourselves." His eyes looked glassy, and he smelled like he'd had a few.

"For what?" I asked.

He leaned in. "For spilling the beans and letting my wife know I was fired."

"Of course, we assumed she knew. She's your wife." Antonia lifted her brow. "How did you find out we mentioned it, anyway?"

"She called me, told me you were both here shooting off your mouths. Wrong move. It's none of your business."

"You've really got quite the temper, haven't you?" I said. "Look at you. You don't have any control over yourself at all. It isn't hard to believe you killed Kim. I'm sure you blame her for your getting fired. Guys like you never take responsibility for your troubles. No, it's always someone else's fault."

"You know, that's twice now you've pushed your luck with me. Take a tip from the old lady here, and shut your mouth."

"Old lady? Old lady?" Antonia stiffened her spine, and anger snapped in her eyes. "You're addressing me? Answer her question! Were you angry on the train too? Angry with Tara, angry at seeing her with someone else? I mean, how could she reject your advances? I'm sure you consider your-self quite the catch."

I thought we'd gone too far.

With both hands he gripped the edges of the table, holding it so tight his knuckles strained.

Barb came up behind him and grabbed him by the arm. "Seth, stop. I'll get fired too if you make a scene, and then we'll really be in trouble."

Slowly the color came back to his face and his eyes focused on me. "I'll go now. I don't want to interrupt my wife at her place of work." He placed a hand on her shoul-der and she flinched. "You think you know everything. I'm not sure you have any business giving other people advice, especially when you can't even see what's going on right under your nose."

"Sorry." I shrugged. "I have no idea what you're talking about."

"I think if you go out through the front door all your questions will be answered, including what Connor and Chantal are up to this evening."

Twenty-five

C ONNOR and Chantal having dinner together for the second night in a row didn't thrill me, but I wasn't about to let Seth know it.

"Good. They decided to grab a bite." I forced a smile. "Chantal's been so upset and we were unavailable to take her anywhere. Connor's been such a trouper."

Seth's smile faltered. "He looks pretty cozy for someone who's just being a Boy Scout. Anyway, she doesn't look very upset. She's all over him."

"Connor and Chantal? An item? Oh, please." I forced a light laugh. "They grew up together. We all did. Don't be silly."

Seth turned, pushed Barb aside, and left through the back door.

Barb trembled slightly and I stood, grabbing her as she dropped into a chair.

"My dear," Antonia said, "we will be happy to go with you to the police station. I, for one, intend to inform them that he behaved in a threatening manner toward us just now."

Barb paled. "Oh, please don't. My boss will find out. He's told me before he doesn't want Seth in here. I'll be fired for sure."

"He might have killed two women, Barb," I said. "You must realize that."

"But what would I tell them? I don't know anything about how Tara or Kim died," Barb whispered, "and I'll never think Seth capable of murder. Never. He has a temper, I know"—she looked at her nails, raw and bitten down to nothing—"but he couldn't have done those things. He just couldn't." She stood. "And if the police ask me, that's exactly what I'm going to tell them." She turned and walked into the kitchen.

"Well, we tried," Antonia said. "At some point the police will talk to both of them. They'll have to, now that they know Seth had a motive for wanting Kim dead. At that point, surely they'll reconsider Seth for Tara's murder as well." Antonia stood. "Chantal will be cleared and then we can go home."

"Right. Chantal. Thanks for reminding me." I pushed back from the table. "I say we leave by the front door. See how Connor and Chantal are making out." I bit my lip. "Not making out. That isn't what I meant."

Antonia raised a brow. "Maybe you did. Maybe it's a sign you've finally decided to let your feelings for Connor out."

"And maybe you want to go back out the way we came in." I stood and started across the room.

She practically leapt across the room and was next to me in a flash. "Ha! Try and get rid of me."

The patio glowed from candles and moonlight. It took a moment for my eyes to adjust, but I finally spotted them at a corner table. Actually, I spotted Chantal, wearing a top in a red shimmery fabric that hugged the way no fabric should. She leaned in, resting both elbows and most of her chest on the edge of a table much too tiny, while Connor perused the wine menu.

"Well, isn't this a pleasant surprise." I pushed my way past the few tables between us. "What a coincidence." I bit my lip in an effort to stop talking. It didn't work. "So many good restaurants in town to pick from, and yet here you are at this one."

I grabbed a chair from the people at the table next to them. "Are you using this? No? Terrific!" I swung it around and took a seat. "So, what are you doing? I mean, of course, I know what you're doing. You're eating and drinking. I just mean how did you end up here?"

Connor stood and offered Antonia his seat. "I looked for you earlier, but I must have just missed you two. I was hungry and wanted to get out of the hotel for a while. Chantal decided to come too. We were just about to order."

"And there really isn't enough room at this table for all of us," Chantal said.

"Well, there would be if you removed your—"

"Penny, that's enough," Antonia cut me off.

"Elbows! I was going to say elbows."

"Penelope and I just ate," Antonia said. Penelope. I was being reprimanded, but I wasn't finished.

"I think a cappuccino would be terrific," I said.

"I agree, and we'll get a couple of those at that cute little bar over there." Antonia pointed across the street, stood, and pulled at my arm. "Join us if you like after your meal."

I had little choice but to follow, getting the signature wave from Chantal. We crossed the street in silence and entered the bar, a red-leather, dark-mahogany sort of place, probably once a local hangout for the regulars that none of the regulars could now afford.

After we had been seated, Antonia turned to me. "What on earth is wrong with you? You sounded like a loon. Are you trying to get a date or get committed?"

"I know!" I smacked my forehead. "Do you think I can't hear myself? I don't know what happens. I haven't had a lot of experience dating. I was never settled in one place long enough. I get nervous and then I start blabbering. Chantal always makes it worse. I'm a mess."

Antonia let me stew for a moment, then patted my hand. "Yes, well, it wasn't that bad. Maybe he didn't notice, or he finds it endearing."

"Sure, that's what I was going for. Endearing."

"Do you really want a cappuccino?" Antonia asked.

"No! I'm stuffed with chocolate and chicken. I can't breathe."

"Well, I have no idea what we're doing here then. Before they ask us what we want, let's leave." She stood to go.

"Or we can join him." Olympio Berninni sat in the corner with several friends.

He saw my glance and stood the moment he spotted Antonia. He hurried across the bar.

"My dears, my dears, I am so glad to run into you this

way." He beamed at us. "The two brightest stars have fallen from the sky."

"Oh, please." Antonia shooed him with her palm, but her eyes were shining and her cheeks flushed a pretty pink. "I suppose you can join us if you wish."

"I'd like that. I'd like that very much indeed." He glanced over his shoulder. "Let me tell my friends my change of plans. I will return."

He hurried back to his friends and in less than a minute rejoined us.

"That was pretty fast," I said. "I guess they didn't mind."

"On the contrary. They're jealous I'm able to spend time with such lovely companions. May I?" He pulled out a chair at Antonia's nod. "So tell me, are you enjoying yourselves in our beautiful little town?"

"Yes, yes, St. Katrina is lovely," Antonia said. "I'm enjoying the visit, as much as can be expected under the circumstances. However, you should come to Monterey and Cypress Cove sometime. Especially Cypress Cove. If you ever want to see a town overflowing with charm, that's it."

"Okay, you two, let's not have a competition over which town is cuter. Antonia is right"—I stopped at Olympio's mournful gaze—"not about the town being cuter . . . Now, Antonia, don't you start. I simply meant that I agree with Antonia in that we can enjoy the visit only so much considering the murders and the cloud of suspicion over Chantal." I rubbed my eyes. "And what just happened at dinner with Barb and Seth didn't help any."

Olympio drew his chair closer. "What has he done now?"

I recapped the scene with Seth as Olympio listened,

silently shaking his head. "Barb's in complete denial about it," I said when I finished. "She's clearly afraid of him but refuses to denounce him for what he is: a bully and possibly much worse."

"I don't know what else I can do," Olympio said. "Her father was the most faithful employee I will ever have. Barb was such a sweet child. It breaks my heart."

Antonia patted his hand. "The day will come when she turns to you. I'm certain. Barb has put up with a lot, but she was really angry that he hadn't told her he'd been fired. Different people have different ultimatums. Keep your heart and front door open. She may walk through both of them yet."

"Antonia, you are a marvelous woman." He squeezed her hand, letting his touch linger. "And now, enough of the problems of others. Let me have the bartender bring us some of our brandy. Something new we are trying at Berninni."

"I couldn't really. You try it, Antonia."

"I intend to. I didn't overindulge in chocolate."

"So." Olympio returned moments later with two snifters and took a seat. "Before I go any further"—he turned to me—"I wouldn't want you to think I'd forgotten your fright at my dinner party. I want to apologize again for any distress caused to you. I want you to know I've locked the system. Now it's impossible for there to be any other accidents like the one that befell you."

The fear I'd felt in that total darkness descended on me once again, but I forced a small smile.

Olympio had concern in his eyes. "Please, my dear, tell me you have recovered from your scare."

"I'm fine, Olympio. Honestly." Whatever the killer intended for me at Berninni Winery wasn't Olympio's fault. I held his gaze until his shoulders relaxed.

"You are most kind, Miss Penny. Now," his gaze included Antonia, "what should we talk about?"

I raised my palm. "No talk about who has the better earth, wine, seafood, town or anything else. You both get too competitive. It isn't becoming."

"What nonsense," Antonia said, but Olympio's eyes shone.

"I think Penny is right. We are competitive, Antonia. It's in our nature. We both enjoy it, and I have a proposal you may find interesting."

"Isn't it a little soon in your relationship?" I said.

Antonia kicked me under the table. "What is your proposition?"

"I suggest we have a blind wine tasting. A competition, tomorrow, at your hotel." He leaned in. "You are stranded in my town through no fault of your own." He took Antonia's hand. "Or your daughter's fault either, as I'm sure the police will soon prove."

Antonia inclined her head. "Thank you for that, Olympio." She straightened. "But what about this tasting? Surely you wouldn't be bold enough to put your wine where your mouth is. I mean, all this boasting I've had to listen to this week, actually put to the test?"

"That is exactly what I am proposing. We can have the hotel invite guests to attend and vote without knowing which wines belong to you and which belong to me." His eyes twinkled. "Until they taste them, of course. That will make everything clear, and they most certainly will vote for me."

"You windbag," Antonia said, but there was a lightness in her voice I'd never heard. "I'd clearly love to take you up on your little, and I mean very little, challenge. You're forgetting something, though. I don't have any stock here."

"Ah, but I do!" Olympio grinned. "Didn't you think I'd be curious, seeing you again after so many years, to try your wine? I ordered four bottles of everything you offer. I only just received it and haven't opened any of them. So, no excuses, Antonia Martinelli. Berninni Winery challenges you to a duel!"

"I'll probably regret egging you on," I said. "But you aren't going to let him get away with it, are you?"

"I can't imagine why you think you'd have to ask me that question. Of course I accept his challenge. Not only that," she leaned in toward Olympio, "I have every expectation of winning."

Twenty-six

I DIDN'T see Chantal and Connor finish dinner and leave, but it wasn't because I'd forgotten about them. They had looked pretty cozy at that corner patio table, in the dark, Chantal's accoutrements spilling out all over the place . . . I turned to gawk out the window so many times Antonia finally reached over and closed the blinds.

I spent the rest of the evening listening to Olympio and Antonia flirt with each other, which, considering my frame of mind, was both disheartening and a little weird. I followed that up with another restless night, giving up around four in the morning. I fought off the tangled sheets, threw on some slippers and curled up on the chaise. The chill in the air signaled cold winter weather was on its way, and I flicked on the fire. In the dim light, I thought about what Antonia had said the night before. Someone was in a panic. Mistakes happen when people panic.

Reaching over, I flipped on the desk lamp and grabbed a pen and notepad. I made two columns, listing in the first column exactly where everyone had been on the train when Tara died. I then made a second list of everyone's location during the time when I'd found Kim. It wasn't a coincidence that Seth was at the top of both columns. His behavior earlier had been frightening and almost certainly contributed to the reason I was now awake. I was doodling a box around his name when I heard a soft knock. Wrapping myself in the comforter, I padded to the door.

"Who is it?"

"It's me," Connor said.

"What are you doing?"

"Standing in a hotel hallway talking to a door. Can I come in?"

Perfect. I had on an oversized T-shirt, pull-on granny travel slippers, and my hair looked like I'd been electrocuted.

After a bit, he knocked again. "You still there?"

I smoothed my hair. "Yeah, yeah. Hang on."

I twisted the dead bolt, threw open the door and stood back. He might as well know what he was passing up when he was with Chantal and her accoutrements.

He stepped in and looked at my feet. "Cute slippers."

I shut the door. "What are you doing loitering in hotel hallways in the middle of the night?"

"I was going for a run and saw your light on."

For the first time I took in what he was wearing: little blue shorts, a sleeveless tank and running shoes.

"I couldn't sleep." Master of the obvious.

"I know. Me neither." He picked up the list of suspects.

"I take it this is what you've been doing." His eyes scrolled down the page. "One of these people is a killer. One of them is trying to kill you."

I shivered. "Wow, and here I was thinking I might sleep again someday."

"I just want you to understand the danger you're in."

"I get it! I'm wide awake in the middle of the night listing names."

"You can't blame me for spelling it out for you. Don't forget, this isn't the first time you've been in this position."

"Thanks so much for stopping by. Cheering me up." I shivered.

He reached over to rub my arms through the comforter. "You're cold. Here." He dragged one of the armchairs closer to the fire. "Take a seat and let's go over these names together."

"What about your run?"

"I was only going because I couldn't sleep. This is more important." He studied the list. "So you're feeling pretty strong about Seth here."

"He's the only one with a motive to kill both women— Tara for rebuffing his advances and Kim for getting him fired."

Connor rubbed his eyes. "In Seth's crazy world, of course it's Kim's fault he was fired, not the way he treated his wife."

"I know, right? That's what I told him."

"What do you mean that's what you told him?"

I fiddled with the edge of the comforter. "We saw Seth last night at the restaurant. He came up to our table, and I basically said the same thing you just did."

"He's dangerous and you're taunting him?"

I tried a little deflection. "Antonia came right out and asked him if he'd killed Tara."

He shook his head and muttered something. We sat in silence as he studied the other names.

"Have you narrowed it down any more than this?"

I shook my head. "It could be any of them." I grabbed the list. "Big Dave swears he wasn't worried over the possibility Tara might leave him and take half his money. But does a man really get that successful being careless with his money?" I threw up my hands. "It's hard to believe, but he seems sincere."

Connor rubbed his eyes. "He didn't have any reason to kill Kim, but if he thought it was you and he needs you to stop digging around . . ."

"Exactly," I said. "And he doesn't have an alibi for when Kim was killed. He said he'd been in his room watching a movie."

He tapped the list. "Why do you have Bill on here? He wouldn't have killed Tara, especially on his own train. On top of that, she wanted to invest. And he wouldn't have any reason to kill Kim either, unless he was trying for you."

"I'm leaving him on, along with Jim."

"Jim didn't have any reason to kill Tara, and he couldn't have killed his wife. He was with me at the time, playing bocce ball."

"In principle, I agree with you," I said, "but for now I want to leave all of them. The only one left is Vance."

"He had the perfect motive with his stepmother."

"He sure did. And the way he pitched that tennis ball

the other night, barely missing me, shows what he's capable of."

"I wonder where he was when Kim died," Connor said.

"The police found him at the tennis courts. I saw them go and get him for questioning. He could have killed Kim, thinking it was me, and been back on the tennis court in less than ten minutes."

Connor's eyes were dark. "Either Seth killed both women, or someone killed Kim instead of you by accident." He shook his head. "If the killer did mistake Kim for you, she'll just be considered collateral damage. It doesn't change the fact that someone still wants you dead."

The world started spinning and Connor grabbed my shoulder.

"Are you okay?"

I dropped my head between my knees. "Not really." It came out muffled by the comforter. "In the last four days I've found two bodies, and one of those was supposed to be me. I've been chased, gassed and threatened." I sat up, my voice louder. "I haven't slept since we got here, and now you're making it painfully clear that none of this is going to be improving anytime soon." The last part was practically a shout. I exhaled and lowered my voice. "I've been better, actually."

Connor knelt in front of my chair so our faces were close. "You aren't alone."

The room was still spinning. "I'm certainly not alone right now. There are about twenty of you." I buried my face in my palms and waited until my head stopped its inner twirl. When I opened my eyes, there was only one

Connor, and his face was just inches from mine. His brows were drawn together, and he wouldn't let go of my gaze.

"I mean it. You aren't alone." He moved closer.

My heart started thumping around, and I closed my eyes again, ready for what was coming next.

Knocking. That's what came next. Not my knees. The front door.

"No kidding, I'm not alone. It's Grand Central in here."

Connor sat back on his heels. "You expecting anyone?"

"Oh, sure. It's the middle of the night. When else would I be expecting someone?"

I peeked through the peephole. Antonia stood there. I opened the door.

"What are you doing here?"

"I heard you yelling a couple of minutes ago. Both of our terrace doors are open."

"You could have called."

"You want me to call first? I thought I was listening to your murder." She moved into the room. "The thought has occurred to me that someone might feel a greater need to silence your inquiry."

"I get it. Someone is trying to kill me."

Antonia turned and spotted Connor. "Oh, I didn't know you had company." She turned sideways so Connor couldn't see and gave me the facial equivalent of two thumbs-up.

I rolled my eyes.

"Connor was going for a run and saw my light on." I looked at the both of them. "I appreciate all this concern, but we need to channel that energy into action." I pointed to the list. "What we need is a trap."

It was Connor's turn to roll his eyes. "Oh, this should be good."

"I'm not kidding. Force someone to show his hand."

"I think it's an excellent idea, Penny," Antonia said.

"Of course, you do." Connor sighed. "Okay, let's hear it."

"Hear what?"

"Your 'trap.'" He used the air quotes. "I hope it's better than the 'plan.'"

"It's not as well developed as the 'plan.' It's really more in the idea stage."

"And your idea is what?"

"My idea," I said, "is that someone must really want to get out of here. They can't pick up and run because that would prove their guilt, but they must want to. Someone needs to push them over the edge."

"And that someone is you?" Antonia asked.

"Exactly. Let's say I let it slip that I've found something."

Antonia raised her palms. "What?"

"It doesn't matter. As long as we make that person think they're out of time, maybe we can force them to act."

"I don't know. Seems a little weak," Antonia said.

"Do you have anything better?"

"Twenty minutes ago I was asleep," Antonia snapped. "Give me some credit for just following along."

"Okay, okay." I rubbed the back of my neck. "The next time, and probably the last time, we'll all come together will be at the wine tasting tomorrow." I looked at the gray sliver of dawn through the curtains. "I mean later today."

"What wine tasting?" Connor asked.

"I forgot to tell you. Last night Olympio challenged

Antonia to a taste-off. Berninni Winery versus Martinelli Winery."

"Oh, this should go well. It's the North versus the South all over again."

Antonia sniffed. "I can handle it if Olympio can."

"My point is that we're out of time," I said. "Harding is going to release us to go home soon. He's going to have to, and once people leave, this same group will never be together again. Something has to happen now."

Connor shook his head. "Back to the trap. You let it be known that you've found something out. Then what?"

"No clue yet, but I'm working on it." I walked to the terrace door and stepped into a gray and sullen morning. "I'm working on it."

Twenty-seven

I WASN'T any closer to a solution when I entered the restaurant later that morning. A chilly breeze had kicked up, and the restaurant was crowded. The server recognized me and brought coffee to my table.

"You're busy." I cradled the warm cup.

He indicated the patio. "Too windy to eat outside. Looks like everyone staying at the hotel is in here."

I scanned the crowded room. Antonia and Chantal sat in silence in the back corner, while Big Dave and Vance shared a table on the opposite side of the room. Vance leaned back in his chair with his arms crossed, while Big Dave kept his head down and just drank coffee.

The mood of disillusionment and fatigue that clung to both tables spread through the rest of the room. All the guests knew about Kim being killed at the spa, of course; the police had interviewed most of them, and the building was still sealed and taped off. Conversation this morning was sparse and mixed with an uneasy silence. It was into this that Jim walked.

It was clear the diners knew who he was when he entered the room. The smatterings of remaining conversations dropped like stones. People seated in his path moved to give him more room, although the aisles were all more than wide enough for him to pass.

"It isn't logical, but they don't want to catch whatever he has." Connor came up behind me and pulled up a chair. "His wife being murdered somehow marks him."

I nodded. "Even though he has an alibi, he'll never quite get rid of the doubt in some people's minds."

Jim moved through the dining room. As though he sensed what was expected of him, he avoided eye contact and settled alone at the end of the coffee bar. His cheeks were hollow and there were bags under his eyes.

"He should try and eat something," I said.

"You can't stay out of anything, can you?" Connor gave me a nudge. "But if it makes you feel better, he's ordering now, and we should too."

The conversation slowly resumed as we plowed through a breakfast of crepes, fresh fruit—with cream, of course—and dark French roast. I plowed, anyway. Connor didn't finish his, and I swiped a cream-covered strawberry off his plate.

"Not hungry?"

"Sure," he said. "But if you recall I didn't get my run in this morning. I try to be careful on those days."

His lean muscular torso verified the sensibility in that approach.

"How very wise of you." I filched the last spoonful of cream. "I'm stress eating."

Connor raised a brow.

"What? It's a real thing. And apparently I'm not alone." Jim was polishing off a large plate of food.

"See that? His wife was killed and it hasn't bothered his appetite."

"No, it hasn't." Connor watched Jim. "That surprises me. If you were to meet your end the same way Kim did, I wouldn't be able to tuck into a plate of food like that."

"I'm touched. Nothing says 'I care' more than turning down hickory smoked bacon."

"No need to be sarcastic," he said.

"Another symptom of my level of anxiety."

"So, now that you've finished both of our breakfasts, let's discuss what happens next. Have you made any progress with the 'trap'?"

"Enough with the air quotes!" I lowered my voice as several people shot us a look. "I admit nothing is coming to mind."

"That isn't entirely bad news, since it wasn't a good idea to begin with." He looked around the room. "It might be time to let the police take over. I mean, trying to get an entire group of people to do something in the hopes of exposing one of them as a killer. What could possibly go wrong?" He tapped my hand. "I said, what could possibly go wrong?"

I didn't answer. I think I only heard about half of what he said. The idea sort of jelled as I stared off into space. I don't know how long I was like that before he tapped once again on my arm.

"Are you okay?"

"I've got it. I know what to do."

Connor sighed and rolled his head, stretching out his neck. "Okay. Let's hear it."

I looked around the room. "Not now. We need some privacy."

I slid my chair back and motioned for Connor to follow. We threaded our way through the diners and into the main lobby.

"How about outside?" Connor asked.

"It's too cold." I spotted the library. "In here."

We were at the door when I heard my name. I turned.

Antonia was scurrying across the lobby. "What are you two up to?"

"How do you know we're up to something?" I asked.

"I know you better than you think, Penelope Lively. Now what's going on?"

"All right!" I grabbed her arm and pulled her into the room, closing the door behind her. "I know what we're going to do."

Connor leaned against the wall, arms crossed. "What's this *we*? I just got done saying I was glad you were going to let the police handle it."

"Oh sure, like they've done such a good job so far," I said. "Just hear me out and then you can decide."

Connor pushed himself off the wall, took a seat and leaned back. "Go ahead."

Antonia took a seat beside him. "Now, how do you propose getting our killer to confess?"

"I haven't the foggiest."

The silence lingered. I walked to the large stone hearth

and turned my back to the flames to face them. "Let me explain."

"Yes, you really should," Antonia said. "Otherwise you need to work on your delivery."

"I've been thinking we needed someone to admit they were guilty. What if we acted like we already knew they were? What if we anonymously sent everyone the same letter threatening to expose them, and demand a meeting."

Antonia bit her lip. "Well, if you're sending it to all of them, I'm not sure what that would do."

"Other than really upset everyone, if you haven't already," Connor added.

"Let me finish. What if I told everyone the same thing? I know what they've done, and before I go to the police, I'm giving them a chance to work something out with me. There wouldn't be any reason for the innocent to show up. Only one of them would come. The guilty one."

"That's what I call brilliant." Antonia clapped once.

"That's what I call blackmail," Connor said.

"Well, I suppose you could look at it that way," I said.

"That's because that's what it is! Are you trying to get yourself killed?"

"That's why we send the notes anonymously. I don't need to be seen. We only need to know who shows up. And anyway, it isn't like I'd be there alone. I'd have someone there, you or the police."

"Oh, I'm sure Chief Harding will love this one," Connor said.

"If I tell him exactly what he needs to know, even someone that bumbling can prevent me from getting killed."

"Maybe, if you draw him a road map," Connor muttered.

"I don't think you're grasping the beauty of this. I don't have to actually know who the killer is. I just need for them to *think* that I know."

Connor made a slicing motion with his hand. "Stop. I understand exactly what you're saying, and it's a bad idea. Someone else is going to get hurt if you go through with this. Probably you. I want you to think long and hard about how you proceed and, at the very least, I'm not going to support this. You can count me out." He stood. "Antonia, you understand what I'm saying, right?"

"Absolutely. One hundred percent. Although I do suppose whoever is responsible will continue to come after Penny, even if she does manage to keep out of trouble—"

Connor took a deep breath and Antonia rushed ahead. "But, of course, you're right. This is a crazy idea and nothing good can come from it."

Connor exhaled and rubbed his temples. "I'm going to leave now, before I say something I'll regret later. Of all the crazy . . ." He turned to the door. "I need to go for that run I missed earlier."

Connor pointedly closed the door without a sound, and Antonia turned to me.

"I assume we are still on course."

"Damn skippy. Now help me write the letters."

Twenty-eight

"HOW does this sound?" Antonia cleared her throat. "'I know what you did on the train.'"

"Like a bad summer teen movie."

She crumpled the page and tossed it into the fire. "Well, then, what do you have?"

I read from the sheet in front of me. "The train. Tonight at six. You left something behind. I'm willing to discuss returning it."

Antonia tilted her head back and forth. "That isn't bad, actually. It leaves the possibility open that the killer left a clue at either Tara or Kim's murder, making it more likely that you actually have something."

"Here, help me write these up," I said. I handed her several sheets of hotel stationery.

"Why meet them at the train?" she asked.

"I admit it's a little theatrical, but I needed a place that everyone knows."

"Why not somewhere here at the hotel?"

"Too exposed. If you're a murderer, you don't want an audience when you confirm it. Also, here it's more likely someone innocent might show up, just out of curiosity."

She nodded. "Makes sense." We wrote in silence for a few moments. "How many do we need?"

I counted out suspects on my fingertips. "Big Dave, Vance, Jim, Seth, Barb and Bill. Six."

"Okay, here are my three." She handed me the folded sheets. "Now what? How, for instance, do we distribute them?"

"Right. Delivery. I hadn't gotten that far."

"Oh, for heaven's sake, Penelope. What is this, amateur hour?"

"Yes," I snapped. "That's exactly what it is. And I don't want to hear any complaining. Either help me figure out a way to do this or let me think in peace."

"Fine. I'm sorry. I'm just frightened for Chantal and frightened for you, and I think we're running out of time."

It was the first time I'd ever heard Antonia apologize for anything. It was a strong measure of the fear she must be feeling.

I squeezed her hand. "Don't worry, old girl. We're going to come out of this just fine."

"Old girl? Old girl?" Pink flushed her cheeks. "Do you know when you can call me that? Never. I'm not sure what I find more offensive, the 'old' or the 'girl.'"

"Fine. Forget I said anything and let me think. What

we need is to get the notes delivered without any connection to us. Three are to hotel guests: Big Dave, Vance and Jim."

Antonia nodded. "Yes, and the other three are going to be here this afternoon for the tasting. Bill said he was coming, and Olympio already told me he hired Seth and Barb to serve during the competition." She shook her head. "I don't know how you can possibly pull this off without any of them seeing you. We need someone else to do the drop-offs."

The drop-offs? "Good idea, Columbo."

"Well, then, you think of something."

"No. You're right. And I know just the person." I gathered up the notes. "Let me take it from here." I looked at my watch. "The tasting is scheduled for four. That gives me five hours."

"YOU'RE trying to solve the murders, aren't you?" I'd kept the purpose behind the messages vague, but George had put things together. "Of course, I'll try to help you. Ever since I heard you found that poor woman in the spa I've wanted to be of assistance."

"If you think we should leave it to the police, I understand," I said.

George huffed. "Harding? If you're waiting for him to solve anything, you'll be waiting a long time. Just ask the locals."

"So I gather."

"I'm just delivering messages between hotel guests. I don't need to know what the contents are."

"Thank you for this."

"Anything for the guests, after all." He rubbed his hands together. "Working in a hotel you'd be surprised the things I see and hear. I've always suspected half the population's secretly crazy. The goings-on here this last week only confirmed it." He paused. "Now tell me again exactly what you want me to do."

"All I need is for you to take each of these six envelopes to the addressed recipient." I handed them over. "Say they were left at the front desk when no one was about."

He flipped through the pile. "So these are our suspects, eh?" He leaned in closer. "My money's on Big Dave, for what it's worth. I saw the way that young wife of his, Tara, flirted with the guys around the pool. No man puts up with that for long, I can tell you."

"George. Can you promise me you'll just deliver them? Deliver them without comment or making any observations."

He drew himself up. "I'm a professional. You can't possibly imagine the outlandish things I've delivered to these rooms with a straight face." He rapped the envelopes against his open palm. "This will be a piece of cake."

"Okay, so let's be clear. Three are guests and three will be here this afternoon for the taste competition between Berninni and Martinelli wineries."

He glanced around the room and slowly tipped his head. "Simple. I can deliver three now and the other three this afternoon."

"It's crucial they each think they're the only one getting an envelope."

"Ah," George's eyes lit up. "This will require a little more cunning on my part. Excellent."

"Let's not turn all cloak-and-dagger. You just need to deliver them without being seen."

George tucked the envelopes into an inner pocket, then stuck his head outside the library door and scanned the lobby. He turned and touched the side of his nose before departing.

"DO you think George can be trusted to deliver the letters?" Antonia posed the question some time later as we sat in the lobby having coffee. The wind continued to blow and most of the guests were availing themselves of the interior activities, which included a number of chess sets and, in the far corner, a billiard room.

"I hope so. All he has to do is get the letters in the right hands. Hopefully the rest will fall into place." I pinched between my eyes. "I mean, what could possibly go wrong?"

"You jest, but we both know plenty can go wrong. For example, what exactly do you have planned at the train, on the outside chance that someone actually shows up?"

"It's impossible to imagine the killer being able to stay away," I said. "They can't take the risk. Beyond that, well, I'm open to suggestions. I do know I'll want the police there. I'll leave it to you to call them and tell them what I've done. Connor too."

Antonia raised a brow. "I would have told him regardless. I mean, when it's too late for him to stop you. He'd never forgive me otherwise. How do you plan on getting to the train?"

"The bike path. It's an easy walk, and I can slip away after the tasting."

Antonia looked at her watch. "The competition is to start in less than two hours. With this wind, people want to be indoors. I should expect we'll have a good turnout."

"You know this whole competition thing with Olympio and Berninni Winery is for fun, right?"

She turned to me. "When have you ever heard me joke about the reputation of Martinelli Winery? We have the best wines, and I fully expect to win this little contest."

I shook my head. "It baffles me. One minute, I would swear you have a thing for Olympio, but the next, you two are at each other."

Antonia smiled. "We're both Italian. It feels good to have someone to joust with again. It's been too long." She stood. "I'm going to change." She paused and then reached out to take my hand. She's never been particularly demonstrative, and I think we were both embarrassed, but she tightened her grip as she held my gaze.

"You don't need to do this. If you think it's best to leave it just as it sits, we can put our faith in the police and hope for the best."

I patted her hand. "Whoever is doing this missed me on the bike path, in the wine cave, and then, to the terrible detriment of poor Kim, in the spa. They aren't going to stop, and neither can I. Let's see it through and then go home. All of us."

Twenty-nine

WITH the walk to the train ahead of me, I dressed in black slacks with some built-in stretch, a soft black sweater tunic, and low slip-on shoes. I'd ordered a salad and baguette to the room but picked at the food, my stomach in knots.

I needed company and, to be honest, the person I really wanted to talk to was Connor. I picked up the phone several times only to put it down again, so it was a relief when it rang.

"I hope you aren't upset with me," Connor said without preamble.

"About what?"

"Making it clear I don't want you to pursue this."

My eyes narrowed and the knot in my stomach vanished. "Right, because you've had such tremendous success in the past telling me what to do."

"Somebody needs to. This isn't the first time you've decided to get involved when you shouldn't, and we can both name instances when it went horribly wrong."

"The point is, I get to decide for myself when to get involved." I grabbed the baguette I'd abandoned and jabbed it into the air. "This is a good idea. I know it is." I took a big bite out of the bread, my appetite restored.

On the other end of the line, there was a sharp intake of breath. "Don't tell me you're going through with this, Penny. Tell me you didn't do anything."

"I haven't done a thing." Yet.

"And that ridiculous idea of handing out notes to entice someone to meet you?"

"No, I didn't hand out those either." Take that.

Connor sighed. "Okay, I'm glad to hear it. See you downstairs."

I finished what I had left of the salad, wishing I'd ordered something more substantial.

At a little before four I grabbed a wrap, my room key, and a small shoulder bag for my phone. If the wine tasting went long, I wouldn't have time to come back to the room, not if I wanted to get to the train early.

The wind was even stronger than earlier, and the lobby was busy. Antonia waved me over as I entered the tasting room. It was the same room where less than a week ago, everyone had gathered together for the first time.

"What a great turnout," I said. "There isn't anyone at all on the outside patio."

"Yes. It was pretty handy that Olympio had all of those cases of my wine on hand. I wonder what he had in mind when he ordered them," Antonia said.

"I think he just wanted to know more about your life since you last saw him, but as competitive as you both are, he was happy to stage this little event. Now the only question is, how is the loser of this 'friendly' little competition going to feel when it's over?"

Antonia threw back her head. "I don't know. You'll have to ask him."

I rolled my eyes. "Honestly, you're impossible. You know that?"

She shrugged and nudged me. "There he is. I must say, he is quite handsome, isn't he?"

Olympio looked impressive indeed in a tailored gray suit that set off the silver in his hair. He'd paired the suit with a lavender tie and a crisp white shirt. The smile he shared with Antonia was warm and inviting as he walked up and took her hand between both of his. "Are you ready to have a little fun?"

"Absolutely, and I fully expect to have more fun than you."

He laughed. "Come, let me show you how I've arranged it." He bowed slightly at the waist. "I made certain that I could not later be accused of 'rigging' the results." He gestured toward the tables that lined the room. Each table had a good number of bottles, all bagged in silk covers of either gold or blue. On each table were stacks of tickets and large glass bowls tied with either a gold or blue ribbon. "You see? They taste the wine and vote without knowing which winery they are voting for."

Behind the tables a number of servers milled about, Seth and Barb included. Barb looked pale and avoided looking directly at me. Seth had the opposite response when he spotted me. He stopped unpacking bottles and narrowed his eyes. His jaw clenched and pulsed with each heartbeat. I looked away first, knowing that if I continued to hold his gaze, he was willing to make a scene. Olympio caught the exchange and shook his head at Seth. Only then did Seth go back to his job. Olympio tsk-tsked behind me.

"You know Bill fired him from serving on the train line, right?" I asked.

Olympio leaned in. "Barb told me. I caught her crying this morning as she packed up the wine cases to bring here. If it weren't for her and my loyalty to her father, I'd fire Seth immediately. I just might have to either way. He's getting worse."

If George had delivered Seth's envelope, that could be the cause of his anger. He could also be trying to decide if I was behind it. I took a quick backward glance and his eyes once again rested on me.

Olympio shook his head as though clearing his mind. "Enough of Seth for now. I was wondering, Penny, if I could call on you to act as the master of ceremonies."

I bit my lower lip. "Actually, I do have something else I need to take care of."

"Not until later," Antonia said. "This will keep you occupied and give you something to do. Plus, no one will suspect you of being"—she glanced around—"you know what, if you're up there running this thing."

"Fine." I turned to Olympio. "Antonia says I'll be happy to." I gestured to the tables lining the room. "I think your voting system is perfect, Olympio. It will be easy and casual, with everyone milling around. We can't be very formal with this many people. I can't believe the turnout."

"It's this wind," Olympio said.

Antonia sniffed. "It's the chance to sample some really fine wine, namely, Martinelli wine."

"Already?" I asked. "It hasn't even started yet. Behave yourself."

"She can bluster all she wants," Olympio said. "These people will know what fine wine is, once they taste Berninni wines."

"Stop it, both of you!" I counted the tables. "It looks like we're judging just a select amount."

Olympio nodded. "To simplify, I've brought only four of the wines that each of us produces: Cabernet, Pinot Noir, Zinfandel, and one white, the Chardonnay."

"That's more than enough," I said. "That's eight tastes for each person and, let's face it, everybody in this crowd's going to finish off each glassful. I'm glad they're all staying here." I took a deep breath. "Well, here we go."

I moved to the front of the room and clapped a couple of times. "Okay, everyone, welcome to the Berninni versus Martinelli taste-off. You may be rooting for the local team"—Olympio took a bow—"which is why the bottles and their labels are hidden in silk bags. Before we begin, there are likely various levels of knowledge in the room, so let's go over a few ground rules for the tasting."

I relaxed into the moment. I grew up knowing how to taste wine and occasionally taught wine classes at home in Cypress Cove. "First, this type of wine tasting is called a 'horizontal tasting,' where you taste the same wines of the same year, but from different wineries."

A voice came from the crowd. "I thought it meant drinking until you're horizontal."

The crowd parted, because nobody ever wants to be associated with *that* guy, and I spotted Vance toward the back of the room. He smiled, looking relaxed and without a care. If George had already delivered the envelope to Vance, he was either innocent or doing a good job of acting.

He raised a glass to his lips, a whiskey glass, which he promptly emptied. On the other hand, he could be guilty and just drunk, a likelihood I found more plausible. I ignored the comment and poured a glass from the bottle in front of me, holding the glass up to the light.

"There are actually four main steps to wine tasting. The first is to take time to notice the color. There isn't necessarily a bad color, but the wine should be clear. Jewel-toned.

"Next, twirl the glass. Notice how the wine travels down the sides in rivulets. These are the wine's 'legs.' This will give you an idea of the wine's texture and, usually, the slower the wine travels, the higher the alcohol content."

A number of tasters started to tip their glasses; I raised my hand. "One last thing. The most important thing before you taste. Take a long, deep inhalation. What do you smell? Is it fruity or woodsy? Does it whisper of spices, or is it sweet?" I let them compare notes before I raised my glass once again. "Now you can taste. And remember, above all, wine and wine tasting should be fun, full of new flavors and a chance to make new friends."

I finished off the rest of the wine in my glass. Even with the bottle wrapped in gold silk, I recognized Antonia's Pinot Noir. It was the perfect blend of spicy smoothness. I poured a glass from the bottle wrapped in blue. It was different but every bit as good, with a shorter finish, likely because it was so much hotter in the Napa Valley than along the coast in Cypress Cove.

"Excellent job." Antonia stood next to me.

"Thanks. Everyone seems to know what they're supposed to do."

"By the way, I saw you take a try of both of our Pinots. What did you think?"

"I like them both. Obviously, I love yours, but Berninni's is very good as well."

"But it's a little short at the finish, right? It's too warm here in the summer."

"Oh, no, you don't. I liked the finish. I think it was different than yours, but quite good."

Antonia sniffed. "No need to tell Olympio that. He's virtually impossible as it is."

I scanned the crowd and caught George standing at the main entrance. He touched the side of his nose and ducked behind the door. "I'll be right back." I scooted out the door and into the lobby where George waited behind one of the side columns.

"It would probably be better if you acted a little more natural."

His shoulders sagged. "I thought I was pulling it off."

Great. Now I felt guilty. "You're doing fine. How's it going?"

"I'm finished," he said proudly. "All the letters were delivered with no problems."

"How did everyone take it? Did anyone read it in front you?"

"A couple." He ticked off on his fingers. "Vance read it, but he just laughed. I think he's been drinking. Seth read his, got really angry and tore it up. Big Dave just turned and closed his door. I found Jim in the hall. He thanked me and walked away. Barb looked at hers then shoved it into her pocket. Funny thing about that one."

"What? Tell me."

"She checked to make sure it was addressed to her. Then she asked me if I was sure it wasn't supposed to go to her husband. I didn't tell her he got one too. I simply said that it was left just for her. Sounds like she suspects him of something."

"I'm sure she suspects him of a lot of things." It probably wasn't the first time someone had left a message for Seth at that same front desk.

"The last one was Bill from the train company. He stuffed it into his pocket because he was helping the folks from Berninni set up for this event." George glanced into the room. "It looks like a good time. I myself am partial to Cabernet."

"I think I can find you a nice bottle."

George waved away the offer. "I didn't mean that as a hint."

"I know you didn't," I said. "But it's the least I can do for your assistance."

"Well, let's hope our little plot helps with the search." He touched the side of his nose.

"What is that?"

He looked hurt. "It's our code."

"Well, stop it!"

"But we need a way to communicate without other people knowing."

I slapped my forehead. "Fine. Whatever."

I left him slipping along the corridor, and I reentered the tasting room.

"What did George want?" Antonia asked.

"Just to let me know the notes were all successfully delivered."

"What's with the nose touch?"

I rolled my eyes. "Don't ask."

"Oh, look there." She grabbed my arm. "Big Dave just walked in."

"I'm going to talk to him," I said. Antonia waved me on, and I made my way across the room. Big Dave lifted his hand in greeting when I stopped in front of him.

"Are you going to do some tasting?" I asked.

"I wasn't planning on it," he said. "I didn't even know this was going on. I came downstairs," he patted his coat about chest high, "because someone left a note at the front desk for me."

I kept my face neutral. "A note? Something important?"

"More confusing than anything. It was delivered to my room, but I was told it was left at the front desk. I just came down to see if anyone up front knew who left it for me."

"Did you have any luck?"

He shook his head. "Nobody knew anything about it. Damnedest thing." He patted his coat pocket once again, looking distracted.

"Well, now that you're here, you should at least have a glass of wine."

"I suppose you're right." He took a glass from the nearest table. "I don't have anything to do for the next couple of hours."

"Oh? You have something planned for this evening?" Stress echoed in my voice. "I mean, I'm glad to see you aren't sitting alone in your room, waiting for this to be over."

"Actually, I thought I'd go in to town."

"Any particular reason?" I smiled, going for casual interest.

"Thought I might talk to the police."

Not what I was expecting, which might be what he intended.

"They must have something solid by now. I'd just like to know they're making some progress and that soon someone will be charged in Tara's death. Kim's too, of course." He glanced across the room at Antonia. "I'm sure everyone here is looking for an answer, even if it's not the one they were hoping for."

"Not if you're the killer."

"What?" He patted his pocket once again, then turned his eyes to me. "I'm sorry. I just can't seem to concentrate right now. I think I'm going to pass on the rest of this event here."

He set the glass down and turned toward the door. Antonia joined me.

"Big Dave read his note."

Antonia looked surprised. "He told you?"

"Not what it said, just that someone left it for him. The interesting part is that he's heading into town tonight. Said he's going to stop by the police station to check on any updates."

"Maybe that's not the only stop he's planning on making, and afterward, he's heading down to the train station."

"It's possible," I said. "I need to leave soon. If he does

show up at the train, I want to be there to see it." I scanned the room. "How's it going?"

Antonia sniffed. "I hate to admit it, but they're just about done collecting the tickets, and it's going to be close."

"How close?"

"Very close." She pointed to the front table, where two stacks of collected votes were growing. They looked exactly the same height. "I wonder if he's found some way to rig it."

"Antonia!"

"His male ego will never survive if I win."

"Sure, *his* ego is the problem. Look at those results." I gestured with my palm. "You two are virtually a tie at this point."

"Ha! A tie." Olympio stood behind me. "That would make it easy, wouldn't it?"

"Easy for who?" Antonia put her hands on her hips.

"Well, I was thinking of you, my dear Antonia."

Antonia's cheeks brightened and she took a step forward. I moved between them.

"Stop it! Look, let me go do a quick preliminary count and then you can decide how you two want to proceed." What I needed was a way for both of them to save face.

Antonia tapped her foot. "I'm fine with that. It is obviously closer than I anticipated, but I have absolutely no concerns."

"Nor do I." Olympio winked at me. "Go, count and tell us what you find."

I walked to the front of the room and a solution presented itself. Barb stood just inside an exit door, holding several empty wine bottles.

"Here, let me get that door for you." I scooted around the table and pushed against the center bar.

"Careful," she said. "Just open it a small bit. The wind is ferocious."

I threw open the door as wide as possible. "What? I can't hear you over this wind. It's really something."

Whatever she said was lost in a huge gust that pulled the door from my hands, rolled through the room and lifted the votes into the air, showering them over the room like clouds of confetti.

Thirty

"DON'T think I don't know what you did back there," Antonia said a short time later when we stood at the foot of the bike path. "You knew perfectly well what would happen when you threw open that door."

"I have no idea what you're talking about. And anyway, it was left as it should be. As a tie. I can't help it if it's windy."

"Well, it certainly is that." She peered around in the lengthening dusk. "And it's getting dark." Her brows knitted together. "I'm not sure this was the best judgment call we've ever made."

"*Now* you're telling me you have doubts?" I wasn't feeling that brave either, to be honest. The skies were clear, so I wouldn't have to contend with rain, but gusts of cold air coiled around me and ripped through my sweater. I pushed my hair out of my eyes and wrapped the shawl tighter around my shoulders.

"Tell me the plan again." Other than an occasional grimace, Antonia didn't look fazed by the wind. Her perfect silver chignon remained motionless.

"What kind of hair spray do you use?" I was stalling.

She glared at me. "Have you lost your mind?"

"Okay, okay. The plan. The plan is to get to the train and see who shows up."

"That's it, huh? No wonder Connor was worried. You really aren't much of a planner."

I narrowed my eyes. "If you do your job and the police are there, the hope is that the person will either panic, run or start talking. In any event, they'll need to explain why the opportunity to retrieve something left at a murder scene would entice them to show up."

The trees rattled around us and I raised my voice. "A few minutes before six, you need to call the police and make sure they get to the train. Connor too. If they don't show up, it becomes my word against the killer's."

"Only if you get a chance to repeat it."

My face started to tingle and Antonia tipped her head.

"You just lost every bit of color in your face," she said. "Listen, as long as you're careful, you should be fine. It's entirely possible nobody will show or, better yet, you can see who turns up before you get anywhere near the train. Then you can wait from a safe distance until the police arrive. Look around before you get close to the train, avoid enclosed areas with only one exit and don't take any unnecessary risks."

"All good advice."

Antonia sniffed. "Of course it is." She looked at her watch then abruptly wrapped both her arms around me, pushing me away a moment later. "Now go."

I braced myself and turned away. The night was closing in faster than I'd anticipated, and she disappeared after the first few steps.

The path itself was well lit, with streetlamps every twenty feet. Biking at night was a popular sport, but tonight I was alone. I did a semi-jog just to get warmed up. That lasted about three minutes and I settled into a brisk walk.

The gusts were stronger now, even moving the metal light posts. Dried leaves swirled around my legs, and I tasted grit kicked up from the vineyard next to me. I continued to walk as fast as I could, but it was difficult; the cold wind buffeted me and I was forced to keep my eyes down because of the dust.

"This is crazy," I muttered to myself and after about fifteen minutes stopped to assess my surroundings. I dropped the idea of turning around only because I made out the scattered lights of town just ahead.

Moments later I was at the edge of the depot parking area. The train waited on the other side of the lot, silent and still.

When I'd first had this idea, my version had me staying right where I was, well back from the train. Now, looking out over the depot, it was clear that remaining in this spot wouldn't work. Anyone arriving could easily get to the train from the other side, completely out of my line of vision. I needed to be closer.

There weren't any cars in the parking area. It would

be easy to see me if anyone watched. I ran as quickly as I could across the exposed lot.

At the edge of the tracks, I ducked into the covered bench area where passengers normally waited to board. Three sides were protected from the wind. I took a seat.

After rubbing the dust from my eyes and warming up a bit, I felt better. The train stood silent. The inside lights were on but set to low. The entire length of the train was visible, but I didn't see anyone. My watch said I had twenty minutes to decide where to wait and see who'd get there next, if anyone. What had Antonia said? To look around before I got on the train, steer clear of enclosed areas and avoid any unnecessary risks. Right.

It stood to reason that if anyone showed, they wouldn't park in the lot. If they lived in town, like Seth, they'd park at home and walk. If they were visitors, like Vance, that Porsche of his would be easy to spot in the empty lot. If anyone came this far, they would be on foot.

I still had time to walk around the entire train before six. I wrapped the shawl tightly around me, took a deep breath and left the protected enclosure.

Scooting to the edge of the platform, I stepped over the tracks and around the back of the train. Behind the caboose the wind was lighter and I breathed easier, which didn't mean I was able to walk any faster. The gravel crunched under my feet as I stumbled over train ties. Gradually my eyes and gait adjusted and I was able to step from one tie to the next. Without the gravel underfoot and out of the wind, I was able to move silently. Stealthy. Like a cat. Yup. That's me. Catlike.

The thought occurred to me that nothing was going to

come of this, and I might actually get out of this mess in one piece, when I stopped. The unmistakable crunch of gravel from somewhere along the tracks reached my ears. This wasn't good. This definitely was not good. There wasn't anywhere to hide, and the roar in my ears made it difficult to hear. I took a couple of deep breaths and focused on where the steps were coming from. They were behind me one minute, then beside me the next, and I realized it was someone on the other side of the train. I moved closer to the car and scanned between the wheels. A flashlight played along the ground. When it flickered beneath the train and glided toward me, I hoisted myself up on the wheel. My heart was pounding and I struggled not to panic.

It seemed like forever that I clung to the side of the car, but the light slowly moved on and I managed a deep breath. In the quiet, I stepped down and considered my options. I was still reeling that I'd actually gotten someone to show up. Now that I had them, I just needed the police to arrive. I couldn't see my watch, but surely it was near six.

I'd started to retrace my steps when once again, steps came from the other side. Whoever it was hurried now and reached the caboose as I did. I peered around the corner of the caboose and made out a silhouette in the darkness. Whoever it was stood motionless, waiting as I was, for something to happen. It did.

"Looking for something, Penny?"

Thirty-one

I STARTED to turn but the sharp end of something pierced my sweater in the back.

"You don't want to do anything too quickly right now." My bag was lifted from my shoulder. "I feel a phone in here. Don't worry, you won't be needing it. All you need to do is get on the train."

I couldn't recognize the voice through the wind, and turned my head slowly. The jab in my back became a searing heat. "I told you to get on the train. Now you've made me tear that nice sweater of yours."

I was bleeding. I just knew it. The world started to slant. "I'm bleeding, aren't I?"

"It's nothing. Yet. Now get going."

As I turned the corner of the caboose, it was dark. The silhouette I'd seen earlier had vanished. I was propelled forward and grabbed the railing, pulling myself up onto the steps of the platform. There was police tape still across the railing, and an arm reached out, grabbed the tape and pulled it to the ground.

"You know we wouldn't be here if you'd only accepted that your friend was a murderer."

I knew that voice. I was so close . . .

"Oh, look, the safety chain is closed." A soft chuckle as the arm reached around me to click open the lock. "You can't be too careful with these things."

This was the second time I'd heard those words spoken, and from the same person.

"Jim, what are you doing?" My heart thumped in my ears and my voice was far away. "Why would you kill Tara?"

"Don't worry. You want to know everything so damn bad, I'll make sure you get all your facts straight, right before you can't do anything with them."

"You need to tell me if I'm bleeding. I have to sit down. I can't do blood." My throat was tight.

"What's the big deal? It's only a scratch."

Keeping the knife in place, he moved to my side and opened the caboose door. "Get going."

I moved through the caboose, past the spot where I'd found Chantal unconscious. Pushing open the door, I moved into the next car.

He stopped in front of the bar. "This is good." He moved in front of me, dragging the knife across my side and to my abdomen before he pushed my back into a waiting chair.

"So, where do we start?" He set the knife on the bar and reached for a bottle from the top shelf. "Might as well go for the good stuff."

I felt better once I took a seat and my head cleared. It was only a scratch. Only a scratch. A glance at my watch confirmed it was shortly after six. The police must be on their way.

He broke the seal of the bottle. "I should have known it was your idea to send me that note. Okay, why don't you tell me what you found, Ms. Detective."

As he tipped the bottle for a swig, there was movement behind him. Bill walked slowly toward us from the next car.

"I didn't find anything, but I knew the murderer couldn't take that chance," I said.

Bill stopped right behind Jim and picked up the bottle of whiskey.

Jim laughed. "Not bad. I suppose you're feeling pretty clever right about now. Or would be, except you're the one bleeding all over the upholstery."

I sat up. There was a small stain on the upholstered chair. I touched my back and when I pulled my hand away, my fingers were sticky.

My heart started jumping around. "I'm bleeding. I knew it."

"I barely nicked you. Relax." He jutted his chin out and studied me. "Wait a minute. You've got a blood phobia. Not a good thing to have if you're going around butting in where you shouldn't be."

Bill raised the container. I kept my eyes on Jim, not wanting to warn him of what was coming.

"Yup," Jim continued. "I suppose you think you had us pretty well cornered."

Us? I stared slack-jawed at Bill and moaned as he tipped the container to his lips.

"What?" Jim pointed to Bill and started laughing. "You think he was going to rescue you or something? That's rich."

"Jim, knock it off. I don't like this." Bill wiped his mouth with the back of his hand.

"Oh, come on." Jim waved an impatient hand. "You knew what was going to happen."

"Not here. Not on my train."

"Why?" I turned to Bill. "I don't understand what you hope to gain."

"It isn't what he hopes to gain," Jim said. "It's what he was afraid he might lose."

"But Tara wanted to invest. She was thrilled to be here."

"No. Nope." Jim took another swig and waved the bottle through the air. "I guess you aren't as clever as you thought. See, you bought Tara's murder the same way everyone else did. Only it wasn't murder."

"What do you mean? Someone threw her off the train. I saw her body on the tracks. That much at least I'm sure of."

Jim waved away my comment. "The only reason everyone accepted it was murder was because the safety gate was locked when the body was found. I told you that myself."

I thought back. "You did, didn't you? That morning when I found you and Kim at breakfast, you made a point of saying Tara's death had to be murder because if it had been an accident, the safety gate wouldn't have been secured. But it was."

He smiled. "Very clever. Now, keep going."

I stared at him until the answer came to me. "You locked it? She fell off the train and you locked the safety gate behind her?"

He clapped his palms together slowly. "I knew you could figure it out. I took a perfectly good accident and turned it into murder."

"That's enough, Jim," Bill said.

"Don't worry. She won't be repeating any of it," Jim said.

"But why would you let him do such a thing?" I turned to Bill.

Bill raised a fist to his forehead as though trying to push away the memories. "It couldn't be an accident. I couldn't afford to have it be an accident."

"An accident would have been better than murder!"

"Not to my insurance. Not to my investors. A murder could happen anywhere, and this way the company wouldn't be held responsible. I couldn't afford the negative publicity, the bad press. Worse, the accident was a safety violation. I might have lost the line, and if I didn't, my insurance would have come after me personally. I'm the one that didn't secure the gate. It came down to losing everything"—he gestured at Jim—"or this."

"Oh, come on, Bill, this hasn't worked out so bad." Jim smiled. "Of course, I knew the train had some safety issues. It's my business. I can look at a train and see deferred maintenance. That morning I just got lucky and saw something else through the caboose window. I saw Tara hit Chantal."

"We all just assumed the killer knocked Chantal out," I said.

"I know," Jim said. "It's been so hard to keep quiet. You thought you were all so clever. After Chantal hit the ground, Tara dug something out of Chantal's pocket then went back onto the platform to throw it away."

"The note telling Chantal to meet someone in the caboose," I said. "Tara wrote it."

"Yep. I got a chance to read it later, when things calmed down," Jim said.

"How did you get it?"

"Let me tell it." He was enjoying this. He took another swig and wiped his mouth. "So, Tara goes out onto the platform to toss the note off the train and drops it instead. Right there, at her feet on the platform. She was drunk from lunch. Remember her husband telling her to lighten up on the booze?" He didn't wait for an answer. "She should have listened. Anyway, she bent over to pick it up, leaned against the platform gate and *whoosh!*" Jim slid his palms together. "Right off the back."

"What happened then?" A cold sweat dotted my upper lip.

"Then it was easy," Jim said. "I ran through the caboose and grabbed the note, slammed the safety gate shut, this time with the safety pin in place, and got back out in no time. I figured that without the note and Chantal lying there, out cold, she'd be the main suspect, and she is." He shrugged. "See, I wasn't sure at the time how I could use Tara's death, but it seemed like too good an opportunity to pass up. And if nothing came of it other than a little confusion, then no harm."

No harm? He was crazy.

Bill grabbed a towel from behind the bar and pushed it between my side and the chair. "Let's go. I don't want her bleeding all over the train."

My mouth went dry. Perfect. I was going to bleed to death. So much for unfounded fears. My face felt clammy and I closed my eyes.

"Quit talking about blood," Jim said. "She looks ready to pass out. Would you just relax? We've got a couple more minutes." Jim scratched his chin. "Where was I? Oh, right, the safety brake. I needed Chantal found in the caboose to have her taken seriously as the suspect, so I had to draw someone's attention to her and Tara lying on the tracks. I pulled the brake, never thinking it would throw those tablecloths and chairs to the floor of the caboose, blocking Chantal in and making her look even guiltier. I think you pointed that out, Penny." He tipped his head toward me. "Mighty helpful of you."

"But why?" I struggled to understand his motive. "What did you gain?"

Jim sighed. "Don't you get it, Penny? What I gained was leverage."

"Over Bill?"

"That's it." Jim turned to Bill, who stood spinning a coaster on the counter. He saw me watching, and with effort pushed the coaster away.

"It was all on the line for me, Penny," Bill said. "After Tara was killed, I wanted everyone to quit talking about the murder. I needed it all to just go away. Let Chantal get accused. Big deal. She had her mother's money to get her out of it. But you wouldn't stop bringing it up. To the other guests, to the investors. I wanted you to just shut up. I tried to scare you, first on the bike path, then at the winery, but you wouldn't leave it."

A lump grew in my throat. "So you killed Kim, thinking it was me."

Jim laughed. "Try again." He pointed at Bill. "It was him, all right, but he didn't kill the wrong person. No, he got that part right, perfectly. All along it was supposed to be Kim."

I froze at Jim's words. "What? This was all about killing your wife? I can't believe it. You seemed so in love."

"Yeah, I'd been laying it on pretty thick this trip, and at one time we were in love; we really were. I'm sure you know she held the purse strings. She never made it a secret, and lately she's fought me over every nickel I wanted to spend. It was getting old." He tilted the bottle to his lips. "I had a couple of investments go belly-up. So what. That could have happened to anyone."

"So you decided to kill her. It's as simple as that."

"I wouldn't say it was all that simple, but, for the most part, that's about it. I've been waiting for the perfect moment. A time when I'd have a foolproof alibi, and that took some planning on my part." Jim raised both palms. "I mean, how could I have been the one to kill her? I was playing bocce ball with Connor when she died, remember? I have a hotel full of eyewitnesses that will swear I didn't go anywhere near the spa. 'Course, I got lucky too. I mean, there I am on the train, the only passenger able to actually see all the safety violations, and lucky me a drunk passenger takes a spill off the back of the caboose. I couldn't have asked for a better opportunity."

I turned to Bill. "Somehow they'll figure out it was you who killed Kim."

Bill started pacing, but Jim laughed. "How? Bill had no reason to kill Kim. None whatsoever."

Bill grabbed the bottle and tipped it back. "Let's get this over with."

Keep them talking. Just keep them talking. I shook

my head at Jim. "I'm so glad she went without knowing you were responsible. Her own husband."

"Hey, I wouldn't have needed to kill her if she'd been more reasonable."

Bill moved behind me and pushed me forward. "Damn. You're making a mess."

"How bad am I bleeding?" I felt lightheaded.

"Enough." Bill pulled me to my feet, and I leaned against the bar. "It's time to move her. I mean it." He pointed to the cushion. "How am I supposed to get that out?"

Jim gave a dismissive wave. "So get rid of the chair."

"The police better not find any trace of her being here." Bill paced between the chair and the bar. His voice was tight, and his hand was shaking as he wiped the bandanna across his forehead.

"It doesn't matter to Jim what happens to you or this train," I said. "He's done with you. Now you're just as much of a problem as I am."

Bill stopped and turned his eyes to Jim. "You know, if I even thought for one minute . . ."

"Don't let her get to you," Jim said. "She's just spouting off."

"Think about it," I said. "You're the only one besides me that knows the whole story. Sure, you killed Kim, but Jim is the one who benefits. He's the one that planned this. Maybe he decides it's cleaner if neither one of us is around."

"She doesn't know what she's talking about. Let's go. The sooner we shut her up, the better."

Bill massaged the back of his neck. "Now that you're not the one talking, you want to get going? Maybe I want to hear what she has to say."

Jim pushed himself away from the bar and started to stand. "And I say it's time to wrap this up."

"You sit back there and relax. I need to think about what I want to do next."

"Or else what?" Jim gave Bill a quizzical look, one eyebrow raised.

"Or else I might be rethinking my next move. If the police do find anything that leads back here, whatever I go through, I won't be going through it alone."

Jim dismissed Bill with a wave of his hand. "I don't think you're in any position to make threats. See, there's only one person on this train who's actually killed anyone, and it isn't me."

"But I think she's onto something," Bill said. "I think she's right. Maybe I did kill Kim, but you're the only one that gained from it. And in reality, Tara falling off the train really was an accident, right?" He looked at me for a response.

I nodded my head.

"So maybe I could say I was coerced by you. Maybe the only thing that will happen to me is that I lose the train. I mean, sure, at first I was willing to go along, but this isn't what I thought it was going to be. If I tell them everything, they'll listen."

Again, he looked at me, his eyes pleading for me to agree. "I'm sure they'll take that into consideration, right?"

I nodded. Sure. That and the fact that he was out of his tree.

"Well, isn't that something," Jim said. "Now you're going to bare your soul and hope the police believe you. It'll be your word against mine, I guess."

"No. Penny heard everything you said too."

"Well, then, I guess Penny can't be around to back you up." It took a moment to grasp the meaning of his words, long enough for him to grab the knife and step toward me. I tried to back away and instead landed in the same chair I'd been in earlier. Jim raised the knife over his head.

"No!" Bill grabbed the whiskey and swung it, catching Jim in the center of his back. The bottle shattered. Glass and whiskey rained down on me, and I covered my eyes. I froze, afraid to look, then heard heavy breathing and realized it was me. Biting my lip, I peered around my fingers. Jim was sprawled at my feet. He was facedown and completely still.

Bill calmly reached up and grabbed another bottle from the shelf. As he broke the seal, he prodded Jim with the tip of his work boot.

"I think he's dead." I sounded pretty calm, all things considered. "You should roll him over and see."

With a sigh, Bill grabbed Jim by the arm and rolled him over. Jim's head lolled to the side.

"He fell on it. You saw it too," Bill said.

The knife was firmly lodged in the center of Jim's chest. The dark stain spread.

"Not on my train. I told him I didn't want any blood on my train."

The world tilted to the side, and everything went black.

Thirty-two

S OMEONE slapped the side of my face.

"Stop that. It hurts."

"She's coming around now." I recognized Antonia's voice and opened my eyes.

I was in the same chair I'd passed out in. Antonia held a cloth to the back of my neck, and Connor spoke with Chief Harding on the other side of the car. I turned my head slowly to one side and looked down. Jim was under a sheet.

Connor saw me move and was by my side in three long strides. "The police want to talk to you. No passing out, okay?" There was a smile in his voice, but his brows were drawn together. When he took my hands, his pulse was racing.

"Good thing you got here when you did," I said through dry lips.

"Oh, we were here for a while before."

"What?" That sounded a little stronger, and I struggled up in the chair. "When did you get here?"

"I arrived with Antonia right after I found her and made her tell me what you were up to."

I swiveled in the chair toward Antonia. "Why didn't you call him like I asked?"

"I couldn't. The wind was playing complete havoc with both the cell and landlines. No calls."

"Then how did the police know to come here?"

Connor pointed to Big Dave, outside the car, looking in through a window. Big Dave had a grin on his face as he waved through the glass. "He went to the police to report a note he received at the hotel."

I avoided looking at Connor. "A note?"

"Don't pretend you don't know what I'm talking about."

I squirmed a bit and Antonia held up the cloth. "I need to get some more cold water for this."

"You're as bad as she is," he said to her as she retreated. "Anyway, Big Dave thought the note was worth reporting. He convinced Harding to come here tonight to see what was going on. We met them in the parking lot."

"How long ago?"

"Long enough to hear what Jim had to say. Bill too. Harding decided to come in when Jim went after you."

"Pushed it a little close, didn't he?"

Connor's face was white. "Believe me, if he hadn't come in when he did, I would have gone right through him."

"What happened to Bill?"

"He was just standing over Jim, mumbling something about the train."

"Bloodstains. He didn't want to get bloodstains on his train."

Thirty-three

WE'D been allowed to leave sometime after midnight, on the condition that we show up at the police station first thing the following morning. When we walked in a little after eight, Chief Harding leaned against the front counter, waiting for us.

"You know I could arrest you for obstruction of justice." He took a sip of coffee. "I'm sure I could come up with a number of other charges, like trespassing, without giving it much thought."

"You were getting ready to arrest the wrong person," I said. "In fact, the only reason there was justice at all is because of what I did. How do you call that obstruction?"

Connor closed his eyes behind his palm while he rubbed his temples. "Penny, let's see if we can come up with a solution." He moved closer and said in a soft voice, "The goal is to go home, remember?"

Chief Harding crossed his arms. "We were hot on their heels before you pulled that little stunt last night. It might have taken a bit longer, if you'd let us handle it, but Jim might still be alive."

"Maybe, but I might have been dead, so I'll just consider it a win."

"You wouldn't have been attacked if you hadn't been on the train!"

"Wrong. I would have been attacked, just somewhere else!" I was tired, still in shock and needed caffeine so badly even the police station coffee he was drinking smelled good. "Look, you heard Bill last night. You have a confession. Don't you think it's time to just let us go?"

Antonia spoke for the first time since we'd arrived. "Chief Harding, if I may interject, wouldn't it in fact be the best thing for all if we were to leave town? The reality is that no one outside this room knows exactly what happened last night. It could easily be recorded that you were wise enough to act on the suspicious note left for a hotel guest. That decision led you to discover that another hotel guest," she tipped her head toward me, "Penny here, was being held against her wishes. Your quick thinking prevented what might very well have been a third murder from occurring."

"What rubbish." I spoke under my breath. Antonia shot me a look.

"Of course," she continued, "if you need us to return in the future to testify, we'll be more than happy to comply and confirm this perfectly, hmm, plausible version of last evening's events."

Chief Harding moved his gaze across the three of us as

he absently smoothed his moustache. Finally he pushed himself up off the counter. "If you agree to return if necessary, I don't see any reason for you to remain here. In the meantime, looks like you folks should get going."

A short time later we were back at the hotel. Antonia was still outside and I pulled Connor into a corner of the lobby.

"I just wanted to make sure we were good, since, you know, you sounded a little testy at the police station."

He nodded. "Sure. I just thought at that moment our best course of action was to get out of there, not point out all of the mistakes that he'd made as an officer of the law."

I sniffed. "Fair enough. I just like it better when we present a united front. You know, I have your back, you have mine, that kind of thing."

Connor smiled and my heart did a little whirly dance. "Yes, Penny. I'll always have your back."

My cheeks felt hot but before I managed to embarrass myself Antonia joined us. "What a relief that that's behind us," Antonia said. "All I want to do is grab Chantal and our bags and start for home."

"That might be delayed a bit, although I'm sure you won't mind," I said as Olympio pushed through the hotel's front doors. His smile was subdued.

"I called and the hotel said you had not checked out, which is very fortunate for me."

"I would have called you to say good-bye," Antonia said. "You didn't need to come down here."

"And forfeit a chance to see you again? I miss you already, my friend."

Antonia tipped her head in accord. "Next time I would love to host you as a guest at my winery."

"I will hold you to that and will visit soon. In the meantime, I have some good news to share. Barb has decided to leave Seth. She is moving into one of the cottages on my property this afternoon."

"That's wonderful," Antonia said. "She's lucky to have you."

Olympio shrugged. "She was once a very happy woman. I think, with time, she will be again."

I saw Big Dave across the lobby and excused myself.

"I didn't get a chance to thank you last night," I said when I reached him. "It was a good thing you insisted the police follow up with a visit to the train. You saved my life."

Big Dave shook his head. "You found out what happened to Tara. I reckon we're even."

"Where's Vance?"

Big Dave grimaced. "Waiting in the car out front. He offered to give me a ride to the airport. How in hell I'm supposed to fit in that thing, with all our luggage, is beyond me, but it seemed like an offer of goodwill on his part, and I didn't want to turn it down."

"You're a good man. I knew it the moment I met you."

"Good thing I didn't let you down. Bye, Penny."

I gave a small wave as he turned toward the main entrance.

There was one last person I wanted to see before I left, and I spotted him a few moments later. George was crossing the lobby with the next suitcase, the next guest behind him. I caught his eye, nodded my thanks and touched the side of my nose before departing.